C000261974

To Fiona,

Best wishes,

gillian

VISION OF LIGHT

Gillian Poucher

instant
ap[]stle

First published in Great Britain in 2023

Instant Apostle
104A The Drive
Rickmansworth
Herts
WD3 4DU

This is a work of fiction. Names, characters, businesses, places, events and incidents are either the products of the author's imagination or used in a fictitious manner. Any resemblance to actual persons, living or dead, or actual events is purely coincidental.

British Library Cataloguing-in-Publication Data

A catalogue record for this book is available from the British Library.

This book and all other Instant Apostle books are available from Instant Apostle:

Website: www.instantapostle.com

Email: info@instantapostle.com

ISBN 978-1-912726-73-8

Printed in Great Britain.

Dedication

During summer 2004, while training for ministry, I was privileged to participate in an exchange programme between the United Reformed Church and the United Church in Jamaica and the Cayman Islands. I was placed at Duke Street United Church in Kingston where Rev Sylvan Hinds was minister.

That cross-cultural experience was formative and deeply enriching. This novel is dedicated to Sylvan and his wife, Rosie, with fond memories and gratitude for a friendship sustained across the years by our annual exchange of news at Christmas.

I have given my character Sonia their surname of 'Hinds' in acknowledgement.

Another UK participant would subsequently be ordained and serve alongside me in the East Midlands Synod. Rev Louise Gee is an indefatigable colleague and dear friend whose unstinting service and generous spirit are truly inspirational. So this book is also for 'The Bionic Rev'.

> For our struggle is not against enemies of blood and flesh, but against the rulers, against the authorities, against the cosmic powers of this present darkness, against the spiritual forces of evil in the heavenly places. (Ephesians 6:12)

I'd only planned to help the ones who are very confused, beginning with Elsie. That was before I found out that the old man had seen me.

It was lucky for me he got a water infection. Otherwise I wouldn't have had a clue what he's been saying. The manager asked me to check on him. The doctor had been in two days earlier, and started him on antibiotics. I found that pregnant carer Kylie in the room with him, the one who's already got two sons by different men.

'I'll just open the blinds wider, Reg,' she was saying when I went in. 'So's you can see the birds.'

He saw me and his eyes bulged. His cheeks were flushed with fever. 'Get out,' he quavered.

Kylie had her back to us as she adjusted the blind. 'But you like to watch the birds, don't you?' she coaxed.

'Get out!' he said again.

She wheeled round and saw me. 'Now, Reg, it's not like you to be rude.' But she was half-smiling, like she was pleased he didn't want me there.

That's because I caught her smoking by the kitchen door last week. 'When's your baby due?' I asked, staring pointedly at her bump.

She pulled a face and dropped the fag on to the gravel, squashing it beneath the heel of her scruffy trainers. 'I know I shouldn't. It's just hard not to.' She looked me up and down, then tossed back her long brown ponytail. 'You wouldn't understand. You professional women have no idea.'

How rude! What does she know about my life?

Anyway, back to today. I ignored the old man's agitation. 'I hear you aren't well,' I said, approaching the bed. 'The manager asked me to see how you're doing.'

He shrank back against his pillows. 'Don't come any nearer! I saw what you did!'

9

'Shall I stay?' the carer asked. 'Reg has been ever so agitated the last couple of days, haven't you, duck? Keeps muttering about Elsie. He's missing her terrible.'

'I'll manage,' I said. 'Is that the buzzer?' I hadn't heard anything, but was desperate to get her out of the room before he said anything else.

'Elsie,' said Reg. 'She did for Elsie.'

You might imagine how that turned me cold, but the carer paid no attention to the old man. Fortunately, one of the other residents happened to buzz at that very moment, and the carer lumbered towards the door, cradling her bump. 'Try not to upset yourself, Reg,' she said. 'It's the infection talking. Nurse is here to help you.'

She's not very bright, that woman. Even so, if the old man gets better and speaks to her again, or if she runs over that conversation the way you do, hours later – well, that's a risk I can't afford to take.

And we both know it's not a good start for a kid to be born into a single parent family, don't we, Mum? What chance would this one have with two older brothers? The poor thing wouldn't be healthy either, not with her smoking habit.

So I've worked it all out. I know exactly what I need to do.

Chapter one

Noel stares out across the river. The lights in the flats on the opposite bank waver in the rain.

He takes another slug of beer from the bottle he bought in the pub, and wipes his mouth with the back of his hand. He can't remember how much he has drunk and couldn't care less. Shrieks of raucous laughter reach him on the wind and he guesses that the landlord has finally called time on the hen party. He stumbles along the tarmac path until he is out of earshot. Here the only sounds are the wind whistling through the reeds and the rain bouncing on the path.

Laughter has no place in the world he plunged into when the two policemen turned up on his doorstep and broke their devastating news. He's sure it was Susan Weatherall who put them on to him, even though they refused to say. *But surely Susan didn't think that he could ever...?*

The older policeman, DI Pritchard, invited Noel to accompany them to the station. 'Just procedure,' he said, with a smile which didn't reach his eyes. Staring numbly at the two men, Noel registered that they were watching him carefully, gauging his reaction. Everyone knows that partners past and present are top of the list of suspects in a murder case.

Now Noel nearly loses his footing where the tarmac runs out. The track is slick with mud. He drains the beer, then rotates the bottle in his hand, before tossing it half-heartedly into the reeds. He tries to ignore his inner censor. Litter is no longer relevant. He screws up his eyes to follow the trajectory of the bottle, but it is swallowed up in the darkness. There is a faint plop as it lands, and he wonders how long it will take to be sucked down into the bog.

He shivers. Maybe there's an easier way for what he plans, but he reckons that coming down here, tanked up, might make it look more like an accident. *Who'll care anyway?* Still, it will make it easier for his ex-wife to explain to their daughter, Jade. Better for Jade, and Carol too. Not that he expects his sister to be anything other than indifferent. But nor does he want to add to her burdens.

Tears of self-pity mingle with the rain coursing down his face, blurring his vision. Somehow, he'd managed to maintain his self-control at the police station. They'd made him wait in the bare, cramped interview room for what seemed an age before they began to question him. Tactics, he supposed. He'd wondered about calling a solicitor, but when he suggested it, DI Pritchard said it might waste valuable time.

'The first few hours after the murder are crucial for progress,' chimed in his colleague, DS Smythe. He'd leaned forward in the chair into which he'd folded his tall, lanky frame, hazel eyes earnest behind trendy aviator specs. 'I'm sure you wouldn't want to cause any delays in the hunt for Kylie's killer, would you, Noel?'

First, they asked where he was at 7.30 that morning. Relief swept through him. He had an alibi: he'd been at the corner shop buying bread and milk. But they'd persisted with other questions: *Where were you earlier, Noel? In bed, alone? So no one can vouch for your whereabouts overnight? Tell us about your relationship with Ms Weatherall. You hadn't seen her since April? You'd tried to phone her, but she changed her number? How did you feel about that, Noel? Did it make you angry...?*

On and on until he'd asked them to contact Mr Ahmed, who owned the corner shop, or get him a solicitor. Mr Ahmed had confirmed his whereabouts. 'Not far from there to Kylie's house though, is it?' observed DS Smythe. 'Ten-minute drive max, wouldn't you say?'

Noel massaged his pounding temples. 'I walked straight home from the shop,' he repeated dully. 'I said "Morning" to the postman. I told you that already.'

A constable entered the room asking for a word. DI Pritchard followed him out on to the corridor. Noel stared down at the desk, ringed with coffee cup stains, avoiding Smythe's stony gaze.

Pritchard came back in. 'We'll be in contact with Royal Mail to locate this postman. And we'll be checking with the victim's sons that they're sure about the time. You're free to go. For now.'

Shakily, Noel scraped back his chair. DI Pritchard led him down a corridor and through the reception area. The policeman opened the glass door, then thrust his ruddy face with its bulbous nose close enough for Noel to smell his sour breath. 'Don't go making any plans to leave Trentby, will you?'

Noel had left the station and wandered aimlessly through the town on the wet October evening. Then the tears came, not only for Kylie, but for her poor boys, who'd found their mother's body in the kitchen ten minutes after she'd opened the door to an unseen visitor.

Kylie. If I'd tried harder, maybe you'd still be here. I should have gone round when you changed your phone. I shouldn't have given up.

Given up. The story of his life. The pub was the obvious destination, and the pints of indifferent lager fuelled the idea that had been forming during the hours since he had learned of Kylie's murder.

He blinks away his tears and tries to focus on the task in front of him. He'd wondered about collecting stones and filling his pockets with them, to make it quicker. Then he rejected the thought. It would look deliberate. Besides, his feet haven't made contact with any stones along the path, and it's too dark to search for them. The rain is easing, but mist is creeping across the marshes, further reducing visibility.

He looks back the way he has come. The river path bends round from the pub, invisible in the misty darkness. The lights on the opposite bank have vanished. He squints at a patch of mist in front of him. It appears denser, more like fog. Maybe it's the beer, but as he peers into it, the mist seems to take on a definable form. Drawn in by the swirling shape, Noel steps down from the path towards the river.

The mist soon envelops him. He's already soaked through, but the fog seeps into him, penetrating his bomber jacket, polo shirt and trousers. He begins to shudder uncontrollably. He has the oddest sensation of losing body weight with each step he takes, as if he is dissolving into the vapour. Something cold and wet slaps his face. Disorientated in the darkness and fog, he realises he has wandered into the reeds. There is a stench, a putrid odour, which makes him gag. He tells himself that it can only be rotting vegetation, even though he has never before smelled such foul decay.

He seems to hear a voice whisper, *'Not much further.'* Involuntarily, he pauses mid-step and turns his head to listen. There it is again. *'Not much further. So easy.'*

He gives himself a shake, trying to dispel the voice, to convince himself that the words are his own thoughts. He peers into the vaporous darkness, but can't see anything, not even his hand when he lifts it to his face. *Is this what happens once you've made the decision? Does everyone feel like someone is speaking to you, urging you on to the final act?*

Noel sets down his left foot. There is a gurgling noise and he lurches forward, grabbing wildly for the reeds. Somehow, he pulls his foot free of the bog, miraculously retaining his trainer.

The sudden movement jolts him from the despair that has engulfed him since the police hammered on his front door with the news of Kylie's murder. He shakes off the self-loathing which has assailed him throughout the hours in the airless interview room. 'Help me!' he cries.

His voice is muffled in the fog. Although he knows it's hopeless, he shouts again, 'Help me!' Rationally, he knows that last orders had been called when he left the pub. There will be no one by the river at this hour or in this filthy weather. There is no one to hear him. No one to save him.

Confronted by annihilation, Noel discovers how desperately he longs to cling to existence. The irony that he now wants to escape the death he was seeking chokes another desperate cry in his throat.

Yet – is he alone? That insidious voice again. *Just a few more steps.* With sickening clarity, he realises that he won't be able to find his way back to the path. His chest tightens as the abominable stench seeps down his airways into his lungs.

'So much easier to keep going. It will all be over soon.'

'Help me,' he whispers. Then, 'Help me, God.' The final desperate plea of the man facing extinction.

The mist dissolves as soon as he utters that prayer, and the foul odour is replaced by a beautiful floral fragrance. Noel gasps to find himself in daylight. In front of him is a river, far wider than the muddy river that runs through the town. This river is so wide that he cannot see the opposite bank. The water runs azure beneath a cloudless sky. The crests of the waves sparkle like diamonds in the sunlight.

A cloud hangs over the river downstream. It is like no cloud he has ever seen. There is a brightness about it, a many-hued radiance. The cloud seems to be moving towards him, as if carried on the current. Noel shields his eyes with his hand as the brightness intensifies around him. He is simultaneously captivated by the rainbow haze and fearful of its strangeness.

As the cloud draws nearer, he sees that the vapour is solidifying, resolving into some other form. Its shape is that of a man, but the dimensions are remarkable. The emerging figure towers far above Noel. The broad shoulders almost span the river.

The giant figure is clothed in a sleeveless linen robe. A belt of gold encircles the waist. The muscular arms and legs gleam like bronze. A mane of lustrous black hair ripples in waves from the leonine head to the shoulders. The face blazes like lightning. From the open mouth thunderous words roar forth.

Above the aquiline nose, the eyes flare like flames. Sparks fly from them as they alight on Noel. He draws back, gasping, certain that the sparks are capable of piercing his very soul.

All strength drains from him. He collapses to the ground. The words pouring over him are spoken in a melodious language he has never heard. He closes his eyes. His body jerks violently and then lies still beneath the torrent of the strange tongue.

The roaring continues above and around him, the words continuing to roll over him like the river. It is only when he feels the firm but gentle touch of a huge hand upon his shoulder that Noel rouses from his trance.

A sudden silence falls. The Being has stopped speaking, and the absence of the sound of the flowing waters of the river is uncanny. Then a voice says softly, 'Do not fear, Noel. Stand on your feet.'

Trembling, Noel obeys. He rises, his eyes fixed on the emerald grass. Again, he hears the whisper, as soothing as honey: 'Do not fear, Noel. You are safe. Be strong and courageous, for the Master has chosen you.'

He opens his mouth to speak, but no words come. He feels the gentle, firm touch again, first on his mouth and then beneath his chin.

The touch emboldens Noel to look up, but he recoils immediately from the burning gaze. He would have fallen again if the Being had not placed a strong hand on his shoulder.

'You are safe,' the liquid voice repeats. 'Only remember: you have been chosen.'

Noel swallows. Not daring to raise his eyes above the bronze feet beside him on the grassy bank, he whispers, 'What for? What have I been chosen for?'

'You have been chosen to right the wrongs in this place, to shine as light in the darkness. First, you will find your own healing.'

Noel's mind reels. 'I don't understand. What wrongs? What darkness? What healing?'

His companion sighs deeply. Emitted by such an enormous creature, the sigh is like a gale-force wind. Noel is certain that if it weren't for the bronze hand grasping his shoulder, he would be blown away.

'Do you not have eyes to see or ears to hear?'

The words are spoken more in sorrow than frustration, but Noel finds himself quaking even more. His teeth are chattering. 'I don't know,' he whimpers.

'Then you must trust,' replies the Being. 'Trust and you will understand, because the Master has chosen you.'

'But why me?' asks Noel. 'Why have I been chosen? Who is your Master?'

'It is not for me or you to question the Master,' answers the Being sternly. 'The Master's ways are perfect, beyond understanding.'

Noel hangs his head.

'Now come,' says the Being. 'Let me take you to safety.' He places gigantic bronze hands beneath Noel's arms.

Noel shrinks back, gasping, and closes his eyes. Words in the strange musical tongue boom over him. He feels himself being lifted and set down gently. Then silence falls, and he is released. He opens his eyes.

He finds himself back in the pub car park. Rain is falling softly. The door of the brightly lit pub opens and a group of women emerge, shrieking with laughter. Noel scratches his head and checks his watch: 11.20. The women totter, giggling, towards the road, and he trails over the bridge after them in a daze. He is sober now, and exhausted.

The women straggle left towards the town. Noel crosses the street and heads in the opposite direction. As he squelches along, turning off the main road into the maze of terrace streets where he lives, he tries to understand what happened after he left the pub. He remembers hearing the rowdy women when he was on the riverbank, but that must be hours ago. How is it still only 11.20pm?

He hasn't made any sense of it by the time he staggers over the threshold of his rented house. He dumps his ruined trainers and sodden jacket on the hall floor and stumbles upstairs. He's tempted to fall into bed as he is, even though he is soaked to the skin, but has the presence of mind to strip off his wet clothes and take a hot shower. Then he drops into bed and sinks into a deep and dreamless sleep.

The radio alarm rouses him at 7am. He leans over groggily to switch it off, then sits bolt upright in the double bed when he hears the local headlines. 'Police are continuing to investigate the murder of Kylie Weatherall, a single mother with two young children.'

Noel flicks off the radio. He sinks back against his pillow and covers his eyes with his forearm, wishing he could erase that sentence which has exploded into his consciousness. Snatches of scenes from the previous day replay on the internal screen of his mind, and soon he is weeping.

Then he remembers what happened by the river. What is he to make of it? He rubs his damp cheeks with the back of his hand and stares up at the Artex ceiling above his bed, pondering the river of his vision, and the radiant appearance of his companion. The words about the Master's call echo in his mind. On one level they are a welcome distraction from the terrible news of Kylie's death, but on another he finds them deeply troubling. *You have been chosen to right the wrongs in this place, to shine as light in the darkness. First, you will find your own healing.*

Dragging himself into a sitting position on the edge of the bed, Noel asks himself whether it's reasonable to believe what was revealed to him when he was on the verge of taking his own life. Could it have been some kind of psychotic episode?

He rises and plods to the bathroom. Surely the Being's Master must know that he is the last person to be trusted with any responsibility? Could anyone be less worthy?

'Who are you?' he shouts on the narrow landing. 'Who are you? Give me a sign if you're real!'

He is unsurprised when there is no response. In the bathroom, he reaches out to turn on the cold tap at the sink. Then he pauses, his hand suspended in mid-air. A lock of lustrous black hair is lying in the basin. Noel blinks hard and passes his hand over his own blond head. He opens his eyes again. The glossy tress is still there. He looks up at the frosted glass window above the sink, remembering that he closed it yesterday morning when the rain was hammering down, just as it is today. The window is still shut. Feeling foolish even though he is alone, he inspects the ceiling. There is nothing there except a cobweb stretching across the right-hand corner. Noel gazes down at the black curl in the sink and takes a deep breath before cautiously picking it up.

He gasps on contact. The coil of hair scalds his hand like a burning coal. He jumps back and drops it to the floor. A red mark is already spreading across his palm. He turns on the cold tap and thrusts his hand underneath.

Sluicing his scalded hand with cold water, Noel acknowledges to himself that he has his sign. However impossible and outlandish, he has received the confirmation he requested. For some incomprehensible reason, he has been chosen by some unknown Master to right the wrongs in this obscure town.

'Why me?' he whispers, staring down at the shining strands of black hair which lie like seaweed on the tiled floor. 'Why me, when you know how I failed them all?'

When the burning sensation in his hand has reduced to an intermittent throb, Noel takes another shower. His tears flow with the soapy water as he scrubs himself with a ratty sponge. He feels better afterwards, even though the warm water has no power to cleanse him from the guilt of believing that if he hadn't left Kylie, she would still be alive. Her two sons would still have their mother. In a few weeks, he would have become a father to his and Kylie's child.

But the possibility that he might be able to influence what is yet to happen, if he follows the mysterious Master's call, offers Noel his first glimmer of hope since the police brought him news of her death.

Chapter two

On Monday morning, Noel is eating cornflakes in front of the TV in the kitchen when his mobile beeps. He ignores it, shovelling more cornflakes into his mouth. It could be his sister with news of the inevitable, and he isn't ready for that. All weekend, he has avoided making the journey which Carol suggested when she rang on Thursday.

If it's someone ringing about a job, he plans to take a few days off to get his head straight. He'd been working all hours until Friday, leaving home early and returning late. As well as needing the money, work had been an anaesthetic against the creeping guilt about leaving Kylie and the kids when she'd told him she was pregnant. Of all the disturbing thoughts which have tormented him since he heard about her murder, imagining her swollen belly has haunted him the most.

The cornflakes taste like soggy cardboard as he pictures Kylie six months earlier. It was a warm sunny April evening. Bradley and Liam had left the house after tea to have a kickabout with their mates in the street. Noel was planning to cut the grass in the scrubby back garden after washing up. He got up from the kitchen table and took his plate over to the sink. Behind him, Kylie asked, 'How'd you feel about another kid?'

Noel remembers the cutlery rattling on the plate, how he almost dropped it into the bowl. He ran water over it before answering.

'You mean, you and me have a kid?' He squeezed out the last of the washing-up liquid with a belch.

'Yeah. Who else?'

There was a teasing note in her voice, but he registered nervousness too. He turned the tap on full, swishing the water around as the bubbles formed, releasing lemon fragrance into the air. 'We've not talked about it really, have we? Still early days.'

Kylie rose from the table and came up behind him. She put her arms around his slim waist and looped her fingers through the belt of his jeans. He didn't relax against her as he usually would, his back stiff as he picked up the dish brush and scoured the brown sludge of Bolognese off a plate.

She released him and grabbed a tea towel from the hook by the back door. 'It's three months since you moved in. You're great with Bradley and Liam.'

'That's easy. They're great kids.'

'You get on really well with Jade too, when you see her.'

'Yeah. When I see her.' He couldn't keep the bitterness from his tone.

'Gemma'll come round.'

'You think so?' Noel scrubbed the frying pan vigorously. 'I just don't get it, why she's got a problem with you, when she left me for that idiot two years ago. Jade came every other weekend until she found out we'd got together.'

Kylie threw some cutlery into the drawer next to the sink with a clatter. 'I know, babe. It doesn't make sense, but I reckon she'll change her tune when she hears from your solicitor.'

Noel grunted and rinsed the frying pan.

'So, what do you think?' she pressed.

'About Gemma coming round?'

She sighed, flicking the tea towel at his arm. 'No. Keep up! About me and you having a kid of our own.'

Noel turned to her, struck by the anxious note in her voice. Through the open window he could hear the boys shouting, and the distant thrum of a motorbike. 'I don't know, love. What with Jade, Bradley and Liam, we only just cover the bills as it is.' He laid the frying pan in the rack and emptied the dirty water from the bowl.

'Right.' Kylie took a mug over to the cupboard above the kettle.

Water gurgled down the plughole. 'Shall we leave it a couple of years?' he suggested, running fresh water into the bowl. 'The business should be set up then. That'd make sense. I mean, you're young enough. We've got plenty of time. There's no rush, is there?'

Kylie didn't answer immediately. Noel sloshed his right hand around in the water, watching as she rearranged the mugs in the cupboard. She turned the handles of those at the front outwards with uncharacteristic precision.

She turned and took a deep breath. 'The thing is,' she said, not quite meeting his eye, 'I'm already pregnant. About nine weeks.'

'Oh.' He turned off the tap and washed a fork with elaborate care, poking the dishcloth between each silver tine.

'Is that all you can say?' She came back alongside him.

'It's just… a bit of a shock.' Noel placed the fork in the cutlery basket, then reached for a knife.

'Can you leave that?' Kylie seized his arm.

Reluctantly, he dropped the knife back into the water and looked at her. Her wide brown eyes searched his face, and he forced a smile.

'I know it's a shock,' she said. 'Not what we were planning yet. Maybe it's not great timing, maybe it'll be a bit of a struggle financially, but we've got each other. We can manage, can't we?'

'Yeah. Course we can,' he said hollowly, thinking about the debts his ex-wife had saddled him with. 'How did it happen, Kylie?'

She pushed a strand of thick chestnut hair behind her ear. 'How do you think?' She smiled coyly.

'You know what I mean.' He turned back to the sink and retrieved the knife. 'You're on the pill, aren't you?'

'I ran out. Around the time you moved in. You know how hectic it was. And, well, I thought it wouldn't matter too much if... So here we are.'

'You didn't think to mention it?' It was an effort to keep his voice even. 'You didn't think we should talk about having a baby?'

He sensed her tense alongside him and take a step away.

'There was a lot going on,' she said. 'You'd just moved in, were getting to know the kids better. I thought about it, course I did, but I just didn't get round to it.'

Noel processed this, watching the shadows lengthen across the uncut grass.

'It's OK, isn't it? You're happy about it?' Her voice wobbled.

He chewed the inside of his cheek. 'I don't know, Kylie,' he said honestly. 'I need a bit of time to get my head round it. I didn't expect it, that's all.'

'And I didn't expect you to be like this!'

He didn't answer immediately, wanting to avoid a row. The sun was sinking behind the houses on the parallel street, another row of uniform 1950s local authority housing. He thought longingly of his old cottage with its view across the fields. He had been forced to sell it when he and Gemma divorced.

'You could have told me,' he said quietly, trying not to sound accusing. 'You could have told me that you'd come off the pill.'

She tossed back her hair and raised her square chin. 'You don't want this baby, do you?'

Noel looked round the cramped kitchen with its cluttered counters and dated mocha kitchen units. 'It's not as simple as that. One day, maybe. But you have to see that the timing isn't great. I was hoping to get some money behind us once the repairs business is up and running, pay off the debts, maybe think about buying our own place. I wanted to get to know

Bradley and Liam better, see how we –' He broke off when he saw her expression harden.

'See how we get on, that's what you were going to say, isn't it? And what's wrong with this house? You were happy enough when you moved in! Kept telling me how we'd be better off paying rent and bills on just one house instead of keeping your place going as well.' Her voice rose and her lower lip trembled. 'I should've listened to Mum. She said you only got with me for the house. That way you could save money and afford child support for Jade and pay your debts. That's what Mum said.'

He took a breath. 'That isn't why I moved in, Kylie.'

She was crying now, fat tears sliding down her cheeks.

'Come on, love. It wasn't like that.' Noel took a step towards her but she backed away, shaking her head.

'I don't believe you. Mum said we wouldn't last the year, that you'd soon get fed up with me and the boys, that you'd never love them like your own.' She cradled her lower abdomen. 'That's why I didn't tell you I'd come off the pill.'

He stared at her. 'You don't mean you thought that if we had a baby now it'd keep us together? Kylie, I've been happy these last few months with you and the kids. I didn't move in to save on rent, I promise. Why did you have to listen to that poisonous –?' He stopped before he said something very rude about Kylie's mother. Kylie knew well enough that he and Susan were only ever going to tolerate one another. Susan had made it abundantly clear that he, Noel, wasn't a patch on Kylie's brother-in-law, an accountant who didn't come with the baggage of an ex-wife and daughter. 'We don't need a baby to keep us together,' he finished, then cursed himself inwardly when Kylie's eyes brimmed over again.

'You don't want it!' she sobbed. 'You're no better than the boys' dads! As soon as Liam was born, off Russell scarpered with that twenty-year-old blonde piece who worked with him at the call centre, no screaming baby to keep him awake at night! You don't want the responsibility, and you won't want me when the baby comes!'

He shook his head vehemently and started to move towards her, but she whipped the tea towel through the air at him. 'Get out!' she screeched.

'Kylie, I don't mean…' He caught the damp tea towel and twisted it between his hands, searching for the right words.

She gulped hard. 'Go and pack your bags. Get out of my house,' she hissed.

Noel looked at her helplessly and reached towards her. But she had already spun round and was marching out of the kitchen. On the threshold of the sitting room she said, without turning, 'If you're quick, you can be out before the boys get in. Best if I explain to them on my own.' She slammed the door. Seconds later the *EastEnders* theme filled the house.

Noel has never watched the soap since, though he'd hardly missed an episode over the previous twenty years. Even now, six months after leaving Kylie's, he finds himself grabbing the remote to mute the TV. The sleek brunette presenter is turning her attention to an *EastEnders* actress who's starring in this season's *Strictly Come Dancing.*

His mobile beeps again. Two calls in ten minutes and it's only just gone eight. He glances at the screen and sees that it isn't his sister. Maybe it's one of his regular customers, one of the old folk who rely on him to do all kinds of odd jobs. Or maybe – and Noel feels his heart beat faster under his striped navy and white polo shirt – maybe this is the mysterious Master calling? As soon as the thought crosses his mind, he dismisses it. There's no chance, surely, that the Master of the radiant Being would contact him by mobile. Even so, he picks up the phone and presses the green icon.

'Reilly's Repairs.'

'No job too small, right?' a woman asks without preamble.

Noel places the accent as Caribbean. He is immediately assailed by another memory, this one of the last family holiday which he, Gemma and Jade had spent together in Jamaica.

'A once in a lifetime holiday,' Gemma had said triumphantly, after they'd booked the package deal at the travel agents with their friends Damian and Mandy. They were celebrating the booking over lunch at the local Italian restaurant. The holiday cost an eye-watering amount, and Noel had been tempted to suggest that they could ill afford a meal out. But he hadn't wanted to put a dampener on things.

'It'll be so much fun for Jade to have Megan to play with,' Gemma enthused, twirling spaghetti around her fork. 'Why ever didn't we think of it before, going on holiday together?'

At the time, Noel hadn't thought anything about the way she batted her blonde eyelashes at Damian across the table, or how Damian grinned back at her as they clinked their glasses of Prosecco together.

But the memory came back to mock him months later, when he discovered that it wasn't only Jade and Megan who enjoyed playing together in the creamy sands at the James Bond Beach on the north coast of Jamaica. On the fourth morning of the holiday, Gemma had complained of a headache and stayed behind at the hotel. Noel took Jade down to the beach where she was soon digging in the sand with Megan. Mandy was stretched out on a lounger with a paperback, and said Damian had gone off for a walk along the beach. Discovering he'd left his sunglasses behind, Noel went back to the hotel. Mindful of Gemma's headache and thinking that she might be sleeping, he'd crept into their room and disturbed Damian and Gemma in bed together.

'Hello? Hello?'

The woman's voice recalls Noel sharply to the present.

'Yeah. Sorry.' He presses his temple, trying to dispel the memory of that excruciating moment when he realised that his marriage was over. 'How can I help?'

'I have a few things need fixing in my kitchen. A cupboard door, broken handles, some tiling. A leak in the bathroom. A bit of gardening, maybe some painting. Are those the kinds of repairs you help with?'

'Sure.' *Definitely not an assignment from the Master.* 'What's the address?'

The woman gives an address on the estate where Kylie lived. His hand clamps sweatily around the phone.

'You know where I am? You can come today?'

'Um –'

'I'll see you at ten.'

Before Noel has time to reply, she has hung up. He stares at the blank phone screen, thinking about ringing to cancel and sticking with his plan of taking time off. Then he considers how the hours will stretch in front of him with only daytime TV for company. Time to dwell on Kylie. Time to wait for his sister's phone call, or obsess over whether he should make the journey he's been putting off since she rang last Thursday.

There are chores he could do in the house, but he won't get paid for those. Chances are that this woman's odd jobs won't take long, and he'll get some money for doing them. Money that is much needed since he is still paying off the disastrous Caribbean holiday in addition to contributing child support to Jade. Most likely it will do him good to get out of the house where he has been holed up for the weekend, unable to face going out after the turmoil of Friday. He'll have to face Kylie's estate some time. He might as well get the first visit over.

Ninety minutes later, Noel draws up in his battered maroon van outside a compact council house which looks very similar to Kylie's. There's even a blue ceramic pot of autumn flowers on the front patio. Kylie loved growing flowers in her tubs. He couldn't cope with passing her house on the main road through the estate, so he took a circuitous route around the side streets. Even so, his hands are shaking as he switches off the ignition. He takes a few deep breaths to steady himself before climbing out of the van. He locks it and makes his way up the path to the front door.

His customer is evidently looking out for him, and opens the door before he has a chance to knock. She's small and skinny, with short silver curls, and wears a flowery blouse with faded jeans. Bifocals enlarge her dark eyes, which rove over Noel and his van.

'You need to move your van,' she says, by way of greeting. 'Bin day today, and the street is narrow. My neighbour needs to buy a new wing mirror. He left his car out on the road last week. Silly man should have kept it on his drive.' She tuts and nods towards the neighbouring house. Noel sees a red Peugeot with the nearside wing mirror precariously taped on.

'OK.' He half-turns, but she raises a hand.

'First, see what jobs need doing. Follow me.'

He trudges obediently behind her through a narrow hall into the kitchen at the back of the house.

'I would like you to fix the kitchen.'

Noel looks around. At some point, the old-fashioned units have been painted blue. The paint has begun to peel, revealing patches of the original cream underneath. Two drawers have lost their handles. A cupboard door adjacent to an old gas stove is hanging off its hinges. The tiles behind the sink are askew, with two propped roughly into place.

It strikes him that a new kitchen would be the best solution, but perhaps his customer can't afford that. He glances at her, and is disconcerted to find that her large eyes are fixed on him. She is smiling, revealing a row of yellow teeth as uneven as the splashback tiles, with three visible gaps.

'You won't know where to start, will you?'

He thinks back to their phone call. 'Well, I can certainly hang the cupboard door and fix the drawer handles. You mentioned a bit of painting?' He looks up at a damp patch

29

above a cupboard in the corner, and then surveys the walls which are papered with nicotine-stained anaglypta. The faintest smell of stale cigarette smoke lingers in the air, and he suspects it's a while since anyone smoked here.

Unnervingly, the woman seems to read his mind. 'No point decorating when my husband was alive. Chain smoker.'

'Ah.'

'I been too busy to get on with these things,' she elaborates, waving a scrawny arm around. 'He was in the hospice seven months. I visited every day, till he passed eight weeks ago. No time for house maintenance.'

Noel rubs the back of his neck. 'I'm sorry.'

'He is with the Lord,' says the woman. 'Better place than this, huh?'

'Well, yes, I guess so.' The last person Noel heard speak about the Lord was his grandmother, and she died thirty years ago. He wishes he could believe Kylie was now in this 'better place', but he abandoned any faith in God and heaven when he was six. That was the Christmas Eve when he saw his dad creeping into his bedroom dressed in a Santa suit. Faith in God disappeared with his belief in Santa. Nothing has happened since to persuade Noel that the deity is any more real than the legendary Christmas character.

'I still miss him, of course,' the woman says. 'We never spent a night apart in fifty-two years.'

'That's a long time.' He cringes at the inadequacy of his reply.

'There again, he wasn't always a good husband.' Her tone is matter-of-fact.

He fixes his eyes on the damp patch on the ceiling. 'I'm sorry,' he repeats. 'Would you like me to do some painting for you too, Mrs...?'

'Mrs Hinds. You can call me Sonia.' She cocks her head on one side, assessing him.

Noel is reminded of the beady-eyed robin who regularly visits his bird table, and immediately feels guilty. He's been so wrapped up in his misery over the weekend that he hasn't even been out to the yard to top up the seeds. He makes a mental note to do so as soon as he gets home. Meanwhile, his new customer is keen to pursue a line of personal questioning which he could do without.

'Are you married?'

'No. Divorced.'

'Ah. Shame. But you must have a girlfriend, a good-looking man like you?' She begins to laugh, unexpectedly loudly for such a slight woman.

Noel feels colour rush to his cheeks. He stares down at his feet.

'Now I've embarrassed you!' chortles Sonia. 'My daughter, Michelle, she is always saying, "Mum, you ask too many questions."'

'It's OK,' he mumbles, thinking her daughter has a point. 'It's just… I did have a girlfriend, but we split up, and now…' His voice trails off. He can't bring himself to say that Kylie is dead, just like this woman's husband. But unlike Sonia's husband, Kylie didn't live to a decent age. Nor did she have a partner who stuck by her. There is a lump in his throat and he is breathing rapidly, something that has happened several times over the weekend since he learned of Kylie's murder. He digs his fingernails into his palms.

'Now you regret that?' Sonia has stopped laughing, and her voice is unexpectedly gentle.

With an effort, Noel gathers himself. 'Something like that,' he mutters.

'Maybe you could speak to her?'

If only. Noel shakes his head and jiggles the key to the van in the pocket of his jeans. 'I'm sorry,' he says. 'I was going to take some time off this week. Maybe I could come back some other time.'

'No, I am sorry,' replies Sonia instantly. 'I shouldn't pry. I would really appreciate you making a start on these jobs. Since my husband died, and I am at home every day, this kitchen is bugging me. That is why I phoned you early this morning. Besides, where would you go on a day like this?' She gestures towards the window. Rivulets of rain run down it, and it is steaming up on the inside, a tell-tale sign that the double glazing is failing.

Noel glances again round the shabby kitchen, and back at Sonia. He detects anxiety in her expression, and has a sudden intuition that she would appreciate having someone around on this dismal autumn day.

There is somewhere he could go, should go, but being here is an excuse not to make that journey. 'OK. I'll fetch my tools and move the van.'

She brightens. 'Good. Park the van in front of the garage with the green door at the top of the street. That belongs to me. We will have a cup of tea together before you start work.'

'I don't want to put you to any trouble –'

She raises a hand, and he notices her swollen fingers. 'It's no trouble.'

'Well, thank you. About the painting – I could do the ceiling and walls, as well as the units, if you like. I should take a look at that damp patch first. Is your bathroom above it?'

'Yes.' She lifts a battered kettle off the hob and carries it across to the sink. 'Please, take a look. The bathroom is through the door straight in front of you at the top of the stairs.' She laughs suddenly, the same surprisingly loud chortle. 'It doesn't matter if you stumble into the bedrooms by mistake. I have nothing to hide.'

'Right.' Sonia strikes him as very trusting. Had his mother lived to her age, he wouldn't have been happy to think of her letting an unknown tradesman move unaccompanied through her house on his first visit. His chest tightens as he climbs the uncarpeted stairs. Thoughts of his mother lead inevitably to anticipation of his sister's phone call.

All three doors off the landing are ajar. Noel pushes the one opposite and finds himself in a small bathroom. The sanitaryware is an unfashionable dusky pink. He swallows hard. It's the same colour as the sanitaryware in his childhood home. The fragrance is familiar too. He spots a tin of talcum powder on the corner of the bath, picks it up and reads the label. Lily of the valley. His mother's favourite.

He inhales the scent, the scent of his mother. He remembers saving up his pocket money to buy her some of the powder for her birthday, and pictures himself sitting on the edge of his bed unlocking the green elephant money box to count out his coins.

He hadn't needed the money after all.

Noel drops the tin of talc onto the tiled floor as if it burns like the coil of black hair in his bathroom earlier. Puffs of powder rise up like smoke. He coughs and flings himself out of the bathroom and down the stairs.

Halfway down, he trips.

Chapter three

Sonia cries out when she hears the crash. She rushes out of the kitchen and claps her hand to her mouth at the sight of Noel spreadeagled across the lower half of the stairs.

Dazed, he stares up at her. After a moment, he places his hands on the edge of the step beneath him.

'Take your time,' she urges.

He gingerly levers himself into a sitting position and winces.

'Have you hurt yourself?'

He rubs his right flank. 'Here,' he groans, 'and my shoulder.' The lily of the valley scent is still strong in his nostrils. He thinks he might throw up.

Sonia sniffs. 'What is that smell?' She peers up the stairs behind Noel and frowns. 'Is it my powder?'

Noel drops his gaze to Sonia's thick-soled burgundy slippers. 'I dropped it. I'll get you some more.'

'Don't worry.' Sonia hesitates. 'I heard a thud just before you ran down the stairs. Was that the talc?'

'Yes. I'm sorry. I'll clean up the mess.' He rolls his shoulder experimentally. He is relieved to find that it rotates fully, despite the pain.

'That doesn't matter. Did you find the leak?'

'Um, no, I –' He flounders, then starts when a whistle pierces the air.

Sonia turns towards the kitchen. 'The kettle. Tea will be good for you after your shock.'

'I think it's better if I leave. I can get some tea at home.'

'You shouldn't drive yet,' she calls, above the shrieking kettle. 'You are in shock. A tumble like that, you're lucky you weren't badly injured.'

Noel grabs the handrail and pulls himself to his feet. His legs are weak. Sonia must have removed the kettle from the hob since the whistling has stopped, but his ears still ring with the shrill sound. He traipses into the kitchen where he leans against the door jamb, shaky from the fall.

Sonia is placing the lid on a china teapot. It's the same teapot his mother owned, commemorating the 1981 wedding of Prince Charles and Lady Diana Spencer.

'Are you OK?' Sonia picks up a wooden spoon from a saucer and stirs something simmering on the hob. It looks like some kind of broth, and smells delicious. 'You should have waited for me to help you.'

Noel takes a deep breath. 'I'm all right.' He manages a smile. 'Like you say, just the shock.' *Not just of falling, but of these connections with Mum.* It could be imagination, but he thinks he can still smell the talcum powder mingling with the odour of the broth. He pinches his nostrils.

Sonia is watching him intently and he shivers. He has the oddest feeling that she senses something of his inner turmoil. She turns and reaches up into a corner cupboard. 'Is it the shock that's making you shiver? Or something else?' She takes out cups and saucers, a sugar bowl and milk jug.

Noel doesn't answer immediately, surprised how tempted he is to tell her everything, this elderly woman who is little more than a stranger. For a fleeting moment he imagines telling her about Kylie, about his mother, about the decision he needs to make before his sister phones again, even about his strange experience by the river. He shakes his head to dispel the ridiculous idea.

'It must be the shock.' He looks over at the condensation on the window and aims for a jocular tone. 'I mean, there's no way I could be cold in here, is there?'

'My daughter always complains how hot it is.' There is a note of disappointment in her voice at his superficial response, but her expression is bland as she gestures towards a small table to the right of the door. 'Please, take a seat.'

Noel sinks down onto a dated padded dining chair. His hostess carries over the teapot and sets it down on a ceramic stand. She hums softly to herself as she retrieves a carton of milk from the fridge. He considers saying that she needn't trouble with the jug, that milk from the carton will be fine, but he can see that she is enjoying herself. She brings the jug and sugar bowl across, then the cups and saucers.

The crockery matches the teapot. A young Lady Diana Spencer and youthful Prince of Wales stare blankly up at him. Noel looks away and surveys the damp patch on the ceiling. From his truncated visit to the bathroom, he suspects there is a leak below the bath. He decides to go back up there after his tea to clear up the powder. Watching Sonia pull out a drawer missing its handle to find teaspoons, he feels ashamed that he was going to leave her to deal with the mess and charge out of her house without any explanation.

Sonia gives the tea a stir before pouring it out. She passes a cup to him, then sits down and smiles across at him. 'It's good to have company,' she says. 'I made tea every afternoon for my husband before he went into the hospice. I don't enjoy making it for myself. Too much trouble, you know?'

Noel nods. He does know. He had enjoyed sharing the cooking with both Gemma and Kylie. Since he left Kylie's, he has lived mainly off convenience food and takeaways.

She slides the milk jug and sugar bowl towards him. 'Please, help yourself.'

'Thanks.' He pours a splash of milk into his cup, then two teaspoons of sugar. He studiously avoids looking at the royal couple emblazoned on the tea set.

Sonia adds milk and one sugar to her drink. The kitchen is quiet apart from the hum of the fridge. Noel glances towards the window. The rain has subsided to a gentle drizzle. He takes a few sips of the hot sweet tea.

Sonia nods approvingly. 'You see, you feel better already, don't you?'

'I do.' He stretches his legs out.

'Such a small thing,' she says musingly. 'A shared cup of tea. My daughter, she never has time. Always in a hurry.'

'That's a shame,' says Noel sincerely. Sonia's calmness is very restful. He realises he is beginning to relax for the first time since he heard of Kylie's murder.

'Ah, well.' She contemplates her cup. 'She works hard. She has a few cleaning jobs, and fits them around her work in the residential home on the hill, the one with the dementia unit. Freshfields.'

He sits up straight, nerves jangling. The sudden movement sends a spike of pain up his right flank. He grimaces. Kylie worked at Freshfields. Sonia's daughter will know her, know about the murder. He gulps some tea. The hot liquid burns the back of his throat.

'I wish she could find other work, but she says she has no time to retrain. Michelle did well at school, and was thinking about teaching. Then she got involved with a boy.' Sonia sighs. 'He left her after she fell pregnant at eighteen. A common tale.'

Noel opens the two buttons of his polo shirt. The heat in the small kitchen has become suffocating and his underarms are damp. Immersed in her story, his hostess seems oblivious to his discomfort.

'My husband was furious, but he calmed down when the child was born. A beautiful baby boy.' Her face softens, and Noel catches a glimpse of the pretty young woman she had once been. 'They lived here with us until she met another man.' She takes a long draught of tea.

He wipes his clammy forehead and inhales deeply now that the subject has moved away from Freshfields.

Sonia wraps her hands with their swollen knuckles around her cup. 'They got married. Six years ago, Michelle had a second child. Another boy, Joshua. They were very happy.' She pauses.

Noel notes the past tense and prepares to hear of another broken relationship.

Sonia bites her lip, her silver head bowed over her cup before she continues. 'Then one night, the baby was running a temperature. He wouldn't settle. Michelle sent her husband to the late-night chemist in town for some medicine. He parked by The Bell Inn. You know it?'

He nods. It was his old boss's favourite pub, and they would often meet for a pint there on a Friday evening to plan the next week's building work. Noel has missed the ritual since his boss retired and he set up on his own.

'My son-in-law got caught up in a drunken brawl outside the pub that night. He suffered terrible head injuries. He never recovered consciousness, and died in hospital three days later.' Sonia unlaces her hands and drinks more tea, staring towards the window.

Noel catches his breath. The words 'Wrong place, wrong time' form in his mind. But they seem ridiculously trite, just as they did all those years ago when his mother died, and he'd overheard their next-door neighbour murmuring them to the woman across the road when he cycled by. He pushes the unwelcome thought away, focusing on what Sonia has told him.

He has a vague memory that the incident happened during the Caribbean holiday that ended his marriage. He was so wrapped up in his matrimonial turmoil when he returned home that he barely registered the news, although he remembers being shocked that such a thing should have taken place in this quiet market town. Neither he nor his friends had known any of those involved. Now, contemplating the mother-in-law of the dead man whose family had been torn apart by the tragedy, his lack of engagement strikes him as complacent, even callous.

'No one was ever charged in the end, were they?' he ventures, setting his empty cup down in the saucer.

Sonia turns her head towards him, her eyes dark wells of sadness behind the large bifocals. 'No. Two men were arrested, but they were soon released. No charges were brought.' She compresses her lips into a thin line. 'My husband believed that if our son-in-law had been a white man, the investigation would have been more thorough.'

Noel shifts in his chair. 'What did you think?'

She looks down and twists a fabric button on her floral blouse. 'I don't know,' she says wearily. 'All I know is that a baby lost his father and a woman lost her husband. All for the sake of a bottle of medicine.'

Noel rubs his temple, aware of pressure building inside his head. Blood pounds in his ears and his breathing is ragged. Here in the widow's kitchen, he is overwhelmed by a sense of grief which he has never known before. It is a grief that extends beyond his own personal sorrow, stretching back across the years to the death of his mother when he was a boy, and erupting again with the recent shocking loss of Kylie. Sonia's story has awakened in him a profound insight into the sadness and suffering in other lives. Needless sadness and suffering, caused by terrible wrongdoing in the cases of both Kylie and Sonia's son-in-law. He lowers his head into his hands and closes his eyes, hoping that this might calm the throbbing in his head.

He feels as though he is pitching forward into darkness, and is powerless to stop himself. He hears again the words of the Being from the mysterious vision which left him in such confusion. *You have been chosen to right the wrongs in this place, to shine as light in the darkness.'* The words reverberate in his mind until he is roused by another voice calling his name.

Opening his eyes, Noel finds himself face down on the kitchen floor, the lino cold beneath his forehead. He groans.

'Thank God.' Sonia places a hand beneath his elbow and helps him to his feet. He sinks back into the chair, rubbing his nose.

'I hope you haven't broken it,' she says.

'What happened?' he asks groggily.

'I think you fainted. Maybe an after-effect of the tumble.' She looks at him with concern. 'Let me pour you some more tea.'

He doesn't argue, and nods when she offers to add milk and sugar.

She sits back down. 'Are you sure you're all right?'

'Yes.' Noel is still shaky, but wants to allay her concern. 'I'm sorry to have been so much trouble,' he says, reaching for his cup.

'Ah.' She waves her hands dismissively. 'I am sorry if the story of my family tragedy upset you.'

'It was a terrible thing that happened.'

'Yes, and that wasn't all. It was the spring after Jonathan died that my husband was diagnosed with cancer. I always wondered if the stress contributed. My daughter thinks that is just me being fanciful. But who knows how the emotions and body are connected?'

She considers him with her penetrating gaze. Noel bends his head over his cup and drinks the stewed tea. He wishes his hands would stop trembling. He replaces his cup carefully in the saucer and folds his hands in his lap.

'I don't know,' he murmurs.

She raises a black eyebrow threaded with silver and sips her tea delicately. Silence blankets them. Noel stares down at his clasped hands, suddenly exhausted.

It is Sonia who speaks first. 'It's true that there is a time to keep silence, and a time to speak, isn't it?'

Her words echo in a distant chamber of his mind, like the forgotten words of a once familiar song. 'I suppose so,' he says uncertainly. He touches his nose, which is beginning to swell.

'I haven't spoken of these things for many months,' she goes on. 'It would only make my daughter sad. I think she keeps herself so busy to avoid facing it all. Not long after her husband was killed, Michelle began to take the cleaning jobs. We suggested she come back here, but there wasn't really enough room. Not with the baby, as well as her older son who was no longer a little boy. There are only two bedrooms. Maybe we could have adapted the sitting room for her eldest, but she said it was time she stood on her own two feet. Ah, well.'

Sonia stands and stretches, gritting her teeth. 'Arthritis,' she explains. 'I shouldn't sit too long.' She limps over to the window. The condensation is clearing. Outside the rain has stopped and the sky is pearl grey. Sonia's voice too is brighter when she says, 'My friend is here. Come, see the collared dove who keeps me company.'

Noel rises and joins her, circling his injured shoulder. A wooden bird table stands in the small back garden. The grass would have benefited from a final cut before the winter, and the bird table is badly in need of a coat of preservative. A grey bird is pecking on the tray. When it lifts its head between bites, Noel sees the distinctive black collar on its neck. After a while, it finishes feeding and rises on to the roof of the table. Unmoving, it stares towards them.

Sonia clasps her hands in front of her small, sagging bosom. 'Isn't she beautiful?' she whispers. 'Her eyes are red, you know. One day in the summer, when I was watering the tubs, she flew on to the fence. I hardly dared to breathe. We looked at one another for what felt like a long time, but was probably only seconds. That's when I saw that her eyes are red. Then she flapped her wings and was gone. Whoosh.' She parts her hands, smiling a little sadly, and looks up at Noel. With her head tilted to one side, she bears an uncanny resemblance to the bird.

'How do you know she's female?' he asks.

She chuckles. 'I don't,' she admits. 'Just a feeling. I don't even know if she is the same bird who visits, or if different ones come and go. Two days ago, three doves arrived together. I realised then that I can't distinguish between them. I like to think when one pays me a solo visit that she is my regular companion. Perhaps you think that is foolish, an old woman's sentimentality?'

'No, I don't,' he says instantly. 'There's a robin comes to my bird table. I'm sure it's always the same one.'

'Ah, but robins are solitary and territorial, aren't they?'

'I guess so. I must put food out for him when I get home. I've neglected him these last few days.'

'Have you been away?' Sonia gazes out at the dove who has started to groom her feathers.

Noel shuffles his feet. 'No. I've just... had my mind on other things.'

'Ah.' Sonia continues to look out of the window, leaving a pause which Noel doesn't fill. The bird beats her wings and flies over the low fence, settling on the roof of the terraced council house behind the garden. They watch her in silence for a moment. Then Sonia says, 'Your tea will be cold now. Would you like me to make a fresh pot?'

He hesitates. 'I should be making a move. And I still need to clear up the bathroom.'

'Ah. The talc.' She moves across to the kettle. 'If you want to tell me something about what happened up there, what led you to rush down the stairs as if the hounds of hell were after you, please feel free. Besides, I think you should rest a little longer, after the faint.'

Noel swallows thickly. His legs feel wobbly again, and he rests his hand on the counter to steady himself.

'I am not prying,' Sonia continues, running water into the kettle. 'Sometimes it helps to talk. You have listened to my story. If it will help you to share yours, I am very happy to listen.'

He regards the dove perched on the rooftop of the house behind Sonia's garden. The bird lowers her head, and he has the strange fancy that she is encouraging him to stay.

'Another cup of tea would be great, thanks,' he hears himself say.

The dove flaps her wings and soars into the sky. Noel watches until she disappears from view. Then he settles back into the old dining chair and waits for the kettle to boil.

Chapter four

Four hours later, Noel is driving slowly along Shakespeare Road in Oldford, his palms clammy on the steering wheel. Parked vehicles line both sides of the street, hampering his progress, but he's in no hurry to reach his destination. Shakespeare Road is the same mean street of red-brick terraces he remembers. Maybe even meaner, he thinks, as he pulls up at a pelican crossing to give way to an old man wheeling a dilapidated maroon and grey checked shopping trolley. Peering through the streaks on the windscreen left by a failing wiper blade, he sees cracked pavements scattered with litter, weed-infested front yards strewn with overflowing refuse sacks and paint peeling off doors and window frames. The lights change to green and he crawls along, passing three houses with boarded up windows. Each is advertised 'To Let'.

You'd have to be desperate to move down here, he thinks, but then reminds himself that the neighbourhood where he rents in Trentby is hardly an improvement. Not that he had much choice when he left Kylie's, with finances tight. The realisation that twenty-five years after leaving the squalor of Shakespeare Road he's wound up in a street of comparable scruffiness in a similarly depressed post-industrial market town thirty miles away does nothing to lift his mood.

A skinny tabby cat shoots out in front of the van. Noel stamps on his brakes instinctively, without checking his mirror, and incurs a beep from the car behind. The cat dives under a black car with a dented boot parked on the other side of the street.

44

Noel finds he is shaking after the near collision. He tries to calm himself by chanting the names of the side roads he is passing: Marlow Street, Keats Road, Tennyson Street, Wordsworth Street. Less poetic-looking streets would be hard to find. Not that he'd known anything about poetry when he came down here as a little boy, delivering newspapers with his dad. He liked it just being the two of them, 'men together', his dad used to say, and it was a relief to get away from the delicate baby sister who never seemed to stop crying. His mother seemed to have forgotten his existence once the squalling infant burst into their lives two months earlier than expected. Before that they'd been everything to one another. He'd never minded when his dad called him 'Mummy's boy'.

Noel squeezes the van into a space a few doors down from his childhood home and switches off the engine. He takes some deep breaths before climbing out. A bus is lumbering up the street towards him, its indicator lamp flashing for the stop opposite the house. It's still the 34, the same number as when he was a boy. The bus trundles past as Noel counts out the paces to his childhood home, head down against the driving rain. His heart thumps against his rib cage as he pushes open the rusting black metal gate.

He raises his forefinger to the doorbell. This is it, no turning back now. Besides, he's promised Sonia he'll see this through, after telling her that he left home when he was sixteen. He hadn't fully explained why, concentrating on his shock at losing his mother when he was a small boy, and how the family had struggled to come to terms with her death. The knowledge that she is praying for him is oddly comforting, although the offer took him by surprise. There's a lot about the last few days that has been surprising, not least the weird experience by the river. *Time enough to think about that later.* He squares his shoulders when he sees a shadow moving towards him through the familiar diamond-patterned glass inner door.

'It's you.' The woman who opens the door flicks green almond-shaped eyes over him, then looks past him to the street. The eyes are the best feature of her prematurely lined face. The scrawny adolescent sister he left behind has grown into a skinny woman. She reminds Noel of an underfed cat, not unlike the one he nearly ran over. 'You could've walked in, you know. Everyone else does. We keep the door unlocked for the nurses.'

'Oh.' He swallows. 'It's good to see you, Carol.' He realises how false the words must sound and chews his lower lip.

Carol twists her thin mouth and arches plucked eyebrows. 'Is it really? Well, you could've seen me any time in the last twenty-five years if you'd wanted.'

Claws out already. What else did he expect? He changes tack. 'How is he?'

'I told you on the phone, didn't I? Dying. Not long now, the nurses say. Maybe today, maybe tomorrow. Who knows? He's hung on longer than expected. Like he's waiting for something.' She stares at him hard before adding, 'Or someone.'

Noel drops his head and rubs his shoulder. The hour's drive has intensified the pain from his tumble down Sonia's stairs. He has a sudden insight of what it must have been like in the trenches of the First World War, knowing that the enemy was so close, waiting for the next round of battle. The unswept doorstep of his childhood home could be no man's land.

'You coming in or what?' She turns on her heel.

Noel closes the front door and plunges into enemy territory. A weight in his chest is making it difficult for him to breathe. He casts a glance up the staircase in front of him as he traipses behind his sister, remembering his childhood bedroom. Carol passes through a frosted acrylic door to the right of the narrow hall. He remains on the threshold, gazing down at the moss-green carpet he recognises, worn thin over the years.

'Visitor, Dad,' says Carol.

Noel surveys the dated furniture. There is a teak sideboard cluttered with newspapers and envelopes together with a matching drop-leaf dining table and chairs. The table used to be left up, but it has been folded to make way for a medi-bed. A plastic bag hangs over the foot of the bed. Bile rises in his throat as he realises that the small amount of rust-coloured liquid inside is urine. He averts his eyes quickly, but the faint odour of ammonia lodges in his nostrils, along with the musty smell of damp. Aware of his pulse throbbing in his neck, he finally looks at the man lying on the bed.

Slowly the man turns his head and gazes at Noel with eyes that protrude from his wasted yellowing face. He takes a deep shuddering breath. 'You came,' he croaks.

Noel barely manages a nod. He wouldn't have recognised his once stocky father in the shrivelled figure outlined beneath the pale-blue cellular blanket.

'Sit down.' Carol points to a battered teak dining chair placed alongside the bed.

Noel's stomach lurches. He'll stand all day rather than sit on that. He unzips his jacket, but doesn't remove it, although the room is uncomfortably warm.

'I'm fine, thanks. Long journey.'

'Never heard thirty miles called a long journey,' sniffs his sister, 'though it might as well be 3,000.'

He doesn't rise to the bait. Is it possible she doesn't remember? She was out of the house that last time, the night he left for good. She had a friend, Jessica, whose mother would often invite her to stay over after school on Fridays. Jessica's mother worked in the library where Noel used to do his homework on Saturday mornings. One time she'd asked him if everything was all right at home. He'd hesitated before he nodded. The hesitation was a giveaway, and he remembers the sympathy in her eyes when she told him that he knew where to find her if he ever needed help.

Noel had never gone to the library again.

Now their father is struggling to speak. Finally, he gets the words out. 'Cup of tea?' The ghastly attempt at a smile in Noel's direction reveals the last two brown teeth in his upper gum. The sick man rolls his eyes towards Carol.

'Forgot I'm playing mother,' she says ungraciously, then claps her hand to her mouth as her father screws up his face. 'Nurse'll be here soon, Dad.' She glances at Noel. 'He needs more morphine.'

Noel nods, wondering if it hasn't occurred to her that the dying man's pain might not only be physical. The word 'mother' had become as unmentionable as any four-letter word in the household after her death.

Whatever is going through Carol's mind, her attitude seems to have softened. 'I'll get you some tea. How do you take it?'

'Spot of milk and two sugars. Thanks.' Being alone with his father even for five minutes hadn't been on his agenda when he came for this last visit. He steps back into the hall to allow his sister to pass. When she closes the door into the kitchen, beads of perspiration break out on his forehead.

'Come here, son,' his father gasps, lifting a skeletal hand with an effort. It seems impossible that it could ever have been the heavy fist of Noel's memory. And 'son'! His father used to call him that when he was a small boy before that terrible day. Noel treads slowly across the room to stand midway along the bed.

Another bus clatters down the street. The old silver-edged mirror, green-spotted with mildew, shakes above the two-bar electric fire as the bus goes by. Noel's chest tightens.

'Still the 34?' He knows the comment is banal, but is desperate to avoid silence.

Another spasm of pain creases his father's face. After it passes, he nods. 'Aye. Still the 34.' Then, with even more effort, 'You don't like that bus, do you?'

'No. I never use the bus.'

His father licks dry, pale lips. 'You know why, don't you?'

Noel shakes his head, bewildered. Whatever he'd expected from this conversation, he hadn't thought that buses would feature.

'You've forgotten.'

Forgotten what? Since Noel came into the house, he has been assailed by memories, none of them good. Most involve him cowering away from his father when he arrived home drunk from the pub. His blue eyes would be bloodshot when he came charging up the stairs to Noel's room and set about his son without any provocation. Noel had tried staying out once, when Carol was round at Jessica's, but the beating he got when he came home the next day was even worse than usual.

He had coped with the punches and kicks, but on that last occasion his father had hurled a chair identical to the one by the medi-bed into his face. Even at sixteen, Noel had been no match for his father. He'd packed a few essentials in his rucksack that night, blood dripping everywhere from his broken nose, before going to the hospital. His one regret had been leaving Carol behind, but his dad had never laid a finger on her, and he had hoped for the best. He'd become a sofa surfer before the term was even invented. He touches his nose now, its contours swollen from the contact with Sonia's kitchen floor when he fainted.

The phone rings, and Noel hears Carol's 'Hello?' on the living-room extension.

His father continues, taking laboured breaths between staccato sentences. 'It was the 34 that killed her. Your mum. They said you darted out across the road in front of it. She ran after you. Remember?'

Noel's heart is hammering as if it will explode. He shakes his head. Outside, the bus thunders on its way.

'Day like today. Miserable, grey. October school holidays. The doctor said you'd blocked it out. Dr Leach. Always had a pipe, remember him?'

'Yes,' says Noel slowly. He stares into the antique mirror, summoning his lost memories, and has a clear image of Dr

Leach in his green tweed jacket sitting behind a large mahogany desk drawing on his pipe. Noel's coat would smell of tobacco for days after a visit to his surgery. He has dreamed of Dr Leach over the years, and always woken fighting for breath. The scent of tobacco has nauseated him for as long as he can remember. His father's next words explain why.

'Used to be sick after you'd seen him. I only took you four or five times. Didn't help. I had my hands full with you and Carol and the shop. Got too much for me.'

The latter is an understatement Noel doesn't need to hear.

'Then there was the guilt.' His father's voice has dropped to a hoarse whisper.

Noel finds his own voice, trying to piece it together. 'You mean, my guilt, because if I'd not run out, Mum wouldn't...?'

His father's body jerks under the blanket and he gives a low bestial moan. 'Where's that nurse?'

'Carol said she's on her way.'

The dying man closes his eyes and falls quiet. Just as Noel wonders if his father is sinking into unconsciousness, he sees his bloodless lips move.

Noel leans over the bed. 'What is it?'

His father's eyes open. They are shining with unshed tears. The monster of Noel's nightmares is dissolving in front of him.

'Not yours. Mine.' Seeing the blankness in Noel's expression, he gasps out, 'My guilt.' Noel drops his gaze to the blanket covering his father's withered body. His father is plucking at it with his bony fingers.

Carol comes back into the room. 'Eileen rang, Dad. She's on her way.'

Noel frowns. 'Eileen?' The name rings a distant bell.

His father's hand becomes still on the blanket. He balls it into a fist.

'Eileen Baxter. She came by last week after hearing how ill Dad was. She said she was one of Mum's best friends. I don't remember her. Do you?'

Eileen Baxter. The name flashes neon lights inside Noel's head. He kneads his temple, which is throbbing like it did in Sonia's kitchen earlier. Suddenly he knows why he hates buses, why his father is talking about guilt. His legs begin to shake uncontrollably. He drops down into the hated chair.

'What's wrong?' Carol's voice is sharp.

Noel glances at his father. His eyes are screwed up in pain. Noel thinks he shakes his head.

Noel inhales deeply, gripping his hands together so the knuckles are white. 'Nothing,' he says tonelessly. 'Cup of tea would be good, if the kettle's boiled.'

Their father lolls back against the pillows. Carol grunts and retreats to the kitchen.

Noel rests his pounding head in his hands. There'll be time enough to tell Carol later, once their father has gone. Time enough to tell her that Eileen Baxter was there on the bus, the 34, that dull October afternoon long ago. Noel had been trailing along in the wake of his mother and the navy pushchair. Carol was inside, wailing as usual.

Noel remembers looking across the road when the green bus came down. He wished he was on it, going somewhere away from his mother and sister. He'd like to go with his dad, 'men together'. He'd been hoping his dad would take him somewhere that Wednesday afternoon, which was half-day closing at the shop. But his dad had disappeared after lunch, muttering about an errand in town.

As Noel looked across the street, the bus drew level with him at the red light. It was as though he'd conjured his dad up, because there he was halfway down the bus. Next to him was Mum's friend, Eileen.

Noel's dad had his arm wrapped round Eileen's shoulder. As the little boy watched, he saw his dad kiss Eileen on the lips, long and deep, the way he used to kiss Mum before Carol came along.

Noel hared off down the street, not understanding what he had seen, intent only on reaching the bus and his dad. The lights changed and the bus moved off towards the stop outside the clinic where his mum was taking Carol. Noel ran faster, desperate to reach the stop before the bus. He heard his mum shout his name but ignored her. He plunged into the road. The bus was coming faster than he expected. He tumbled over the kerb on to the opposite pavement just in time. Behind him a screech of brakes from the bus was followed by a loud thud.

The next thing Noel remembers is a piercing shriek of a child breaking the uncanny silence of the previously busy street. He knew the child was Carol, even though she was screaming louder than he'd ever heard her scream before. The traffic was at a standstill. Motorists had turned off their engines.

In the stream of people climbing out of the bus, Noel saw his father, his face white, his voice urgent. 'What are you doing here, son? Where's Mum?'

Noel turned his head to look back up the street. People were gathering around some kind of bundle a few yards in front of the bus. Between their feet Noel saw a flash of turquoise, the same colour as his mum's mac.

Then a woman who lived up their street, Mrs Johnson, was standing in front of them. When she spoke, her voice was shaky. Noel wondered why she was crying. 'Oh, Mr Reilly, I am so very, very sorry.'

The rest is a blank, although Noel is sure Eileen wasn't with them on the street. And he is certain he never saw her again afterwards.

'Here you are.' Carol plonks a mug of tea on the table, recalling him to the present. 'So, do you remember her? Eileen Baxter?'

Noel turns his head and meets his father's eyes. 'I remember her.'

Gathering all his strength, the old man raises his wasted body as best he can, then gasps out, 'It was the 34 that did for her. Your mum. And I blamed you. It got worse as time went on. Because I couldn't face what I'd done. Me and Eileen. You know.'

'I know.'

His father closes his eyes and sinks back on to the pillows with a sigh. Noel takes hold of his skeletal hand.

'What are you talking about?'

Carol's tone is harsh, but Noel hears uncertainty too. With a pang, he remembers the frightened little girl who followed him around the house like a lost lamb in the weeks after their mother died. He looks up at her and mouths, 'Later.'

She glowers at him. Noel thinks she is about to start an argument, when their father's stertorous breathing halts. They both jerk their heads towards him.

Noel grips his hand more tightly. 'Dad?' he asks, the name clumsy on his lips, as if he's trying to speak a foreign language.

There is no reply, just one long, rattling breath.

Carol steps forward and lays a hand gently against their father's cheek. 'I think he's gone,' she whispers. She moves away from the bed and lowers herself wearily into the dining chair by the table. 'I knew he was waiting for you.' She takes a tissue from her jeans pocket and dabs her eyes.

Noel releases his father's cold hand and bows his head.

Brother and sister sit in silence until a squeal of brakes outside announces the arrival of the 34 bus carrying Eileen Baxter.

Noel is instantly on his feet. 'I'll go.'

An old woman has her hand raised to the doorbell when he opens the front door. She is dressed in a cherry anorak and holds an umbrella of the same shade above her head. There's just enough daylight left for Noel to see that her wispy hair is tinted pink. Her pencilled eyebrows are the same shade.

She scans his face, then takes a step back. 'It's Noel, isn't it?'

'Yes.' He holds her gaze, and does nothing to keep the hardness out of his tone. 'And you're Eileen Baxter.'

'That's right.' She runs her tongue over coral lips. 'You're the spit of your dad. Slimmer than he was, though.' She looks past him into the dark hall. 'How is he?'

'He died a few minutes ago,' he says coldly.

The old woman gasps and claps her free hand to her mouth, the umbrella wobbling above her. 'Then I'm too late.' Her voice quavers. 'Can I – can I see him?'

Noel is about to refuse, when his attention is caught by a bird swooping from the sky. It lands on the roof of the terraced house opposite, illuminated by the streetlight. He recognises it is a collared dove, like the one in Sonia's garden. The bird turns its head to the left and Noel spots a magpie perched on a chimney pot two houses along. The dove swivels its head back so that it is gazing straight ahead. He has the odd thought that both birds are looking on with interest at the encounter taking place across the street.

He shakes his head at himself. He's obviously losing it after the tumultuous events of the last few days.

Eileen Baxter misinterprets the movement. 'Please, just for a minute? I'd like to say goodbye. Your dad and I were' – she ducks her head beneath the umbrella – 'good friends once.'

Noel contemplates her for a moment, this old woman who had an affair with his dad more than thirty years ago. He wonders what has led her to come back at the end of his father's life. Maybe she still had feelings for him, even if his dad had cut her off when his mother was killed beneath the wheels of the 34 bus that day? Noel's stomach clenches at the thought. He hears Carol emerge behind him into the hall and flick on the light.

Eileen lifts her head. There's no mistaking the plea in her eyes.

He finds himself stepping backwards. 'Come in.'

Chapter five

Eileen shakes raindrops from her umbrella and leaves it upturned behind the front door before following Noel into the house. He glances at Carol, who is standing by the rear inner door that leads to the living room and kitchen. The unforgiving naked bulb in the hall emphasises her pallor and the incipient crow's feet at the corners of her red-rimmed eyes.

Noel looks down at the threadbare carpet, thinking of what she must have been through, caring for their dying father over the past months. 'Mrs Baxter wants to see Dad,' he says, not sure how much his sister heard of the conversation.

Eileen pauses behind Noel. 'I'm so sorry for your loss, duck.' She raises a tentative hand towards Carol.

Pretending she hasn't noticed, Carol steps quickly out of reach into the living room. 'Thanks. Can I get you some tea?' Her tone is brusque.

'That's kind. Milk and one sugar please.'

Noel turns into the front room where his father's corpse lies on the medi-bed. The room feels uncomfortably close, and the current of air flowing in during his brief doorstep exchange with Eileen has failed to dispel the malodorous whiff of ammonia. He finally removes his bomber jacket and drapes it over the back of the dining chair he had been sitting on before Eileen arrived.

He has a dim recollection of his grandmother speaking years ago of opening the window in a room where someone had passed to let their spirit out. He is unsure what he thinks about that, but opens the small upper window of the bay anyway. A movement outside catches his eye. A dove has settled on the low brick wall that fronts the row of terraced houses. It faces Noel, its head cocked on one side. He wonders if it is the same bird that occupied the rooftop opposite.

There is a wheezy cough in the room behind him. Hairs rise on the back of his neck. He spins round, thinking for an unnerving moment that the cough came from his father. Eileen is standing by the medi-bed, her hand to her mouth as she coughs again. She smooths a strand of wispy white hair from his father's creased forehead. 'I'm sorry I missed you, Ron,' she whispers. She looks over at Noel. 'Can I have two minutes with him?'

He hesitates, but finds himself unable to refuse when he sees the tears in her hazel eyes. 'Sure.' He makes his way through to the kitchen where his sister is standing by the kettle.

'A watched pot never boils,' he smiles. 'Do you remember Gran saying that?'

Carol's eyes narrow. 'No. I was only five when she died.'

'Sorry. I forgot.'

'Yeah, well.' She opens a brown plastic caddy, extracts a teabag and drops it into a ceramic mug decorated with two blue flowers.

The mug strikes Noel as the most cheerful item he has seen in the house.

'You remember Eileen Baxter, don't you?' asks his sister.

He walks over to the sink and stares through the window into the back yard, shadowy in the gathering gloom. 'Yes,' he says quietly, his back to her.

'So, what's the story?'

He waits for the kettle to boil. 'Nothing much. She was around back then, when you were tiny.' He keeps his voice light. 'Shall I take Eileen her tea while you ring the doctor's? They'll need to send someone out, won't they?'

Carol sloshes water over the teabag. 'Yes. Best if I ring since they don't know you, isn't it?' She bangs the kettle down on the base.

There's no mistaking the venom in her voice. She stirs in milk and a spoonful of sugar so vigorously that she slops tea on to the dated laminate worktop. From her stifled sob, he realises she is crying again. After a moment's hesitation he places a hand awkwardly on her thin shoulder. She shakes it off as if it stings.

'Sorry,' he mutters. 'I'll take the tea.'

He pauses on the threshold of the front room when he hears Eileen speaking softly.

'I should have told you the other day, shouldn't I? I wanted to tell you how sorry I was about Ann too, but –'

Noel holds his breath at the sound of his mother's name. Then there is a thud, and he erupts into the room.

Eileen spins round, eyes wide with fright, hand clutching her throat. 'Did you see it? The bird?'

'What bird?'

She points a shaking finger towards the window. 'It looked like a magpie. Hard to tell in the dark. It flew right at the window.'

Noel strides across the room, heedless of the brown drips he leaves in his wake. He sets the mug down on the folded table and looks outside. The darkness has deepened in the ten minutes he has been in the kitchen, but the silhouette of the dove is clear.

'There's a dove on the wall,' he says. 'It's been there a while. Could have been that, though it looks like it hasn't moved since it landed.'

'Maybe.' Eileen sounds unconvinced. 'I thought I saw a flash of white, that it was a magpie. I hate magpies. You know what they say, don't you?'

'What's that?'

'"One for sorrow, two for joy." Sorrow enough here today, isn't there?' She dabs her eyes with a crumpled pink tissue.

'Daft thing whatever it was, flying at the window. Could have done itself an injury. Or me, come to that. Gave me such a fright.' She places a liver-spotted hand briefly over her heart.

Noel doesn't reply as he stretches up to close the window. There is a lull in the traffic, and a soft cooing is audible. He can't see a magpie, although he remembers there was one on the roof across the street when Eileen arrived. There's something altogether more comforting about the dove. He eyes it with something approaching affection before turning back to face Eileen. The old woman is still trembling, her face pale beneath her blusher.

'Sit down. Or shall we go into the living room?' He glances towards the corpse.

'I'd like to stay here.' She drops down into the chair Carol had occupied earlier.

Noel places her mug on the sideboard. He angles his chair away from the medi-bed and perches on the edge of it, his face averted from his father's body.

The old woman sips her tea. Noel hears the low murmur of his sister's voice in the next room, presumably on the phone to the doctor.

'Long time since you were over here,' observes Eileen. 'That's what Carol said when I called in last week.'

He folds his arms. 'It's been a while.'

They sit in uneasy silence before Eileen says, her voice quivering, 'I wish I'd caught him. There were things I wanted to tell him. It didn't seem right saying anything the other day. That was the first time I'd seen him in more than thirty years.' She sighs. 'You always think there'll be enough time, don't you?'

Noel hunches forward and contemplates the moss-green carpet. Patches have faded in decades of sunlight. He notices the drops of tea he spilled as he rushed in and vaguely considers fetching a cloth. He rubs his swollen nose, which has been throbbing intermittently since he blacked out in Sonia's kitchen. Eileen's words remind him of what he said to

Kylie on his last evening in her kitchen, that they had plenty of time to have a child together.

And that child is now dead, killed with Kylie.

He clears his throat. 'Yes. You always think there'll be enough time.' Rousing himself, he looks up. 'You said there was something you wanted to tell him?'

Her eyes dart towards the window. She works her mouth, and Noel senses that she is gearing up to tell him something significant. But the moment is lost when Carol comes in to tell them that the doctor is on her way.

Eileen lowers her head, the overhead light brightening the pink tint in her hair. She gulps down the rest of her tea. 'Then I'd best be going.' Standing, she hands her mug to Carol. 'Thanks for the tea, duck. You'll let me know about the funeral arrangements, won't you?'

'I'll phone.' Carol takes the mug and leaves the room.

Turning back the frayed cuff of her anorak, Eileen checks her watch. 'Just in time for the next bus, if I'm quick.' She moves over to the medi-bed and places her hand briefly over the hand of her former lover.

Noel flinches, then tries again. 'There was something you were going to tell him?'

Eileen gazes down into Ron's face one last time and wipes a tear from her lined cheek with the back of her hand. 'Too late now.' She turns abruptly and goes out into the hall where she picks up her umbrella and calls a farewell to Carol. Carol doesn't reply.

Noel follows the old woman outside. The dove has abandoned its post on the wall. The rain has finally stopped, and the air is chill and damp.

'I'll see you at the funeral.' Eileen pauses with her hand on the gate. 'Thank you for letting me see him.'

Noel ducks his head in acknowledgement.

She glances down the street, and he thinks that she is about to say something else, but she merely nods towards a woman locking an executive saloon parked in front of his van. 'There's

Dr Granger.' Taking advantage of a gap in the traffic, she scuttles across the street to the bus stop.

Noel gazes up at the sky as the clouds part to reveal a crescent moon. He wonders what she wanted to tell his father. Perhaps it was linked with the expression of sorrow he heard her utter about his mother; maybe Eileen has carried her own burden of guilt all these years about being on the bus with his father that day. *And so she should.*

The doctor's arrival puts an end to his speculation and he ushers her into the house. It doesn't take long for the young GP to examine the dead man. She advises that the medical certificate needed to register the death will be available for collection at the surgery the following day.

After the doctor has left, Carol phones the undertakers, and brother and sister sit silently beside their father until the doorbell rings fifteen minutes later. Carol disappears into the kitchen. After showing in two sober men who murmur conventional expressions of sympathy, Noel joins Carol.

Carol has the radio on and is wiping down the work surfaces. Noel washes the mugs. They work in silence until one of the undertakers calls that they have completed their task of removing Ron Reilly's body from his home of fifty years. Noel goes to see them out.

When he returns to the kitchen, the local radio presenter is urging his listeners to 'have a good evening'. Noel winces at the bright tone, then cringes even more when he hears himself echo it. 'Six already!'

Carol doesn't answer as she squirts citrus-scented cleaner on the sink and scrubs some stubborn stains. The radio commercials give way to the news. Noel stiffens in the doorway when the male news reader intones, 'Police have no further leads in the search for the murderer of single mother Kylie Weatherall, who was killed in Trentby on Friday morning.'

The item rouses Carol, who stops cleaning and turns towards him. 'Did you hear that woman was pregnant? Who could do such a thing?' Noel looks down at the floor, but she has already seen his stricken expression. 'You didn't know her, did you?'

'Yes.' His voice seems to come from far away.

Carol flicks off the radio. 'Not… well?'

Noel chews the inside of his cheek and nods. He takes a deep breath. She's bound to find out some time. Better if she hears it from him. 'We were together. Until April.'

Carol gapes at him. 'You mean she was your partner?'

'Yes.' He passes a hand over his eyes and retreats into the living room where he slumps onto the brown sofa bedecked with cream flowers. He remembers his mother buying it soon after he started school. He leans forward, his head in his hands, overcome by another bout of the profound exhaustion that has affected him since the police arrived with the news of Kylie's death on Friday.

'That's terrible.' His sister sits tentatively on the edge of the cushion alongside him. 'Worse than terrible. Why didn't you say something earlier, ring me over the weekend?'

'You had enough on your plate.' He looks at her bleakly. It had taken him three years to phone home after he'd left. He used to ring when he knew Carol might be home from school, and their father would still be at work. He remembers the first phone call, how quiet she'd been when she heard his voice, how he'd kept it factual, checked she had pen and paper and given her his mobile number in case she ever needed it. He'd updated her on new numbers whenever he changed his phone, and got in the habit of trying to call near her birthday in April. He always hung up without speaking if his father answered. He'd never mentioned her birthday, and wondered if she ever realised he timed the calls around it. When he'd called last April, Carol had mentioned that their father had lost weight and was having blood tests. A week later, Kylie had thrown him out. He'd neglected to ring his sister back to find out the result of the tests.

When Carol had phoned him the previous Thursday, he'd known immediately that something must be very wrong. She'd never phoned him before. 'It's Carol,' she had said. Her adult voice sounded so similar to their late mother's that for a crazy moment he had thought it was her. 'Dad's dying,' she said bluntly. 'He's asking for you. He's at home. Can you make it?'

He couldn't answer immediately. His hand was shaking so much that he thought he might drop the phone. 'I'll think about it,' was all he could manage.

He heard her suck in her breath. 'Don't take long. The nurses reckon he's only got a few days left.' Then she cut the call.

Now he wipes moist palms on his jeans. 'I didn't feel I should bother you, knowing how bad things were here.'

'I get that.' Carol's tone is the softest it has been since Noel arrived. She seems as if she is about to say something else, then stands and goes over to the sash window. She half-pulls a faded beige curtain across before changing her mind and tugging it back. Her reflection is ghostly in the glass.

She spins round and her next words come out in a rush. 'Do you want to come back to mine and we'll get a takeaway? We could have one here, if it's easier, but I'd really like to get home. I've seen enough of this place the last few weeks.' She glances around the room, unchanged since Noel lived there. Her voice hardens. 'Or is this it, and you'll disappear again, having paid your last respects? I suppose you'll want me to sort the funeral on my own too, won't you?' She juts out her chin in the way he remembers she did as a little girl. 'Will you even come?'

'Of course I'll be there,' he says quietly. 'I can help with the arrangements too, if you like.'

The right corner of her mouth twitches upwards in a half-sneer.

'I'm serious,' he insists.

She stares back at him, then gives an almost imperceptible nod. 'OK.'

Noel clears his throat. 'There are things… Maybe you've forgotten. You were only little when I left.'

She drops her gaze and folds her arms across her narrow chest. She shivers, although she is wearing a thick red roll-neck jumper with her jeans. 'It's always cold in this house, even with the heating on. Must be the damp. Might need to get some work done before we sell.'

He frowns at the change of subject. *Does she remember how their father beat him? Surely if she does, she can't blame him for leaving?* The old nagging guilt, that he left his kid sister behind with a violent man, resurfaces.

'How was he with you?' he asks carefully. 'After I left?'

She doesn't raise her head. Beneath the 1970s pendant glass lamp, he notices a sprinkling of grey hairs among the ginger. 'He was all right. Turned in on himself when you'd gone, stopped going to the pub.' She flicks a glance towards him. 'I had a friend, Jess. I used to go to hers on Fridays. Remember?'

Noel nods. He pictures again the sympathy in the face of Jessica's mother when she asked him how things were at home on that long-ago Saturday morning in the library.

'After you left, Dad wouldn't let me sleep over at Jess's any more. It was like he thought he'd lose me too. Like he'd lost Mum.' She crosses the room, then pauses on the threshold. 'Like he'd lost you,' she throws over her shoulder.

'Oh.' Noel can't think of anything else to say. He stands, registering a dizziness which reminds him that he hasn't eaten since breakfast. He switches off the light and follows Carol into the front room. She picks up a scuffed orange tote bag lying next to the teak sideboard. He notices how she averts her eyes from the empty medi-bed. Some impulse drives him towards it, and he finds himself smoothing the pillowcase. Perhaps it's imagination, but it still feels warm to his touch. He bows his head and closes his eyes, mentally rerunning the final conversation with his father. Unexpectedly a deep stillness settles over him, balm after the emotional turmoil of the last few hours. 'Bye, Dad,' he whispers.

'You coming for takeaway or what?' Carol recalls him sharply to the present.

'Yeah. Takeaway would be good.' He allows his hand to linger one last time on the pillowcase before he picks up his jacket from the back of the dining chair. He slides into it stiffly, but is unable to avoid jarring his injured shoulder. He rubs the spot.

'What's wrong with your shoulder?' asks Carol. 'You've been rubbing and rolling it around ever since you got here. And your nose is swollen too.'

'I fell down some stairs this morning,' he says briefly. His morning at Sonia's seems like weeks ago.

She arches her eyebrows but doesn't ask him any more questions.

Following his sister into the hall, Noel finds himself glancing up the shadowy staircase. He wonders again if any of his belongings are still up there, or if his father threw them away in fury when he left.

Carol reads his mind as she unlocks the front door. 'There's still a lot of your stuff up in your old room. It'll need sorting before the house goes on the market.' She tugs the front door open, letting in a draught of the chill, damp evening air.

Petrol fumes mingle with a smell of burning outside. Noel coughs, stepping past his sister onto the flagged path so that she can lock up. He glances up and down the street to discern the source of the acrid odour.

Again, she guesses what he's thinking. 'Chicken factory,' she says succinctly. 'Opened about two years after you ran off.'

'Right.' Noel watches as she locks the door. *So that's how she sees it. 'Ran off.'* He wonders about explaining more, but the murky street, still busy with commuter traffic, hardly presents the right time and place. Maybe an opportunity will come up over their takeaway, away from this blighted house. He huddles deeper inside his jacket. 'I thought you'd have got rid of it all.'

'Dad insisted on keeping the lot.' Carol raises her voice as a lorry lumbers past. She turns, unzipping the front pocket of her bag. 'Your room's just as you left it.'

'No way.' He gawps at her.

She stows away the key in her bag. 'I told you. He was waiting for you. Been waiting twenty-five years.'

He registers the tightness in her tone, the challenge in her raised chin. He massages his swollen nose. 'Don't you remember?' he asks finally. 'I had to go. I had to get out of here. He could have –'

'Whatever.' She pushes past him on the narrow path. 'Look, maybe takeaway's not a good idea. I'm shattered. I've been with him all day every day this last two weeks except when Jack came round in the evenings to give me a few hours at home.'

'Jack?'

She nods impatiently. 'Yeah. My partner.'

'Right.' Noel kicks a cigarette butt lying between the flags. A thought occurs to him. He told her about Jade when she was born, but that doesn't mean she's shared similar news with him. 'Do you and Jack have any kids?'

She snorts. 'Kids? No thanks! After what happened here?' She sweeps an arm up in the air, taking in the house and Noel.

Maybe she does remember. Noel turns to look along the street as another bus swishes towards them through the puddles. In its parallel row of bright rectangles, he sees it is half full. He thinks of the passengers coming home from shopping and work, students returning from college. *How many others, like Eileen Baxter, set out to visit a dying former lover today and arrived too late?* Carol hasn't pressed him further about what he remembers about the woman, but he suspects she will ask him some time. He ponders the way his father shook his head at him. Was it a mute request that Noel shouldn't tell Carol as he lay dying, or did he mean ever? *Should he tell her about the affair?* Noel hasn't been able to assess the nature of his father and sister's relationship yet. She had cried when he died, certainly, but were they tears of grief or relief? Or both?

He yawns, watching the bus disappear into the darkness down the hill. He wonders if there is any way back for him and Carol, any possibility that they might salvage something of a brother/sister relationship from their damaged past. Looking at the slim figure of his sister swinging the gate squeakily back and forth, waiting for him to say something, his throat constricts. The physical distance he has covered on the drive over may have brought him back to his family, but it's only one small step across the gaping chasm of twenty-five years.

Maybe that chasm will prove unbridgeable.

'I'll ring you tomorrow. I'll help however you want,' he says.

Her face is unreadable in the darkness. 'If you say so. I'm parked up the street. See you around.' She turns on her heel and marches off without giving Noel the chance to reply.

The daughter called in today to collect some of Elsie's belongings. Very tearful, she was. She's an only one, just like me. She said how much she would miss her mother. Of course I didn't say anything like that about you, Mum. I don't think you'd be surprised to know that I didn't shed a single tear over you, given how bad you were at the end.

It was a blessing, wasn't it? You wouldn't have wanted to finish up in a place like Freshfields.

You always said that nursing was a good profession for me, and I've got lots of experience now. Looking after you has helped me spot the early signs of dementia, see when people are becoming more muddled. As they get worse, I can help them, just like I helped you. Help their families too.

I mean, who wants to be a burden on their family? It's selfish, isn't it, to expect your children to run around after you when they've got their own lives to lead?

Not that you ever understood that, Mum. It would have been unfair of me to expect you to, with me being everything to you after my father left you pregnant. Whoever he was. I've wondered about him ever since I found out it was strange not to have a dad when I started nursery. But I soon learned not to mention him, the way it would bring on one of your 'dos'.

You just wanted to keep me close, didn't you? I get that.

Even so, it's strange to think that if I hadn't seen Andy in town the other Saturday, I might not have started helping these poor old souls and their families. First Elsie, then Reg. He wasn't confused like her, but there was the risk someone might become suspicious if he carried on saying things when he recovered from his water infection. And those infections are miserable. He'd had a few this year. At least he's spared any more now.

That carer was dangerous too, she might have worked it out. Collateral damage, I suppose you could call it.

I've not decided who's next yet. But the more I mull it over, the more certain I am that I'm doing them all a favour, them and their families.

Elsie's daughter will be grateful soon enough, even if she's upset now.

Chapter six

The morning after his father's death, Noel is tidying his van when he hears a woman calling, 'Mr Reilly! Mr Reilly!' The voice is vaguely familiar. He drops an assortment of sandwich and crisp packets, chocolate wrappers and drinks cans from the footwell into a black dustbin bag and straightens up, rotating his injured shoulder. It had woken him a couple of times in the night. Otherwise, he'd slept better than he had since Kylie's murder, emotionally exhausted after the visit to his dying father and the draining encounters with his sister and Eileen Baxter. But the conversation with his father had brought him an unfamiliar peace, which hadn't been lost in the charged meeting with Eileen or the loaded exchange with his sister. He was aware of this new calmness when he woke, a glimmer of light in the darkness of the last few days.

He shades his eyes against the bright October sun and recognises the stout elderly woman tapping her way towards him with her walking stick. She lives in one of the 1930s houses on the other side of the street. The semis stand above tiered gardens, looking down on the older terraced housing opposite. He's done a few odd jobs for her since he moved in.

'Morning, Mrs Hadley. What can I do for you?'

She leans on her stick, breathing heavily. 'Have you seen Mrs Mullins?'

'Mrs Mullins?'

'My neighbour. Prone to roaming. Tweed coat with a fur trim and black fur hat.'

'I know who you mean.' Noel hadn't known her name before, but the succinct description matches that of the old lady who regularly patrols the street. Her elegant style marks her out in the down-at-heel neighbourhood. 'No, I don't think I've seen her this morning.'

'Oh.' Mrs Hadley's shoulders sag inside her mustard padded coat. 'Her mind's wandering, and I try to keep an eye on her. We have coffee every morning at ten. This morning there was no answer, and her front door was unlocked. I checked the downstairs rooms – I didn't venture upstairs because of my bad knee' – she taps her left knee with her stick – 'but I did call her, and there was no answer. Her coat was missing from the peg behind the door. I'm wondering if she's gone out.' She grimaces. 'Although she has taken to wearing the coat indoors as well.'

'I see.' Noel slams the van door shut, locks it and picks up the refuse sack. 'Would you like me to check upstairs?'

'Would you mind? Then if she's not there and you think we should call the police...'

Noel notes the 'we' and realises that he is now involved in the hunt for Mrs Mullins. 'Does she have family?' He dumps the bulging dustbin bag over the low brick wall which separates his rented terraced house from the pavement.

Mrs Hadley sniffs. 'There's a daughter, Geraldine. Brings her shopping once a week. Doesn't want to face the obvious.'

'The obvious?'

Mrs Hadley fixes him with a look. 'That her mother has dementia. She's not safe living on her own any more. I tried to have a conversation with her on my way back from the hairdresser last week. She didn't want to know, said she was in a hurry, and that as far as she could tell, her mother was managing very well.' Mrs Hadley harrumphs. 'She's not the one checking the curtains are drawn back every morning, or losing sleep when her mother puts the TV on loud enough to wake the dead in the middle of the night, is she?'

'Well, no.' A disturbing thought occurs to him. 'You said the door was unlocked. Does Mrs Mullins ever go out at night?'

'Not as far as I know.' Mrs Hadley raps her walking stick impatiently on the pavement. 'Anyway, we'd best go and check the house. We're wasting time. She could be anywhere.'

Noel accompanies the old woman across the street. She puffs along, but rejects his suggestion that she should wait at the foot of the steep steps leading up to her neighbour's house. Raising her walking stick, she points out a wooden gate at the top of the garden which leads onto her patio. 'Had it put in five years ago to make it easier for us to get between our houses,' she explains. 'If you don't find her upstairs, I can use her phone to ring her daughter as well as the police. Geraldine's on speed dial.'

'Good thinking.' Noel stoops, pretending to tie the lace in his left trainer so that he can give her a start on the steps.

She pauses twice on her way up. At the top she slumps on to a bench usefully positioned beneath the front bay window. Too breathless to speak, she hands over the key.

He advances into the house shouting, 'Mrs Mullins! Mrs Mullins!' He doesn't expect a reply after Mrs Hadley's report, but calling her name makes him feel less like a trespasser. He is greeted by silence, broken only by the ticking of a grandmother clock in the dining room at the back of the house. In the narrow kitchen, he finds the chrome kettle is warm to his touch. Did Mrs Mullins suddenly decide to take a walk before her neighbour visited? Or – and Noel's heart rate quickens – has she had an accident upstairs? He climbs the stairs, hoping and praying that he won't find her lying unconscious, or worse.

The boxroom at the top of the stairs is used for storage. It is crammed with assorted boxes and carrier bags, a vintage record player and an ancient wooden console TV, suitcases, an old-fashioned aluminium silver Christmas tree and piles of photograph albums. He moves on to the adjoining room, a large, tastefully furnished bedroom. The duvet on the mahogany double bed is pushed aside, and a white lace nightdress lies unfolded on the pillow. The wardrobe door is open, revealing a jumble of dresses, skirts and blouses falling off padded hangers. Mounted on the wall above a chest of drawers is a TV which is no doubt the source of Mrs Hadley's nocturnal disturbance. The final bedroom is sparsely furnished with a single pine bed and matching chest of drawers.

Only the bathroom remains. Noel pauses on the landing, struck by the unsettling idea that he might discover the old lady's body in the bath. Holding his breath, he pokes his head round the door. He exhales in relief to find the bathroom empty.

'Is she up there?' calls Mrs Hadley.

'No.' Noel descends to join her in the hall. 'It looks like she went out recently. Her bed seems to have been slept in, and the kettle's warm.'

'Thank goodness.' Mrs Hadley slouches against the banister. She indicates the phone, set on an elegant cherry kidney-shaped table in an alcove beneath the stairs. 'Can you find Geraldine's number? I don't have my glasses.'

He hesitates. 'You said you usually see Mrs Mullins at ten. Could she have just popped out? Maybe she needed something and nipped to the corner shop on Peel Lane? Or is there anywhere she likes to go? I could go and look for her rather than worry her daughter, and I think it's too early to call the police. They wouldn't count her as missing yet.'

Mrs Hadley considers for a moment, then nods her curly grey head. 'Yes, you're right. What worries me is that this is the first time she's forgotten our morning coffee in twelve years.' She emits a gusty sigh. 'Another sign of her mind wandering, I suppose. She often walks to the river, up Adam Street and Peel Lane, then along the road to the bridge. Used to walk her little terrier up there. Had to have the poor thing put down last year. I'm sure her memory worsened after that. You'll know the way, won't you?'

'Yes.' Noel considers taking the van, but decides against it. Mrs Mullins is unlikely to recognise him, and she might not accept a lift if he does find her. From his sightings of her on the street, he assesses that she is far sprightlier than the sturdy Mrs Hadley. But there's a chance he might catch up with her if he jogs. He could do with the exercise too, as long as it doesn't jar his injured shoulder. Examining himself in the shower earlier, he'd noticed purple bruises developing down his right flank, but apart from being a little stiff, there is no pain in that area. 'Give me an hour,' he says. 'If I don't find her in that time, or she doesn't come back here, we'll call her daughter.'

'That sounds like a good plan.' Mrs Hadley's creased face clears. 'I'll wait here. I have to say this is very kind of you, Mr Reilly.'

He ducks his head, embarrassed. 'No problem,' he says, stepping outside. 'And it's Noel.'

'Well, thank you, Noel. I'm Maureen. I do hope you find her.'

Noel descends the steps and sets off at a steady jog before making the left turn into Adam Street. He pauses to catch his breath under the railway bridge where a train rattles overhead on its way to the county town. Then he goes along Peel Lane, the terraced street that runs down to the main road. There is no sign of Mrs Mullins. He asks a young woman wheeling a sleeping baby in a black buggy if she has seen an elderly woman in a tweed coat and fur hat. The woman barely looks up from her mobile to give a negative response. Mr Ahmed at the corner shop recognises Mrs Mullins from Noel's description, but says she hasn't been in.

Leaving the quiet terraced streets for the main road, Noel heads in the direction of the bridge. He describes Mrs Mullins to a postman, who confirms he saw her about ten minutes ago. 'Very smart lady. She was chattering to herself about the river. Struck me as a bit confused.'

Spurred on by the information, Noel picks up speed and rounds the bend towards the bridge. He nearly collides with a

73

youth cycling along the pavement. The teenager yells an obscenity. Noel doesn't waste his breath on a reply. He can see a figure wearing a hat and tweed coat in the distance. There is something odd about the woman's gait, but he is too far away to work out what it is. He accelerates again, past the vehicles backed up from the crossroads. Traffic is heavier here, with the town centre half a mile ahead, the bridge to the left and the bypass to the right. In front of him, Mrs Mullins crosses the road at the pelican crossing and bears left towards the bridge.

Too late for the green signal at the crossing, Noel runs along the opposite side of the road until a gap in the traffic allows him to cross. He is close enough now to see that Mrs Mullins is skipping up the gentle slope towards the bridge, the movement belying her age. A short middle-aged woman walking a retriever glances at the old lady in amusement, then raises her eyebrows as she passes Noel.

Mrs Mullins halts on the pavement at the crown of the bridge and gazes into the murky depths of the fast-flowing river. Noel draws to a halt a few paces away and catches his breath, bending over and holding his sides. The pavement is narrow, and he straightens up when he hears footsteps pounding towards him. Rubbing his painful shoulder, he wishes he was as fit as the lean older man who jogs past.

He checks his watch. It has taken twenty minutes to reach the bridge, so he should be able to get Mrs Mullins back home within the hour he agreed with Maureen. He waits for a tractor to rumble over the bridge before saying, 'Mrs Mullins?'

The woman is now scanning both sides of the riverbank, and seems not to hear. Noel raises his voice and repeats her name. She turns unfocused blue eyes on him. 'I thought he'd be here today,' she says, 'but I can't see him. Can you?'

Cold beads of perspiration run down Noel's spine. 'I can see the man who just jogged past. He's going down the path by the pub now.' Noel points him out, and Mrs Mullins follows his finger. 'And there are a couple of people walking their dogs further along.'

'Yes, yes, I've seen them,' she says impatiently. 'But what about *him*?' Her voice rises querulously.

'Who are you expecting?' Noel remembers how he used to go along with whatever his grandmother said when she developed dementia in her final years. He's always been certain that it was the death of her only daughter, his mother, that precipitated the illness.

Mrs Mullins scowls at him. 'You know,' she says.

He wipes the back of his hand across his clammy forehead. 'I'm afraid I don't, Mrs Mullins. But I do know it's cold out here. Why don't we go home, and you can tell me who you were expecting on the way?'

The old lady stamps her foot. 'But *he* won't be at home. He's only ever here, at the river.' Her lower lip trembles and Noel is afraid she might cry.

He zips up his bomber jacket as a gust of wind sweeps across the bridge. 'Of course,' he says gently. 'Sorry. Now, shall we go home and we'll talk about it there? Maureen's expecting us.'

Mrs Mullins' eyes spark with sudden clarity. She claps her hand to her mouth. 'Oh, my goodness. What time is it?'

'Twenty-five to eleven. Shall we go?'

'We must!' she exclaims. 'Poor Maureen! I've kept her waiting.' She steps closer to Noel and peers into his face. 'Who are you, anyway? Do I know you?'

'I live on your street. Maureen was worried, so I came to look for you.' He places a hand beneath the crook of her elbow.

Mrs Mullins allows him to guide her down the slope from the bridge and back to the pelican crossing. When they are halfway across the road, she stops abruptly and wheels round. 'He should have been there,' she insists.

'I know,' says Noel soothingly. The crossing beep falls silent and a van driver revs his engine loudly. 'Maybe he'll be there another day.' He raises a placating hand to the glowering van driver.

The old woman's face brightens. Noel sighs with relief as she allows him to steer her to the safety of the pavement. 'Do you think so?'

'I do.' He crosses the fingers of his free hand at the fib. 'Now, let's get home to Maureen, shall we?'

Mrs Mullins is quiet on the walk back to Somerville Terrace. She stops once when the sun disappears behind the clouds. 'He won't come now,' she mutters, gazing up at the darkening sky. She darts an accusing glance at Noel, then fixes her eyes on the pavement. Her pace slows to a crawl. Noel is assailed by memories of dragging his small daughter, Jade, to school. He wonders when Gemma will agree to him seeing her again. It's been nine months. He kicks a stone against a tree, making Mrs Mullins jump. But it encourages her to pick up speed.

Maureen is visible in the bay window of her neighbour's sitting room, and meets them in the hall. 'Now then, where've you been, Florence? You had me so worried. I'll put the kettle on. Have you got time for a coffee, Noel, or have we made you late for a job? Do you realise the trouble you've caused, Flo?'

Mrs Mullins looks between them, fumbling with the buttons on her coat. 'I didn't mean to,' she says, hanging her head.

Noel raises his hand. 'It isn't a problem. I'm taking a day off today.'

Maureen raises a bristly grey eyebrow. 'I'm sure there's other things you could have been doing on your day off,' she says dryly. 'Let me help, Florence.'

Mrs Mullins stands passive as a child while her friend deals with the troublesome buttons, and then helps her off with her coat. 'Do you mind?' Maureen passes Noel the tweed coat, which he hangs on a hook at the side of the door. 'Shall I take your hat, Flo?' Maureen reaches out her hand, but Mrs Mullins bats it away and clamps the fur pill box hat lower on her head.

'All right.' Maureen plods back to the kitchen. She turns on the threshold. 'So where did you get to?'

Mrs Mullins gazes out through the open door, a faraway expression on her face. 'The river.' Her head droops and she hugs herself. 'It's too dull now. He won't be there today.'

'You're not on about all that again, are you?' Maureen rolls large brown eyes at Noel. 'Every sunny day recently, she's been talking like this. Would you close the door to keep the heat in?' As Mrs Mullins edges towards the sitting room, Maureen mouths, 'And her!'

Noel obediently shuts the front door. It seems that he is staying for coffee.

He turns to find Mrs Mullins' face crumpled in disappointment. She is staring at the closed door. 'No, he won't be there today,' she repeats sadly.

He can't resist. 'Who?' he asks. 'Who is it you're hoping to see, Mrs Mullins?'

She transfers her gaze to him. Her eyes snap into focus as they did on the bridge. She moves towards him and thrusts her face so close that a wisp of her white hair tickles his cheek. There is a whiff of mothballs which Noel assumes emanates from the fur hat.

'You know,' she whispers conspiratorially. 'The Bright Giant.'

Goosebumps break out on Noel's skin. 'What does he look like?' he asks slowly. 'The Bright Giant?'

She takes a step backwards and places a veined hand on his shoulder. 'You know,' she repeats. Then her eyes cloud over and she drifts away into the sitting room, leaving Noel gawping after her.

Chapter seven

'Can you take the tray in for me, Noel?' calls Maureen.

He goes through to the galley kitchen at the back of the house in a daze. Maureen waves a milk carton at him. 'Do you take milk? She'd want me to use a milk jug, but I can't be bothered with that palaver.'

'Just a splash, thanks.'

'What's she been saying to you?' Maureen adds milk to three china mugs of coffee set out on a silver tray. 'I could hear her whispering out there.'

'Nothing much.' Noel massages the bridge of his swollen nose. 'It was a bit strange.'

Maureen grunts. 'That's Florence for you these days. Sugar?'

'Two, thanks.'

Maureen heaps two generous teaspoons of sugar from a canister into the middle mug, and adds one spoonful to the others. 'Here you are.' She stands aside. Noel lifts the tray from the counter. 'She wasn't on about that thing she goes to see at the river, was she? Some kind of giant with a gold belt?'

The tray jerks in Noel's hands, slopping coffee over the rims of the mugs.

'Careful!' Maureen reaches out to steady the tray. 'Are you all right? You've turned very pale.'

'I'll be fine.' Noel tightens his hold on the tray. *Get a grip*, he tells himself. *Can't be anything more than coincidence, can it?*

Maureen takes a cloth from the sink. 'Let me mop that up before you take the coffee in.'

Noel sets the tray back down and she wipes the underside of the mugs and the spillage. 'There we are. Take it through. I'll get some biscuits.'

He carries the tray through to the sitting room, where Florence is standing by the bay window. She whisks round when she hears Noel coming in. Her fur hat is perched at a jaunty angle above her white hair.

'Who are you?' she demands. 'What are you doing in my house?'

He places the tray on a walnut coffee table with scrolled legs. 'I'm Noel,' he says patiently. 'I live across the road.'

Maureen pants in with a plate of chocolate biscuits. She sets them down next to the tray and selects one for herself. 'Noel very kindly brought you back from the river.' She gestures to him to take a seat on a claret leather buttoned sofa facing the window, then sinks down into one of two matching armchairs set at right angles to the sofa.

Noel is no furniture expert, but the sofa and armchairs strike him as antique, like the ornate coffee table. They seem out of place in a modest semi on Somerville Terrace. He perches on the edge of the sofa, wondering about Florence's background.

'From the river?' Florence crosses the room, bends, and peers into his face. Noel finds himself inching back on the sofa. She shakes her head. 'I don't remember.'

'Never mind,' says her friend. 'Now, why don't you sit down and enjoy your coffee?'

Florence straightens up, then cocks her head as the grandmother clock in the corner of the room begins to chime. She counts along with it. 'Eleven o'clock!' she exclaims. 'We're an hour late, Maureen.'

'Well, if you will go wandering off, what do you expect?' Maureen crunches into her biscuit and points towards the plate. 'Help yourself, Noel. Come on, Flo.' She waves at the adjoining armchair. 'Chocolate biscuits. Your favourites.'

Noel leans forward and takes a biscuit. Florence grabs one, then returns to her post by the window. The sun has disappeared and the leaden sky is heavy with rain. She sighs. 'It's going to pour. No point going to the river today.'

'I should think not,' says Maureen firmly. 'Not after you've already been. You'll wear yourself out.'

'Have I been today?' Florence massages her temple. 'Then he mustn't have been there,' she says dolefully.

Noel stiffens on the sofa. Maureen shakes her head. 'Now don't start all that again.'

Florence breaks the biscuit in two, scattering crumbs across the windowsill. She rams one half into her mouth, staring out at the threatening sky. 'The Grey One's getting stronger,' she says.

Noel pauses in the action of raising his mug to his mouth. Upstairs a door bangs. He starts, spilling more coffee. Fortunately, the drops of brown liquid land on his jeans rather than the sofa.

'Jumpy, aren't you?' Maureen placidly finishes her biscuit. 'It's only the wind. Flo always leaves the bathroom window open.'

Noel rubs the drips without taking his eyes off Florence. Her forehead is pressed to the glass. 'What do you mean about the Grey One, Mrs Mullins?'

Maureen shakes her head at him. 'Don't ask,' she says in a stage whisper. 'She's been talking about them for years, the Grey One and the Bright Giant. It's got worse lately.'

For once Noel doesn't defer to her, desperate to find out more about the creatures her friend is referring to. 'Who are they, the Grey One and the Bright Giant, Mrs Mullins?'

Maureen tuts and reaches for another biscuit.

Florence doesn't answer immediately. Thinking she hasn't heard him, Noel is about to repeat the question, when she says, 'The Grey One is bad, very bad. He took William.' She spins round, her lips trembling. Tears glisten in her vacant blue eyes. 'The Bright Giant couldn't save him.' She reaches into the pocket of her tartan-checked pinafore and extracts a lace handkerchief.

Noel's scalp prickles.

'It's all a long time ago, Florence,' says Maureen soothingly. 'Don't go upsetting yourself. Now, for goodness' sake, sit down and get your coffee.' She leans towards Noel and says, *sotto voce*, 'William was her brother. Drowned in the river when they were children.'

He shudders.

Maureen notices, but misinterprets. 'Chilly in here, isn't it? Pop the fire on; Flo won't mind.'

Noel crosses to the electric log fire and flicks the switch.

'That's better.' Maureen eyes the glow contentedly. 'Lovely and cosy.'

He sits back down on the edge of the sofa, well aware that the coldness that has spread through him has nothing to do with the room temperature.

Florence wipes her eyes and slips the handkerchief back into her pocket. All energy seems to have left her. She shuffles across the room and drops into the armchair alongside her friend. 'Tired,' she says, licking chocolate from her fingertips.

'You will be, after that long walk,' says Maureen. 'Drink your coffee, you'll soon feel better.'

Obediently, Florence reaches for her coffee and gulps it down in one draught.

'Another sign,' murmurs Maureen to Noel, tapping her forehead. 'People like Flo don't notice things are hot.'

Noel grimaces sympathetically and eats his biscuit. He doesn't want to upset the old ladies, but he feels compelled to ask about how the long-ago tragedy happened. He can't shake off the uncanny feeling that, for all her confusion, Florence might be able to shed some light on his strange experience by the river on Friday evening.

'I'm very sorry about William, Mrs Mullins,' he ventures.

Florence seems not to have heard him. She waves her empty mug to and fro, head bowed.

Maureen sighs heavily. 'Such a sad story. Flo told me about it years ago, soon after we moved here. We were both young married couples then, and our children were the same age. They used to play together, along with Alma's son down the street.' Her eyes take on a faraway look and a wistful smile plays around her mouth. 'Happy days.' She bites into her biscuit, scattering crumbs down her ample bosom. 'Maybe I should have fetched plates after all.'

'I could get some if you tell me where they are,' offers Noel, standing.

'Well, I don't suppose there's much point.' Maureen glances at the crumbs strewn across the carpet. 'Florence's cleaner will be coming tomorrow.'

'Right.' Noel resumes his perch on the edge of the sofa. He crosses his legs and jiggles his foot up and down, anxious not to be sidetracked by domestic arrangements. 'You were saying about Mrs Mullins' brother?'

'William,' says Florence loudly, making them both jump. 'William drowned. The Grey One did it. Jesus saved me.'

Noel nearly falls off the sofa. '*Jesus* saved you? What do you mean?'

Maureen frowns. 'Best not to get her started.'

'Grey One very bad,' mutters Mrs Mullins. 'Bright Giant very good.' Her head lolls forward on to her chest.

Noel sucks through his teeth in frustration as her eyes close.

'That's all you'll get out of her,' says Maureen.

'But what is she talking about?' he persists, as Florence begins to snore softly. 'Why did she mention Jesus?'

'Oh, I don't know,' Maureen sips her coffee. 'It was a terrible accident, that's for sure. I suppose that's why she says Jesus saved her, though she usually goes on about the Bright Giant. Would you like another biscuit?'

Noel doesn't, but takes one anyway to keep Maureen company, hoping she will tell him more about what happened. Sure enough, she picks up another biscuit and settles back into her armchair. After she has crunched her way through the biscuit, she licks her lips and launches into the tale. 'It happened one summer's day when Florence's mother took the children for a picnic by the river. They were over the other side of the bridge. You know, along the path by the pub?'

He nods. That explains why Mrs Mullins' attention had been focused there when he caught up with her on the bridge. He feels a surge of adrenaline, more certain than ever that Mrs Mullins' Bright Giant must be connected with the Being from his vision. *But where does Jesus fit in?*

'Florence told me she was six at the time, and her brother just turned four. After they'd eaten, the children went off to play hide and seek while their mother was reading. Florence said it was a hot sunny day – funny how we always look back on childhood summers and think they were so much better than the summers we have now, isn't it?' She glances at Noel.

He hesitates, struck by how his memories of carefree summer days end abruptly with his mother's death. Seeing that Maureen clearly expects him to agree, and anxious not to distract her from the story, he murmurs assent.

'Florence remembers beginning to count, while William ran off to hide. Before she got to fifty, she heard him screaming. She stopped counting straightaway and ran in the direction of his screams. He was round the back of the old boathouse. She said she could see his little head bobbing up in the reeds, and his arms flailing around. He was gradually being sucked down. She ran into the reeds, thinking she could rescue him. But then she got into trouble herself. Somehow, she managed to get out.' Maureen sighs heavily. 'But her brother wasn't so lucky. Their mother heard them screaming. By the time she got there, it was too late. William had disappeared under the water.'

Noel pictures the scene: the little girl desperately trying to save her brother, then fighting the mud and water herself, and the distraught mother discovering her son drowned. An innocent picnic on a carefree summer's day torn apart by tragedy.

'That's terrible.' He glances sympathetically at Mrs Mullins dozing in her armchair between them. She shifts in her sleep, but doesn't wake, continuing to snore gently. Between her parted lips, he glimpses even white teeth which must surely be dentures.

'It certainly was.' Maureen nods soberly. 'Florence came from a well-to-do family. From what she told me, William's drowning set off a disastrous chain of events. Her mother turned in on herself and took to her bed as an invalid. We'd probably call it a nervous breakdown these days. She died a couple of years later. Around that time, Flo's father made some bad investments. I suppose he wasn't thinking straight after what happened. He had to sell their home. It was a grand-sounding house on the other side of town. He saved what furniture he could, like this suite.' She taps her armchair and nods towards the sofa where Noel is sitting. 'They took a much smaller house in town. Flo never talked about that time much, but I got the impression she must have been lonely, growing up with a father who was a broken man. She married when she was just eighteen, and I think it was a relief for her to get away from home. Her father ended his days in an asylum, poor man.'

They sit quietly for a few moments. Noel stares out of the window. A mist is spreading like gauze over the roofs of the terraced houses across the street below them. Maureen's description of Florence's father as a 'broken man' inevitably leads him to draw a parallel with his own father. Reflecting on yesterday's revelations, Noel has realised how his father was devastated by his wife's death, and plagued by guilt about his affair.

He looks again at the sleeping old lady. No wonder Mrs Mullins has been haunted by these dreadful memories. Is it possible that they have disturbed the balance of her mind, so that she has invented outlandish characters to explain them? Then why does her description of the Bright Giant remind him so powerfully of the Being from his own vision by the river on Friday evening? Could it really just be coincidence?

'What about these creatures she talks about, the Grey One and the Bright Giant?' He clears his throat. 'And why did she talk about Jesus, do you think?'

Maureen shrugs her broad shoulders. 'I don't know what to make of it. They sound to me like things from a fairy tale. The first time she told me about William drowning, she didn't mention them at all. She's always said it was a miracle she survived, so perhaps that's why she talks about Jesus. When she started on about these things later, I assumed she was embroidering things. Maybe early signs of her mind wandering, who knows?'

'When did she first mention them?'

'About ten years ago.' Maureen hoists herself forward in her chair, then winces and rubs her left knee. 'It was around the time when our friend Alma lost her son Peter in the river. He used to play with my Barry and Flo's daughter when they were small.'

'Did he drown too?'

She purses her lips. 'Suicide.'

Noel feels colour flood his face. He begins to tremble, and curls his hands into fists at his sides to try to control the shaking.

Maureen is too immersed in her sad tale to notice anything amiss. 'The shock was too much for poor Alma,' she continues. 'She had a heart attack and was dead herself within a month. Flo and I put it down to the shock.' Her voice wobbles, and she pauses, flicking crumbs off her navy A-line skirt to join the others on the carpet.

'I'm sorry.'

She nods, wiping a tear from her cheek before resuming the story. 'That was when Florence started talking about the Grey One and the Bright Giant. She insisted she had seen someone – or something – dragging her brother down into the reeds all those years earlier, and that the Bright Giant had helped her when she got into trouble. She said it would have been the Grey One who had lured Peter into the river. I asked her why she hadn't mentioned the creatures when she told me about what had happened to William. She said it was because I wouldn't have believed her, and that she'd wondered over the years if she'd imagined them herself. Peter's suicide convinced her that there was something bad – "evil" was the word she used – at the river. That's what she calls the Grey One. She insisted this Bright Giant rescued her.'

'You said you thought she was embroidering the tale?' prompts Noel.

Maureen leans forward to return her empty mug to the tray. 'Yes. What other explanation is there? These creatures can't be real, can they? Only...' She opens and closes her mouth, searching for her next words.

'What is it?'

Maureen folds a pleat into her skirt. 'There was something very strange. It turned out there was a history of suicides and accidents by the old boathouse, and an unusually high number of murders for a small town. I didn't know anything about them, but Florence was a history teacher – not that you'd think it now, poor thing' – she glances compassionately at her sleeping friend – 'and she'd read a lot of local records. Alma and her son died shortly before Florence's husband, Ted. After he died, Florence started to spend hours at the library, going through old books and newspaper cuttings and microfiches and what not. I suppose all the records will be on computer now. To begin with, I thought it was her way of coping with her grief, a distraction, but it became an obsession. I used to say, "Florence, it's not healthy." But she didn't take any notice. Within a few months, she'd got a file together. Evidence, she called it.

'She took the file down to the Town Council meeting and made a presentation, urging them to pull down the old boathouse, saying it was a site of "evil happenings", and that its influence was spreading through the whole town. The council took no notice, probably thought it was a lot of hocus pocus like I did. That didn't stop her, though. She wouldn't let it rest. She tried to get the local clergy involved, even saying the place needed exorcism. Well, who believes in that kind of thing these days?'

She breaks off to look at Noel and catch her breath. Apart from the eponymous film, he knows nothing about exorcists, although the word makes his skin crawl. 'I don't know,' he says faintly.

'Exactly. Anyway, none of the clergy took any notice. Then Flo started writing letters to the local paper. You can imagine how the press lapped it all up. It sounded like a ghost story, and sales of *The Tribune* soared. The journalists featured her research on the suicides and accidents that had happened near the boathouse. The story ran for weeks. It was suggested that Trentby had had more than its fair share of suicides and accidental and violent deaths over the years. They weren't all by the river, either.' She snorts. 'A lot of superstitious nonsense, of course.'

Noel notices that despite her words, Maureen shivers and hugs herself. He rubs the coffee stain on his jeans absently. He thinks about Kylie and their unborn child, murdered last Friday, and Sonia's son-in-law, killed in a drunken brawl. Three violent deaths which he knows about, and now Maureen is telling him about others. Is it just coincidence that he is finding out about these tragedies a few days after he experienced that unsettling vision by the river? He recalls again the Being's words: *You have been chosen to right the wrongs in this place, to shine as light in the darkness. First, you will find your own healing.'*

'Anyway, the boathouse hadn't been used for years by then,' continues Maureen. 'After a few months the Town Council arranged to have it pulled down to put an end to all the hysteria. The landlord of the pub complained that there'd been a fall in customers, with folk not wanting to venture over that side of the river. *The Tribune* moved on to other news. But it didn't end there for Florence. Every now and then she'll start on about these things, the Grey One and the Bright Giant. She's been worse than ever lately, especially since that young woman on the estate up the hill was murdered last Friday. That was awful, wasn't it?'

Noel grips his hands tightly together in his lap. 'Yes,' he says, when he trusts himself to speak. There is a loose piece of skin under his thumbnail, and he tears it back roughly. He looks at the bead of blood forming. It gives him a strange sense of satisfaction.

'I put it down to the dementia,' says Maureen. 'I reckon it's getting worse. I think I should tell Geraldine about her mother wandering off this morning, don't you?'

He licks the blood from his thumb. 'She should know.'

'I'm grateful you went after her like you did. It was very kind of you.'

'No trouble.' Noel bats the compliment away. 'Any time.'

'Thank you.' Maureen eyes him. 'What do you make of it all, then? Flo talking about these creatures? Her take on things, that there was something evil by the river?'

A gust of wind rattles the letter box. The sky has darkened further, and a moment later hailstones batter the window. Noel shudders. Maureen is still watching him, waiting for his answer.

'I don't know,' he says eventually. 'I don't know what to make of it.' His brain pulses with questions, but he can hardly discuss them with Maureen. Is it possible the Being he saw in his vision is one and the same as Florence's Bright Giant, maybe even – his heart races – somehow connected with Jesus? And what about that sense he had of being lured into the water the other night by some unseen presence in the mist? Could that have been a manifestation of the Grey One who Mrs Mullins believes was responsible for drowning her brother decades ago, and who she blamed for enticing Alma's son, Peter, into the river?

It all seems too fantastic. Yet Noel finds himself unable to dismiss the striking connections between his experiences and those of Mrs Mullins.

The grandmother clock chimes the half hour. Florence has slept through the hailstorm, but now she stirs. Her eyes alight on Noel. 'Who are you?' she asks. 'What are you doing in my house?'

He smiles at her. 'I'm Noel,' he says. 'I live across the street. I brought you home from the river.'

'The river!' Florence claps her hands and twists round to look at the window. All animation drains from her face as she takes in the dark sky and the hail pelting the glass. 'The Bright Giant won't be there today,' she says sadly.

Maureen rolls her eyes heavenward. 'Now, don't start again, Flo,' she says. 'I've been explaining all about it to Noel.'

Florence swivels towards Noel. 'He knows already,' she says. 'You don't need to explain to him.'

Chapter eight

An hour later, Noel is chewing the final mouthful of a tuna mayonnaise sandwich when his mobile rings. It's Sonia. He texted her the previous evening to tell her his father had died, and remembers that he promised to call her earlier.

'Are you OK?' she asks.

He wipes his mouth with a square of kitchen towel. 'I think so.' He stifles a yawn. 'Sorry I didn't phone earlier. I've been out looking for an old lady.'

'Ah. Did you find her?'

'Yes.' Noel drops the kitchen towel into the pedal bin.

'That's good. Is she all right?'

Noel wanders over to the window. A magpie is perched on the roof of the bird table in the back yard. He recalls Eileen Baxter's dislike of the birds as he watches it lean forward, bending its head towards the tray. Finding it empty, the magpie flaps its wings and rises into the grey sky. Noel reaches for the plastic bag of nuts and seeds he keeps on the counter by the sink, realising he has neglected to put out food again.

'Not really. Her neighbour told me she has dementia and that she often wanders off.'

'The poor lady. You did well to find her. How did you know where to go?'

'Maureen – that's the neighbour – said she often goes down to the river. I found her on the bridge.'

'That doesn't sound very safe,' comments Sonia. 'The roads are busy. And what if she went along by the river alone, and slipped or fell? She could drown!'

Just like her brother did all those years ago. Noel shivers. 'I know. Maureen plans to speak to her daughter about it.'

'Good. Rivers can be dangerous. This one especially.'

Noel's hand stiffens around the bag of bird food as he hears the gravity in her tone. 'Why this one especially?'

'There are stories about it. An unusual number of drownings and suicides.'

She takes a breath, but doesn't elaborate. Her words are remarkably similar to Maureen's report of Florence's research.

'Is that all?' he prompts, the plastic bag slippery in his moist hand.

Sonia hesitates, then says, 'It's difficult to explain. But perhaps it would be wise for me to tell you, if you are concerned about this old lady. Face to face would be better than on the phone. I would like you to tell me about your father too, if you feel able. I prayed for you yesterday afternoon as I promised. Did you sense that?'

'Um...' Noel stares out over the yard. The sky has darkened ominously. 'The visit went better than I expected,' he says at last. 'And I feel... clearer.'

'Praise the Lord!' Sonia's words are so unfamiliar that he drops the bag. Nuts and seeds roll across the counter. 'Are you free now? You would be very welcome.'

Noel brushes some of the bird food into a heap with his palm. 'That would be great.'

'Wonderful! Unfortunately, I have run out of milk. I was planning to go to the shop, but then the hail and rain came. Would you mind fetching a carton for me, semi-skimmed?'

'Sure. I'll be about twenty minutes.'

'I look forward to it.' The sincerity in Sonia's voice warms him as they end the call.

Perhaps it's a combination of his eventful morning and the turmoil of his visit to his dying father that causes Noel to drive to Sonia's on autopilot. Where only a day earlier he had eschewed the main road through the housing estate to avoid Kylie's house, today he finds himself halfway along her street before he notices where he is. His breathing quickens, and he keeps his eyes fixed ahead as he passes the house. In front of him, the sky is almost black, threatening a further downpour.

He considers driving a mile further to the supermarket, rather than stopping off at the nearest convenience store where he sometimes shopped when he was living with Kylie. But after sorting out the bird food, he is already running late for Sonia. Having forgotten to phone his new friend earlier, he doesn't want to let her down again.

He reverses the van into a space opposite the shop, hoping that he won't see anyone he knows. He tells himself it's unlikely; he'd only spent three months living with Kylie and the boys, and the sprawling council estate has a population of around 2,000. Even so, he keeps his head down as he approaches the entrance.

Inside, his pulse accelerates again when he sees that the shop has had a refit since he was last there. The fridge is no longer along the left-hand wall. Noel pulls his beanie down low over his forehead. He is conscious of each step he takes as he tries to saunter casually down the aisle, and imagines this is how a shoplifter must feel. He strains his ears, listening for the hum of the fridge above the pop song playing through the speakers.

The fridge is in the third and final aisle. Noel is trying unsuccessfully to open the glass door when a gravelly voice at his side says, 'Let me help, duck.'

He freezes. The voice unmistakably belongs to Kylie's mother, her hoarseness the result of her forty-a-day smoking habit.

Noel keeps his face averted as she slides the door open. 'Thanks,' he mutters, grabbing a two-litre carton of milk. He doesn't bother to check whether it's semi-skimmed as Sonia requested. Taking a couple of paces to the right, he begins to root among the yoghurts, willing the woman to move on. But she doesn't. From the tail of his eye, he sees that her hand is immobile on the fridge door handle. He picks up a random pot of blueberry yoghurt and steps back, turning towards the shelves of biscuits opposite.

Behind him, the fridge door finally squeaks shut. He exhales, thinking she hasn't noticed him. Then her voice rasps, 'You've got a hide, showing your face around here.'

He doesn't turn, continuing to rummage among the biscuits.

'Don't pretend you didn't hear me!'

A young man pauses in his selection of crisps from the adjoining shelf. Noel picks up a packet of custard creams. He didn't bother with a basket, so he clutches the milk, yoghurt and biscuits awkwardly to his chest, hoping that he'll make it to the till without dropping them. He turns slowly to face Susan Weatherall and swallows hard.

'I'm so sorry, Susan.'

She stares at him, her eyes as hard as the hailstones pounding against the glass frontage of the shop.

'About Kylie,' he clarifies lamely. His voice trembles as he utters his ex's name, and he begins to shake. He hugs the groceries more tightly, careless of the moisture from the milk carton dampening his bomber jacket. He darts a glance to his left. The young man has been joined by a curvaceous black woman with a glossy ponytail. A male retiree pulling a cumbersome shopping trolley basket stops behind them.

'So you should be,' says Susan. 'She'd still be here if it weren't for you.'

Colour rushes to his face. *Surely she doesn't suspect him?* 'I didn't –' he begins.

She folds her arms across the chest of her purple fleece. 'Didn't what? Didn't inject her?'

His jaw falls open. 'Inject her?'

'You look so innocent, don't you? Yes. She was injected with a drug.' She spits out her next words. 'When the police told me, I knew that ruled you out. You wouldn't have the intelligence.'

He runs his tongue over his dry lips. 'Then you know I'm not responsible,' he insists, cringing at the pleading note in his voice.

She continues to glower at him, her brown eyes – Kylie's eyes – dark with hatred. He drops his gaze, inspecting the groceries in his arms. He begins to read the list of ingredients of the custard creams, hoping that this might help to slow his rapid shallow breathing.

'You might not have killed her,' Susan Weatherall says slowly. 'But don't think that means it wasn't your fault from where I'm standing. If you hadn't left her up the spout and on her own, she wouldn't be in the mortuary now, would she?'

Noel hears a sharp intake of breath behind him. He doesn't follow Susan's logic, but nor does he want to argue with her in front of the small audience.

The elderly man says querulously, 'What's going on here?' He fiddles with his ear. 'Damn hearing aid. Battery's always going. Paid a fortune for it.'

At least one person doesn't understand what Susan is saying. But the young man and the woman are looking at him with undisguised contempt. News about Kylie's murder will be all round the estate. They will understand exactly what Susan is talking about.

She hasn't finished. 'And my grandsons wouldn't be without their mum, would they? Heartbroken they are, both of them. Bradley won't come out of his room except to eat, and Liam has hardly stopped crying since they moved in with me.' Her voice wobbles.

'I'm so sorry,' Noel whispers again. He focuses desperately on the information about the biscuits. *Carbohydrates 8.2g, of which sugars 3.7g.* Four sharp blasts of the till buzzer distract him from his perusal of fats and protein.

'Too late now, isn't it? I told Kylie you were bad news from the off. Divorced. In debt. A kid you hardly see.'

His flush deepens. 'That's not my fault,' he protests. 'My ex –'

'That's what you all say, isn't it?' interrupts Susan. 'You men sowing your seed and bolting?' She turns to the group behind them. The young man looks away quickly. The woman is glaring at Noel.

'You know what I mean, duck, don't you?' asks Susan.

The woman wrinkles her nose in disgust. 'It's always the woman who struggles,' she agrees.

A stocky man wearing a bottle-green store jacket appears behind the onlookers, presumably summoned by the buzzer. A badge pinned to his barrel-shaped chest identifies him as the store manager. 'Is there something I can help with here?'

'I'm ready to pay.' The old man taps his watch. 'I've got a bus to catch.' The other onlookers step aside. He wheels the basket trolley up to Noel and Susan. 'Excuse me,' he says loudly.

Noel flattens himself against the shelves. Susan Weatherall doesn't move from her position in the middle of the aisle.

'Could you let this gentleman through?' says the manager. 'If you have a private matter to discuss, I'd ask you to continue your conversation outside.'

'There's nothing private about this,' snarls Susan. 'All over the news it is, about my murdered daughter. And this is the useless scumbag who left her.' She steps forward and jabs her forefinger at Noel's chest. He inches further back into the unit, grimacing when the middle shelf digs into the shoulder injured on Sonia's stairs.

Susan begins to cry noisily. She finally moves her trolley aside, her back to Noel and the others. The old man ignores the weeping woman as he trundles past her towards the till.

There is a moment's appalled silence before the manager steps forward. He avoids eye contact with Noel as he nods towards the checkout. 'I think you'd better go and pay.'

Head bent, Noel traipses behind the old man to the till. Behind him he hears the manager offering to make Susan a cup of tea.

The old man seems to take an age to pay, fumbling in his pocket for the exact pence, despite the assurances of the checkout operator that there is plenty of change in the till. Noel considers dumping his items and making a dash for the door, anxious to avoid a further encounter with Susan. But having agreed to pick up Sonia's milk, he waits his turn, hurrying outside after he has paid.

Hail is bouncing off the pavement, but is no deterrent to a youth on a skateboard, who almost knocks Noel over. Noel collapses inside the van with his purchases. Inhaling deeply, he stares unseeingly through the spattered windscreen. The icy stones drum on the roof, echoing the pounding of his heart. He flicks on the wiper, then turns it off again. The perished rubber on the failing blade is no match for the hail.

When he has regained some control, Noel realises that if Susan Weatherall refused the tea offered by the manager, she might make a beeline for his van when she leaves the shop. Galvanised by the thought, he jumps out and wipes the hail off the windscreen roughly with his hands, gritting his teeth as the ice stings his palms.

Back in the van, he wipes his hands on his jeans, then pulls out without checking his blind spot. A horn blares repeatedly behind him. Glancing in his wing mirror, he sees a youth driving a dirty white car, mouthing ugly obscenities. Noel flashes his rear lights in apology, and drives with the utmost care along the remainder of the street, the white car on his tail. The small parade of prefab shops with flats above is drab enough on a summer's day; on a stormy afternoon in late October, he can't think of a more dispiriting area of town.

The near accident precipitates a fresh bout of the trembling that began in the shop when Susan Weatherall laid into him. Noel turns right at the top of the street, and is relieved when the dirty car forks left. The hail has eased by the time he passes the primary school attended by Kylie's sons. Shouts and cries announce the afternoon break. He glues his eyes to the road in front of him, knowing that if he catches sight of Bradley or Liam, he will lose grip of his shaky composure.

Past the school he pulls in again, shuts off the engine and rests his head on the steering wheel. He ponders abandoning his visit and retreating home. But he reminds himself that Sonia needs the milk he has brought. And he does want to hear whatever she has to tell him about the river, intrigued to discover whether it might shed some light on Mrs Mullins' research and his own bizarre experience.

Remembering to check over his shoulder this time, Noel sees the bus that operates the circular route to town approaching. He waits for it to pass before setting off again. Inevitably, the bus makes him think of Eileen Baxter and his recovered memory of his mother's fatal accident, and he drives on aimlessly for a few minutes. The digital clock on the dashboard shows 14:30 when he registers that he is lost in the maze of streets of near-identical local authority housing. Navigating a speed bump, he realises with a jolt that it's twenty-four hours since he arrived at his childhood home. Somehow, he finds himself back on King's Road where Kylie lived. This time he takes the direct route to Sonia's street, and parks outside her garage. The hail has given way to heavy rain as he trudges up the road towards her house.

Sonia welcomes him warmly, clucking about how wet he is. She shows him into the sitting room at the front of the house, and insists he remove his jacket so that she can dry it in front of the kitchen radiator. She bids him to make himself comfortable while she prepares the tea, refusing his half-hearted offer of help.

Two rocking chairs and a sofa have been crammed into the small room. There is a scuffed pine bureau in the alcove next to the window, and a TV mounted in the alcove on the other side of the chimney breast. The fireplace surrounding the lit gas fire is covered with school photos of two boys who Noel assumes are Sonia's grandsons, and a wooden cross stands in the middle of the mantelpiece. A reading lamp behind one of the rocking chairs casts a pool of light on a large book lying open face down.

Taking a seat in the matching rocking chair opposite, Noel feels the tension of his encounter with Kylie's mother and his near collision begin to ebb away. He shuts his eyes and rests his head against the back of the chair, swaying gently back and fro. The soothing aroma of baking fills his nostrils, and he drifts off to sleep.

Noel starts when Sonia wheels in an old-fashioned trolley with a gold trim. She positions it between their chairs. 'You're tired,' she says. 'Bereavement is exhausting. Losing your father, that difficult visit, it will take time to get over it.'

And losing Kylie. Sonia doesn't know about the other source of his grief, or the guilt that accompanies it, heightened by his encounter with Susan. Noel passes a hand over his head.

'I made a sponge cake. You will have a slice, won't you? Oh, I am so sorry! I didn't mean to upset you,' says Sonia, as Noel dashes away tears.

He gathers himself. 'You're too kind,' he says thickly, overwhelmed by her kindness after Susan's tirade. The woman's accusation, '*She'd still be here if it weren't for you,*' echoes around his head. 'I don't …I don't deserve it.'

Sonia regards him without answering. Then she cuts two generous slices of cake and places them on her Charles and Diana side plates. She slides a plate across the trolley towards him and pours the tea, adding milk and sugar to Noel's. Even the fact that she has remembered how he takes his tea touches him, and he lowers his head, blinking back further tears.

Sonia moves the book lying open on the other rocking chair to the bureau. She sits down and nibbles her cake. 'Mmm,' she says. 'One of my better ones. Tell me what you think.'

Noel takes a bite. The cake is still warm from the oven. The two sponges are sandwiched together with a generous layer of strawberry jam. 'Delicious,' he says sincerely.

She beams at him and they sit in companionable silence for a few minutes, eating cake and drinking tea. He wonders how it is that he feels so comfortable with Sonia, a stranger until yesterday. She exudes serenity as she takes delicate sips from her cup, rocking in her chair.

She replaces her cup in her saucer and smiles at him. 'Better?'

'Yes. Thank you.' He finishes his tea and nods when Sonia waves the teapot at him.

'Tea and cake. The best medicine.'

She is pouring herself another cup when the bell rings. 'Ah. That will be Michelle. She rang just after I spoke to you, offering to fetch some shopping. I'd already asked you to get the milk, but there are some other things I need.' She gets to her feet, glancing at the wall clock on the chimney breast. 'I will ask her if she would like to join us, although she will soon need to fetch her son from school.'

Noel nods, inwardly chiding himself for his spark of resentment at having his visit interrupted. He doesn't have the energy to meet a stranger, and it will delay him asking Sonia about the river.

But when he hears Sonia's daughter greet her mother in the hall, he realises that she isn't a stranger. His heart plummets as he recognises the voice of the woman from the convenience store.

'I got held up,' the woman is saying, above the rustle of plastic bags. 'You know my colleague at work who was murdered last Friday? Kylie?'

'Ah yes.' Sonia clicks her tongue against her teeth.

'Her mother was in the shop, having a go at Kylie's ex.'

'A terrible thing. For both of them.' Sonia sighs. 'Now, come in and tell me about it over a cup of tea, if you have time. I'd like you to meet my friend.'

Her daughter hesitates before saying, 'It will have to be quick, Mum. I've got to collect Joshua.'

Sonia enters the sitting room, smiling at Noel. 'My daughter, Michelle. Michelle, this is Noel, the handyman who is going to fix the kitchen and the leak in the bathroom. You remember I mentioned him yesterday?'

He sits rigidly as Michelle follows her mother into the room. Her smile of welcome disappears instantly and her generous mouth settles into a sullen line.

'I know who he is,' she says, making no effort to conceal her disgust. 'You should have nothing to do with him, Mum. He's the reason I'm late. Kylie's mum said that if it wasn't for him, Kylie wouldn't be dead.'

Chapter nine

There is a shocked silence after Michelle's pronouncement.

Noel hauls himself to his feet. 'I should go,' he says hoarsely, not looking at either woman. 'Your daughter's right, Sonia. You won't want me here.'

'Too right. You should go and not come back,' snaps Michelle. 'I can find you another handyman, Mum.'

Noel stares down at the carpet, wishing it would swallow him up, and waits for Sonia to tell him to leave. When she doesn't say anything, he raises his head slowly. The older woman is gazing at the cross on the mantelpiece. Her lips are moving. With a start, Noel realises she is praying. After another long moment, she says, 'Please sit down, Noel.' He is aware of his eyes widening. 'Please, sit,' she repeats, gesturing towards the chair he has just vacated. 'I would like you to stay.'

He lowers himself obediently into the chair.

'What are you doing, Mum? This man should not be in your house,' hisses Michelle.

'Michelle, I would like you to fetch a cup and saucer and join us.'

'You got to be kidding! No way do I want to join a tea party with a man who ran out on his pregnant girlfriend. Divorced, with another kid he hardly sees. That's what Kylie's mum said. That's exactly what Kylie told me at work months ago, about the loser who'd walked out on her when she told him about the baby. We shouldn't have anything to do with him. You know how I feel about such men.' She glares at her mother.

'It wasn't like that. I didn't –' Noel begins. There is a pressure in his chest, and he is beginning to hyperventilate. *What's the point? They won't want to hear it. Kylie was right. I am a loser.* His body starts its uncontrollable trembling again. The cluttered room, which previously seemed cosy, now feels cramped and claustrophobic. He shuts his eyes and grips the wooden arms of the rocking chair.

'Enough, Michelle!' Sonia scolds her daughter. 'You have heard what the two women had to say. I am sorrier than I can say that your friend was murdered.' She shudders. 'The mother will be heartbroken, as any mother would. But with grief comes anger. You know that. Remember how you were after Jonathan died? This woman is lashing out. That's understandable, but we should hear what Noel has to say as well.'

'Don't bring my business up in front of a stranger!' flares Michelle. 'This has nothing to do with what happened to Jonathan.'

'Doesn't it?' asks Sonia quietly. 'Another violent death in this blighted town?'

Engulfed in his own distress, Noel has barely registered the exchange between mother and daughter, but Sonia's words remind him of the reason for his visit. Maureen had commented on the number of untimely deaths which Florence had discovered in her research after their friend's son took his life. There were others besides Florence's brother who had drowned in the river. *Who else might have met a brutal end recently besides Michelle's husband and Kylie and their baby? Who might be next?* His quaking increases.

'This poor man hasn't had a chance to speak, to give his account,' Sonia continues. 'You can see he is suffering. Now, please join us, and listen to what he has to say.' She limps to Noel's side. 'If he wants to tell us,' she adds softly, placing her hand on his injured shoulder.

The pressure is gentle but firm. *Like the Being's touch*, thinks Noel, then pushes the thought away. Even if Florence's descriptions are remarkably similar, it's possible that the phenomena he encountered by the river are hallucinations brought on by his drunken state. Or even – and he trembles even more at the idea – a psychotic episode brought on by the mental strain he was under after learning of Kylie's death and the police interrogation.

The peace Noel found by his father's bedside yesterday has evaporated, and the glimmer of hope that his healing had begun just as the Being promised has dissolved. He's been fooling himself. There can be no healing from the scars of the past, or the hurt he has inflicted. Michelle's dismissal of him following Susan Weatherall's tongue-lashing have brought him face to face with the damage he has caused to others. Not only to Kylie and her sons, but to his sister too. From their conversation yesterday, he is unsure if Carol understands why he had to leave home, and why he made so little contact over the following years. Even if she does understand, her attitude towards him is resentful, even bitter. And the question that has preoccupied him over the past few days continues to haunt him: if he had tried harder with Kylie, would she have had him back? Would that have meant she would still be alive today, as her mother believes?

Noel doesn't know the answers to these questions, but he is certain of one thing. There is no chance that he is capable of helping anyone, of righting wrongs and being a light in the darkness as the Being told him. No way would any Master choose him, Noel Reilly. He needs to forget all about that peculiar experience and face reality.

But the pressure of Sonia's hand on his shoulder reminds him that he isn't alone in his despair, that there is someone who cares. God knows he doesn't deserve it, but this kind woman wants to hear his story. His breathing begins to slow beneath her touch, and his quivering body gradually becomes still.

Sonia withdraws her hand when she senses him relax. 'Michelle?'

There is a pause before Michelle replies sulkily, 'I've got twenty minutes, then I need to pick up Joshua.'

'Good. Would you put the kettle on again? This tea will be cold now.' Her mother indicates the teapot on the trolley.

Michelle purses her lips and scowls at the teapot as if she is going to refuse. Then she snatches it and marches out of the room. A few seconds later, a cupboard door bangs against the kitchen wall.

Sonia seems unperturbed by her daughter's ill-temper as she settles back into her chair. 'Will it help to talk?'

Noel looks down at his clasped hands.

'You don't owe me any explanation,' Sonia goes on, 'but it would be good for my daughter to hear the other side. This estate has a close-knit community.' She looks towards the window, tight-lipped. The rain has abated to a gentle patter against the glass. 'We were the only black family here when we moved in. People were not friendly. They crossed the street to avoid us, shunned us.'

He twists his mouth. 'That's terrible.'

'Yes, and it got even worse when Michelle fell pregnant with her first son.' Sonia is silent for a moment. Then she gives herself a little shake. 'It's a long time ago, and things have improved.' She sighs. 'Even so, as I told you, I can't help thinking that if Jonathan had been a white man, the police would have pursued their investigation more thoroughly.' She taps her fingernails on the arm of her chair. 'Anyway, that's another matter. What I am saying is that gossip spreads like cancer in this place.'

He digests what she has said, then nods. 'You're right.' He jerks his head in the direction of the kitchen. 'I'm not sure your daughter wants to hear it, though. Seems like she's made up her mind already.'

'Michelle's past means that she is quick to jump to conclusions. But my daughter is fair. You will see. If she can set the record straight at Freshfields, where tongues are wagging after Kylie's murder, that will be a start. It's amazing how many people know, or are related to, one of the Freshfields residents!' Sonia eyes him solicitously. 'I know how exhausted you are. These two deaths within a few days have taken their toll. Perhaps you don't feel like telling us your story now. You might prefer to go home and be alone, to lick your wounds in private. Am I right?'

He runs his hands over his thighs, impressed again by the woman's perspicacity. 'Yes,' he admits, his voice barely audible above the shrill whistle of the kettle.

'I understand.' She pauses. 'But this isn't a private matter. Kylie's mother will continue to spread her version of events. You have your business to think about, and your daughter. You can't afford to hide away, however tempting that is.'

Noel isn't convinced that telling Sonia and Michelle will have much impact, whatever Sonia says. But he dimly comprehends that if he can give his account to someone prepared to listen, he will feel better. The weight he has carried since hearing of Kylie's murder won't lift entirely if he unburdens himself to this kind woman, but it will be easier to bear. Despite Sonia's assurances, he is far from certain that her daughter will show any understanding or adjust her poor view of him. Yet for some reason that he can't define, it's very important to him that Michelle at least hears him out. 'OK,' he says at last. 'I'll try to explain.'

Michelle comes in with a pot of freshly brewed tea and another cup and saucer. She pours a cup for herself before depositing the teapot on the trolley, making it clear that she has no intention of serving either her mother or the despised guest. Plonking herself down on the sofa, she avoids eye contact with both of them. 'So, what are you waiting for? I'm all ears.'

Noel ignores her sarcastic tone and darts a glance at Sonia, who gives him an encouraging smile before leaning over to pour them both fresh tea. He begins to talk, hesitantly at first, then with greater fluency when he gets into his stride. He forgets where he is, the company he is in, as he tells them about Gemma's affair, the debt from the fateful Caribbean holiday and the divorce. He describes how Gemma became awkward about him seeing Jade when he told her he was moving in with Kylie, and that she hasn't relented since he and Kylie separated. He explains that he has started legal proceedings to arrange contact with his daughter. He is honest about his shock when Kylie told him she was pregnant that April evening, and how his immediate reaction was that it wasn't a good time for them to have a child given their precarious financial circumstances. He tells them how she threw him out instantly.

'I just needed time,' he says. 'I'd have come round, but she sent me packing on the spot. I tried to phone afterwards, but she wouldn't pick up.' He kneads his temple. 'After a while I gave up, figured that she'd given up on me and decided that I was no better than the boys' dads. I hoped maybe she'd come round when the baby was born, but it's too late now. Too late for us, and too late for the baby. *Our* baby.'

A low noise, like an animal in pain, breaks the silence of the room. It takes a moment for Noel to realise that he made the sound, keening the death of his unborn child and his ex-girlfriend.

He is barely aware of Michelle gasping, '3.10! Mum, I have to go!' and her scrambled departure, the door slamming behind her. Then Sonia is kneeling beside him, murmuring, 'You poor man. You poor man.' She cradles him as he weeps, heedless of his tears dampening the shoulder of her pink and white striped nylon blouse.

When the storm of grief has abated, Noel lifts his head. Sonia uses the arm of the rocking chair to lever herself up. She hobbles over to the bureau and picks up a box of tissues which she passes to him. Resuming her seat, she remains silent as he blows his nose and recovers himself. He is worn out by weeping, too exhausted to be embarrassed at his loss of composure in the home of this woman he only met a day ago.

Sonia sips her tea before asking, 'Better?'

He nods and manages a half-smile. 'Yes. Thank you for listening, for giving me a chance.'

She smiles back at him. 'That is my privilege. I am grateful to you too, for sharing your sad story. What you have experienced is terrible.' She rocks herself to and fro before continuing, 'I would like to pray with you presently, if that is all right.'

'Pray with me?' he echoes, bemused.

'Yes. But first – something happened in my bathroom yesterday which upset you, and then you had the difficult task of visiting your father who you hadn't seen for many years. I wonder if the visit helped to heal something for you?'

Noel jerks forward in his chair. He'd avoided telling Sonia anything of the physical abuse he had suffered at his father's hands after his mother died, focusing instead on the shock of losing his mother. Now he gazes at her mutely.

Her eyes are soft. 'I don't need to know the details,' she says, 'but I could sense there was something troubling you from your past, and that it was more than your grief at losing your mother when you were only a little boy. The Holy Spirit revealed this when I was talking with you yesterday, and when I prayed for you during your visit to your father.'

The Holy Spirit. The term is vaguely familiar, stirring up memories of the church he attended with his grandmother when he was a small boy. Or was it the Holy Ghost? Noel frowns, trying to remember. He sees the thickset, ruddy-faced vicar in his cassock, the kneeling figures of the predominantly elderly congregation, smells the incense which used to make his asthmatic grandmother cough. But he has never heard of anyone chatting about the Holy Spirit in such a personal and matter-of-fact way as Sonia.

He raises his hand to his mouth to stifle a yawn. This morning it was Mrs Mullins talking about the Bright Giant and the Grey One, the Bright Giant sounding uncannily like the Being in his vision, whom she somehow associated with Jesus. Since his experience, he had been tempted to dismiss the

Being as a symptom of his disturbed mental state, but the coincidence of Mrs Mullins' descriptions have set him wondering again. Now here is Sonia talking about a Holy Spirit. But where Mrs Mullins is undoubtedly unwell, Sonia strikes him as very well balanced. She is watching him with her penetrating gaze.

'You don't know the Holy Spirit?'

He crosses and recrosses his legs. 'No,' he admits. 'I mean, I remember it – or the Holy Ghost – was mentioned in church when I went with my grandma, but that's all.'

Sonia doesn't seem surprised. She rises and goes over to the bureau. She picks up the book that was previously lying on her chair and taps the front of it. 'If you read the Bible, you will find out about the Holy Spirit who came when Jesus ascended into heaven after His resurrection.'

Darkness is falling quickly on the gloomy October afternoon. Sonia switches on the light before returning to her chair and placing the Bible on her knee.

Noel blinks. '*Who?* You sound as though the Holy Spirit is a person!'

Sonia claps her hands, throws back her head and laughs her rich laugh. 'Of course! Father, Son and Holy Spirit. You know, Michelle asked me the same question when she was a teenager, questioning so many things, before she fell in with that young man and had her baby.' She sobers and shakes her head regretfully. 'She could have gone far, my daughter. Anyway, that's done. Past.' She lifts her hands, signifying that the direction of Michelle's life is long since out of her control.

Noel's mind is spinning. He glances over at the Bible in her lap. It has a colourful cover, unlike the imposing black Bible he remembers on the brass lectern in the church, or the smaller black leather-bound one his grandmother owned. Sonia's Bible is clearly well used: there are papers poking out of it, and the page edges are yellow. He looks from the Bible to the simple wooden cross on the mantelpiece and shifts in his chair.

Sonia is watching him. 'The Bible and the cross. Two of my most precious possessions.'

'Right.' Noel rubs the back of his neck. He is aware of warmth spreading through him, and the accelerated beating of his heart.

'The cross reminds us that Jesus died to take away all sin, all the wicked things of this world,' she continues. 'He forgives all who ask. He heals all in need who believe.'

That word again. *Heals*. And now *forgives*. 'Forgive us our trespasses, as we forgive them that trespass against us,'[1] he murmurs. Sonia hears and nods approvingly. Noel remembers his grandmother teaching him the Lord's Prayer, scandalised that children no longer learned it at primary school. Apart from the few occasions he has been in church as an adult – baptisms, weddings and funerals – he hasn't said the Lord's Prayer in years. But those words... He thinks of holding his dying father's hand the previous day, of recovering the memory of how his mother died, of how he surprised himself by allowing Eileen Baxter into the house. There was something mysterious about the peace that came to him during those hours. He intuits that somehow that peace is related to what Sonia is telling him now.

'You asked about what happened with my father yesterday...'

She leans towards him attentively.

'I think I forgave things from the past,' he says slowly. He lowers his head and swallows. 'My father,' he mumbles. He dashes away another tear. 'I forgave him. And now, I wish...'

'Yes?' asks Sonia gently. 'What do you wish?'

'That I could be forgiven.' The words come out in a rush. 'Forgiven because I left my sister with my father. She was only a child, but I had to go, I had to leave. He hit me... I was so frightened he might...' He shakes his head, unable to say any more.

---

[1] From *The Book of Common Prayer*, 1662.

Sonia raises her hand, showing she understands.

'I wish I could be forgiven because I didn't try hard enough with Kylie. I gave up on her and the boys too easily. We were getting on really well until she told me she was pregnant. Maybe, if I'd gone round to see her, told her we'd cope with the baby, maybe then she and our baby would still be here, like her mother says.' Noel wipes away more tears and reaches for another tissue.

She gives him a moment to collect himself, and he senses that she is weighing her words carefully. 'You mustn't blame yourself for Kylie's death,' she says. 'Her murderer alone is responsible.' She speaks more sternly than he has ever heard her speak before, and her lips are tightly compressed. Then her voice softens. 'It sounds to me as though you did try with Kylie. Her news about your child came as a shock to you, and she didn't give you time to digest it. You phoned, and she chose not to pick up. I suspect she wouldn't have let you in if you had visited.'

'But we don't know that,' he points out. 'Although her mum...'

'Yes?'

He sighs. 'Her mum didn't reckon much to me. She tried to put Kylie off me when we first got together. I just wasn't good enough.' He runs his tongue around his dry lips, remembering difficult occasions with Kylie's family. Her sister's wedding reception, when they had been relegated to sit with some distant cousins rather than placed at the top table. Kylie had laughed it off, but Noel could tell how hurt she was. Bradley's birthday party in the local soft play centre, where Susan Weatherall had blanked him completely. When they'd moved in together, her mum had stopped calling the landline, and would only phone Kylie's mobile. Kylie's comments about her mum's view of him on their last evening together hadn't come as any surprise. He'd suspected when they separated that Susan had done her best to urge her daughter not to listen to anything he had to say, and not to respond if he tried to contact her.

'Then her mother was a fool,' says Sonia unexpectedly.

Noel blinks. 'What makes you say that? You hardly know me!'

Sonia smiles. 'I know a good man when I meet one,' she says. 'And you – you are a good man.'

'But after what I've told you…'

'I understand you have been scarred by your experiences,' she answers softly. 'Yet you still had the courage to go back to see your father yesterday. This morning, despite all your troubles, you went in search of an old lady who was a stranger to you. These are things I know within just a day of meeting you.'

There is a lump in his throat. The warm sensation he was aware of when Sonia talked about her cross and Bible, about healing and forgiveness, has spread throughout his body. He feels like he is floating on a sun-kissed ocean.

'Look at me, please,' she says.

He glances towards her, shyly.

'Now listen. I will say it again, and I want you to believe it: you are a good man, Noel Reilly.' She holds his gaze. 'Like every good man, every human, you have had your struggles. You have made mistakes. You have suffered.' She gets up, takes the simple cross off the mantelpiece, and caresses the wood. 'You talk about wanting forgiveness,' she says. 'This is where you will find it. This is where we *all* find it. Our Lord Jesus took all our sins – all the sins of the world – upon Himself on the cross. In doing this, He made right our damaged relationship with His Father, our heavenly Father, God Himself. If you ask our Father God for the forgiveness that comes through the cross of Jesus, and believe, then you will find it. Jesus once said, "Ask, and it will be given to you; search, and you will find; knock, and the door will be opened for you.'"[2] She pauses and considers the man in front of her as he stares at the cross in her hands. 'Would you like me to lead you in prayer?' she asks. 'A prayer for you to know this forgiveness?'

Noel dashes fresh tears from his eyes and nods. His voice trembling, he repeats the words Sonia offers to the Lord she loves. They are simple words, but he senses at the end of the prayer that something profound has happened to him as he echoes her 'Amen'. The glow inside has deepened, and his heart is lighter than it has been for years, since early childhood when his mother was still alive.

---

[2] Matthew 7:7.

You know, Mum, I can't stop thinking that if it hadn't been for that lad whizzing about on his skateboard, I might never have seen Andy that Saturday. Or more like bumped into him. There he was, coming out of the florists just as I ducked into the doorway to avoid the lad. Andy was carrying the most beautiful bouquet. (I know it isn't kind, but I wished afterwards our collision had squashed it. Sadly it survived intact.)

'I'm sorry,' he said, even though it was my fault. He's one of those who always apologises first. I suppose you'd have said it was good manners. But it irritates me, seems a sign of weakness.

You should have seen his mouth drop open when he recognised me!

I'd dreamed of that moment so often, how one day we would meet. We'd lock eyes and know we were meant to be together. We'd agree that splitting up was a terrible mistake that we'd both regretted ever since.

But it wasn't a bit like that. His cheeks reddened – you know how he's prone to flushing with his ginger colouring – and his eyes darted up the street as if he was looking for someone to rescue him.

'Sharon. It's been a long time.'

'Hello, Andy.'

'How are you? Still nursing?'

'Yes. And you? I heard you'd made professor. Congratulations.' (I hadn't heard any such thing; I keep up with his career online, but I wasn't going to admit that.)

He smiled then. He always lapped up praise. Most people do, I've noticed, for the smallest things. You weren't one to give praise, were you? Always on the lookout for the tiniest fault: the cushions out of place if they weren't exactly symmetrical on the sofa; the picture slanted even when it looked straight to me; the books needing to be kept in alphabetical order on the shelves. And on it went. Everything just so.

'Thanks. Anyway...' Andy glanced up the street again.

I was determined to prolong the meeting, give him the chance to realise how much he'd missed me. 'Beautiful flowers.' I nodded at the red roses and white carnations, the pink lilies and gerberas, and stretched my lips into a smile. 'Someone's a very lucky lady!'

That's the moment when he should have swept me into his arms and said, 'They're for you, Sharon. I've never met anyone like you. I'm so sorry we've been apart for so long.'

But instead, he said, looking down at the bouquet, 'They're for my wife. It's our anniversary.'

I kept my smile pinned in place. That's something I learned from you, how to look like everything is fine, put on a good face. 'Really? Congratulations!' I said, as if it was news to me that he was married. 'Any children?' (And I knew the answer to that one too. You don't have to dig around much on the internet to find out personal information.)

He smoothed the cellophane over the flowers, leaving a damp patch with his sweaty palm. 'A son. Oscar. How about you?'

I shrugged. 'Me? No ties,' I said airily.

He nodded, his flush deepening as I continued to smile at him. I could see he was still attracted to me.

'Footloose and fancy free.' I giggled flirtatiously.

He swallowed hard, his Adam's apple bobbing up and down, making his feelings for me even more obvious.

'Still on George Street,' I added, so he'd know where to find me.

'Right. And how's your mother?'

'She died three years ago.'

'I'm sorry. You must miss her.'

'It was for the best. The dementia had taken her over by the end.' I let a beat fall. 'I don't miss her that much. I expect you understand why.'

'Dementia's a dreadful illness,' he muttered.

'That wasn't what I meant. All those years looking after her. I can't get those back, can I?'

He lowered his head over the bouquet. 'Um...'

I placed a hand on the arm of his olive wax jacket. 'You'd have appreciated the quality of that coat. 'If you have any free time during your visit, you know where I am,' I said softly.

He jerked backwards, nearly dropping the bouquet. 'I'm sorry, Sharon. That won't be possible. Like I told you, I'm married.'

'Oh, I didn't mean that!' I exclaimed, widening my eyes and raising my hand to my throat as if horrified. 'Not that!' I enjoyed watching him squirm with embarrassment, beads of sweat breaking out on his forehead.

Then, because I might never see him again, I had to say what I've been thinking all these years. 'I mean, I know that if it hadn't been for Mum, we would have –'

'Good to see you,' he broke in. 'But I need to go and find my family. They'll be wondering where I am. Bye.' And he turned and scarpered up the street towards the car park without so much as a backwards glance.

So that was the cruel end of that dream I'd held on to all these years, of how me and Andy would be reunited one day and spend the rest of our lives together.

I went home and made a cup of tea. I drank it in the living room, staring across at your armchair. I've not touched it, not even washed the antimacassar you embroidered when you were a girl. The lilies and carnations reminded me of Andy's bouquet. It seemed that they were taunting me, that you were laughing at me wherever you are now.

I remembered how often one of your 'dos' came on the evenings I was supposed to be going out with Andy, and how I used to cancel our dates, worried about leaving you on your own. The doctor never could explain them, said they might be mini-strokes. They scared me in the beginning, how you would suddenly go completely blank, not even remember who I was. It took me a while to realise your 'dos' coincided with me going out.

Then on the nights I did manage to get out with Andy, you used to phone or text, didn't you? Did I know where you'd left your glasses? What time would I be home? Could I pick up some headache pills for you? You'd fallen but not hurt yourself too badly, though your head *hurt. You'd heard a noise of breaking glass and thought someone might have broken in... But you rang me, didn't you, not the police?*

I thought about all this while I drank my tea. Afterwards I fetched your sewing basket from the cupboard under the stairs and found your dressmaking scissors. I took your cloth into the kitchen and opened the bin, and very slowly and deliberately I cut your precious handiwork into tiny shreds. How you'd have hated to see those fragments of material mingling with the leftovers and veggie peelings, blackened banana skins and mashed teabags!

The shreds floated down like the tears I never shed for you.

And that's when I decided that no one else would have to ruin their life the way I did.

Chapter ten

Two days after Sonia led him to faith in Jesus, Noel is again
driving towards Oldford. The late October sunshine reflects
his mood as fields and farms flash past. He brakes to join a
queue of traffic following a tractor. The tractor slows on a
bend, causing the vehicles behind it to decelerate further. Noel
lowers the window and savours the fresh air blowing through
the van. A rising thrum alerts him to a motorbike approaching
from behind. He watches in his wing mirror as the rider
zigzags up the hill and settles on his tail. Overhead a
thunderous boom announces the presence of the Red Arrows.
Noel hunches over the steering wheel for a better view. The
nine Royal Air Force jets roar forward in a graceful V before
splitting off, performing various aerobatic moves on their
descent towards the air base fifteen miles away. The swirling
white plumes in their wake look like a child's first brush
strokes in the pale blue sky.

The road opens out. With no traffic coming towards them,
the motorcyclist takes the opportunity to overtake Noel's van
and the three cars and tractor in front. Noel grins to himself,
struck by the thought that the motorbike and jets are playing
in harmony on the earth and in the sky, showing off their
grace and speed. He flicks on the radio, tuned to a station
playing nineties' music. He turns up the volume and sings
along to the Meatloaf hit at the top of his voice.

The tractor forks left down a farm track before the next
village. He picks up speed and turns his mind to his pending
meeting with his sister. She'd texted the afternoon before to

say that the funeral was set for the following Tuesday. Noel noted that she hadn't asked if this was convenient for him, but he wouldn't have felt able to object after distancing himself from his family for so long. A second curt text had followed in the evening: *'Getting house valued tomorrow. Starting clearing. If you want anything, I'll be there at 11.'* He guessed it was the nearest Carol would get to offering him an invitation. The implication that she wouldn't be saving any of his possessions if he didn't show was clear.

He pondered not going, tempted to keep away from the house that held so many disturbing memories. That would have been the easy option, but something has shifted within him since he repeated Sonia's simple prayer two days ago. One aspect of that change is his strengthened determination to seek a reconciliation with his sister. He wants to explain that he felt he had no choice other than to flee all those years ago, and to apologise for leaving her alone with their father. He senses that this visit could be another step towards healing his emotional pain, and maybe his sister's too, if she is willing to listen. Carol might be as evasive as she was on the evening their father died, when she changed her mind about them sharing a takeaway and talking further. But he calculates that this is a risk worth taking, not only so that he will know he has tried, but also because he believes that it might help her.

The digital clock on the dashboard is showing 11:09 when Noel slots the van into a space a few doors down from his childhood home. The street is no more prepossessing in the sunshine than it was in the rain on his last visit. Rays of sunlight glint unforgivingly on broken glass and discarded drinks cans strewn along the cracked pavement. Noel pauses in the gateway of number 249 and casts an eye over the property. It looks even more drab on the bright morning, with the peeling paintwork on the windowsills and drainpipe clearly visible. Two roof tiles have slipped close to the chimney, and he makes a mental note to check for damp in the front bedroom. He still thinks of it as his parents' room, despite his mother's death thirty-three years ago. Pressing his forefinger to the doorbell, he wonders when his father last slept in the room, and if Carol used to help him with the stairs in the later stages of his illness before he was confined to the medi-bed downstairs.

Noel is thinking about everything that his sister has been through, nursing their father, when she opens the front door. She is wearing a shapeless khaki hoodie with jeans. Her ginger hair is scraped back into a high ponytail, and her oval face is paler than ever in the sunlight, which plays on the fine lines at the corners of her eyes and darkens the shadows beneath. She doesn't speak.

'Hi,' he says. 'I've come to help.'

Carol tugs her ponytail. 'Not before time.'

Noel shivers in a gust of wind, a reminder that despite the sunshine, it's still the end of October. 'Sorry I'm a few minutes late. I got held up behind a tractor. Do you need to be somewhere?'

'I wasn't talking about you being late to clear the house.'

He stoops to pull out a weed growing between the flags. 'It must have been tough for you, looking after Dad these past weeks.'

He straightens, and sees her bottom lip curl.

'It wasn't just these past weeks, was it?' She folds her arms across her chest.

'Well, no, but his illness must have made it really difficult for you. Awful.' He takes a step back and surveys the roof, anything to avoid her scornful gaze. He points upwards. 'There are a couple of loose tiles up there, and the guttering and windowsills could do with a lick of paint. Do you think it's worth making a few repairs before putting the house on the market?'

'You going to pay for them?'

He flinches at her sharpness. 'Won't there be money in a bank account or something? I mean, I don't know how you sort these things out, but I'd have thought –'

'I'm sure you've been doing plenty of thinking,' she cuts in. 'Like how you'll get a nice share in everything now he's gone.'

'That hadn't crossed my mind!'

She rolls her green eyes. 'I bet. That's why you've turned up today, isn't it? To find out how much the house is worth?'

'No! Honestly, I haven't given it a thought.' Noel is aware of footsteps and a whirring noise behind coming to a halt. He swings round to see a young woman with a red buggy on the other side of the low brick wall. She holds out a sippy cup to a blond toddler. Noel suspects that she has paused to eavesdrop.

Carol evidently reaches the same conclusion. 'You'd best come in.' She turns on her heel and Noel follows her through to the kitchen. Tins, jars and packets of food are lined up on the work surface. Carol opens the fridge in the far corner. 'I've made a start on the cupboards,' she says, her back to him. 'If there's anything you want, take it.'

'What about you? Have you got what you want?'

'I don't want anything. Help yourself.' She bangs a tub of margarine on to the counter.

Noel pokes about among the cans. Most of them contain soup, beans, carrots and peas. 'Spam! I'd forgotten all about Spam!' He picks up a blue tin emblazoned with the familiar yellow capitals. 'Unless I'm thinking about junk e-mails.'

Carol ignores the joke. 'Take it. I can't stand the stuff.' She tugs the door of the freezer compartment. 'This is iced up. Can you get me a knife? They're –'

He pulls out the drawer in front of him.

'You've remembered,' she says.

'Yeah.' Noel is unsurprised to find the same wooden-handled cutlery of his childhood inside the drawer. He passes her a knife, wondering if this is a good opening. 'Weird what sticks in your mind from when you were a kid, isn't it?'

She grabs the knife and kneels in front of the fridge, scraping away at the ice with vicious strokes.

The harsh grating sound sets his teeth on edge. 'Do you want me to – ?' he begins. Too late. The rest of his words are drowned out as the freezer compartment door thuds to the floor.

Carol picks it up and lays it on the counter. 'You were saying?'

'I was offering to help. Shall I see if I can fix it?'

'Some things can't be fixed.' She glares at him, chin tilted, leaving him in no doubt that she isn't only talking about the damaged fridge.

'I know that,' he says quietly. 'But things can be made better.'

She arches an eyebrow, then turns away, kicking the fridge hard. 'It's years old. Only good for scrap.'

'Right.' Noel rubs the bridge of his nose. The swelling is subsiding three days after he fell down Sonia's stairs, but it still throbs intermittently. 'Did you say there's some of my stuff upstairs?'

'Yes.' Carol squats and reaches along the narrow gap between the fridge and wall. She wrenches out the plug, banging her hand. Cursing under her breath, she gets to her feet and rubs the back of her hand.

The doorbell rings. Noel turns automatically towards the living room.

'I'll go,' she says. 'It'll be the first agent. I'll show him round while you sort your things. I've put some boxes and bin bags in your old room.'

He lets her pass and follows her into the hall. He inhales deeply at the foot of the narrow staircase. Behind him, his sister opens the front door and greets the estate agent. Climbing slowly upwards, Noel hears the man murmuring the standard condolences. The windowless landing is dim, and the four doors leading off it are closed. His breathing quickens. He caresses the small wooden cross in the pocket of his jacket. Sonia gave it to him before he left her house on Tuesday afternoon.

'Help me,' he whispers, stepping towards his childhood bedroom. 'Please help me, God.' He isn't sure if the simple words qualify as a prayer, but as soon as he has uttered them, he feels calmer. He pushes open his bedroom door and enters, gasping when he sees that the room is exactly as he left it twenty-five years ago, except that the single bed has been stripped. Nineties' rock bands stare back at him from faded dog-eared posters taped to the opposite wall. He studies the rugged face of Meatloaf, the lyrics of the song he'd been singing along to in the van running through his head.

Wandering over to the wooden desk, he finds his school exercise books stacked alongside textbooks. He lifts the lid off a rusting biscuit tin. Inside is the jumble of biros, pencils, rubbers, felt tips and pencil sharpeners he remembers. On impulse, he takes out a green felt tip. Opening an exercise book at random, he finds himself looking down at algebra equations. He never made much progress with algebra, and he grins when he sees the teacher's red crosses outnumbering the ticks. He presses the felt tip to the page. Unsurprisingly, the pen has dried out and leaves no trace beyond an indentation.

Noel replaces the felt tip in the tin and runs his finger along the desk. It's covered with only a thin layer of dust, as is the shelf above. With a pang, he realises that someone has been cleaning the room until recently. Carol or his father? He looks along the shelf. His throat constricts when he sees his knitted grey elephant sitting there alongside an assortment of cassette tapes and CDs. He picks up the stuffed toy and turns it over, stroking patches darned by his mother. Still holding the elephant, he peers at the tapes and CDs. Nirvana, Radiohead, R.E.M., Meatloaf, Tracy Chapman, U2, The Beautiful South... He wonders what became of them all as he replaces the elephant on the shelf.

Kneeling, he peers under the bed. His old ghetto blaster is still there, next to a battered cardboard box. He pulls out the boombox and plugs it into the socket beneath the desk. Extracting the Tracy Chapman CD from its case, he inserts it into the machine, presses play and holds his breath. The disc spins, then stops. He takes it out and rubs it against his jacket to remove any grime, then replaces it on the wheel. This time it works, and seconds later he is singing along.

Noel rocks back on his heels, drags out the cardboard box and pulls back the lid. Inside are a miscellany of toys from his early childhood. He rifles through Lego bricks, model cars and a ship, a spinning top, marbles, action figures and plastic farm animals, shaking his head in disbelief that these items have been preserved all these years. Underneath them is an electronic football game he used to play for hours. He'd forgotten how good Tracy Chapman was, and gets to his feet to ramp up the volume on the CD player before turning his attention to the chest of drawers next to the desk. The top drawer contains packets of photos alongside his disposable camera. His hand hovers over the photos. The final notes of the song are dying away when he hears his sister's raised voice.

'This is the second bedroom.'

He spins round. Carol is glowering at him in the doorway. 'Can you turn that down?'

'Course. Sorry.' He flicks off the CD player, feeling like an errant teenager.

A young man wearing a navy suit and waistcoat over a white shirt and blue tie follows Carol into the room, grinning at Noel. Carol transfers her glare to him, and the smirk vanishes. He takes in the room, his eyes widening beneath his floppy fringe. 'Wow. This is like stepping back in time.'

'My brother's sorting it out,' says Carol, without looking at Noel. 'We'll get rid of the furniture before any viewings. And these posters.' She advances further into the room and rips a U2 print from the wall. 'Never could stand Bono.' She savagely tears through the singer's face, then balls up the poster and drops it to the floor.

The estate agent darts an uneasy glance at Noel, then bends his dark head over his clipboard and begins to make notes with a silver ballpoint pen. Carol's hand hovers above another poster, this one of The Beautiful South.

'I can take them down today if you want,' says Noel quickly.

She hesitates, then lowers her hand. 'OK.' She turns and addresses the estate agent. 'You done in here?'

'Yeah.' The young man clicks the pen and backs out onto the landing.

'Just the bathroom to see. It's on your right.' Carol follows him. 'Same as it was in the eighties, like the rest of the house.'

Seconds later, Noel hears the door to the bathroom swing open. He pictures the dusky pink sanitaryware inside as he carefully peels the posters from the walls. The estate agent is right: from what Noel has seen, the house is stuck in a time warp. Nothing seems to have changed since he lived here. From the way Carol ripped the U2 poster down, he suspects that their father is responsible. He sinks down onto the single bed and looks again around his old bedroom, swallowing a lump in his throat. He's heard of people keeping rooms as shrines to children who have died, not allowing them to be touched. That seems to be what has happened here. But surely his father hadn't expected him to come back after the way he'd treated him? Hadn't he realised that the chance of his return receded with every passing year? He raises his hand to his nose, which has started to ache again.

Footsteps retreat downstairs. Noel hears the estate agent ask, 'Would you like me to send your brother a copy of the valuation too?'

'That won't be necessary,' his sister replies crisply.

'OK.' The young man sounds nonplussed. 'I'll email you as soon as I'm back at the office.'

Noel switches the CD player back on, drowning out any more of their conversation, and resumes his task of removing the posters from the wall. He is certain that they are too scruffy to be of any saleable value. But he still folds them neatly before disposing of them in one of the refuse sacks which Carol has left in the room.

The wall looks bare without the prints. Corners of tape hang off the anaglypta. He half-heartedly scrapes at one yellowing edge with his thumbnail, succeeding only in causing further damage to the wallpaper. He turns his attention to the desk. Flicking through the exercise books, he is transported back to the secondary school where he spent nearly five miserable years.

He'd been a loner at school, the only kid whose mum had died when he transferred from the local primary. The other children had avoided him as if he had a contagious disease. He'd made little effort to make friends, knowing that he could never bring them back to his gloomy home. As his father's violence towards him escalated, Noel had become convinced that there must be something very wrong with him. The only lesson he enjoyed was woodwork. He could lose himself for hours whittling away at pieces of wood, watching them transform beneath his fingers. He remembers making a plane, and a pair of bookends carved with his initials which he'd kept on the shelf above the desk. He looks up at the shelf, but the items aren't there. He starts rummaging through the toy box again, wondering if they're buried inside. A handful of marbles falls from his hand when he hears Carol's voice, raised above the music.

'I never listen to Tracy Chapman.' She steps over to the ghetto blaster and switches it off.

'Before your time?' Noel retrieves some marbles that have rolled under the bed.

'Bad memories,' she says curtly. She pokes at the toy box with the toe of her grey trainer. 'Looking for something special?'

He drops the marbles back into the toy box and stands, rolling his injured shoulder. The pain has improved gradually, but it still stiffens up. 'Nothing much. Just some bookends and a plane I made in woodwork at school.' He nods towards the desk. 'The exercise books got me thinking about them. Guess they were thrown out years ago.'

'They're still here. Dad kept them in his room.' She whirls around and disappears, returning a moment later with the bookends and plane. She dumps them on the bed next to Noel.

He picks up the plane, tracing its contours with his fingers. 'Not bad for a twelve-year-old, is it?' His smile fades beneath her stony expression. He takes a deep breath. 'About me leaving –'

'How long do you think you'll be?' she interrupts, turning towards the landing. 'The next agent's due soon, then the last one at 12.30. I've got an appointment at the Registry Office at two.'

'The Registry Office?'

She sighs heavily from the threshold. 'To register the death.'

'Oh yeah.' His hand stills on the smooth edge of the plane. 'Would you like me to come with you?'

Carol doesn't answer immediately, and he realises he is holding his breath. The silence is broken by the peal of the doorbell.

'That'll be the next agent,' she says.

Seconds later, he hears her footsteps receding downstairs. He carefully places the plane in the toy box. He leans back on the bed, resting his weight on his elbows. She hasn't replied to his offer to accompany her to the Registry Office. He picks up the bookends. They are shaped, as he remembered, into his initials. 'NR,' he murmurs to himself. 'Noel Reilly, how are you ever going to fix things with your sister?'

Chapter eleven

Half an hour later, Noel has cleared the shelf and desk. He's added his stuffed elephant, cassettes and CDs to the toy box, and discarded his school exercise books. After salvaging some pencils, he has thrown away the rusted stationery tin and its contents. He plans to take the textbooks to a charity shop, although he suspects they will be rejected for being out of date. Next, he turns his attention to the chest of drawers. He takes out the packets of photographs from the top drawer and sits down on the bed.

Noel opens the flap of the top packet and pulls out the photos. His heart twists when he sees his mother smiling up at him. She is sitting on a red and grey checked travelling rug on a sandy beach beneath a cloudless blue sky. Her blonde hair hangs loose around the shoulders of her striped sundress. One tanned arm is wrapped around her baby daughter, who sits in her lap. Beneath a floppy striped sunhat, Carol's head is angled away from the camera. She wears a pink swimsuit decorated with blue shells, and holds one small fist in her mouth. A five-year-old Noel sits on his mother's left, his head resting against her upper arm. He is dressed in a yellow T-shirt imprinted with a smiley face, and green and red checked shorts. His grin reveals a missing upper incisor.

Noel instinctively runs his tongue over his teeth as he stares down at the photo, trying to work out the location. It must be one of the North Yorkshire resorts, since they always spent their holidays in the area. Bridlington, Whitby, Scarborough or Robin Hood's Bay? He's only been back once, when Jade was tiny, even younger than Carol in the photo. It had been Gemma's idea to spend a week in North Yorkshire. Noel had gone along with it, although he'd had his doubts about raking up memories of the childhood he wanted to forget.

It had proved a difficult holiday. Jade had started teething and was cranky, waking them regularly during the night, just a few weeks after she had begun to sleep through. Gemma developed symptoms of food poisoning on their fourth day, which she put down to some prawns she'd eaten in a Whitby café chosen by Noel. It was unusually wet for early August, so they only made it to the beach once. Even then, they'd had to beat a hasty retreat with all the paraphernalia of windbreak, buggy, nappy bag, rug and beach towels when a storm blew up. They'd cut the holiday short and returned home early, more tired than before they left. Not long after, Gemma's brother and sister-in-law had taken a holiday in the Maldives. Gemma began to talk endlessly about how they went off to exotic places regularly. Noel had pointed out that with their university educations, both of them were in better-paid jobs and unencumbered by a small child. But after a few more annual staycations, with his wife growing ever more discontented, she had finally worn him down.

Gazing down at the photo of his childhood holiday, when he looked perfectly happy on a Yorkshire beach, Noel remembers how Gemma had argued that it would be good for Jade to 'broaden her horizons' and travel overseas. So he had agreed to the expensive and ill-fated Caribbean holiday which had sealed the end of their marriage. And Jade had had her horizons broadened in another way, with the advent of Damian as a stepdad in place of her father.

Jade. Noel feels the familiar plucking at his heart strings, thinking of his nine-year-old daughter. Nine months have passed since he last saw her. Gemma refused all contact after he told her that he was moving in with Kylie. Tracing his mother's face with his forefinger, Noel realises with a start the extent to which his daughter has inherited her paternal grandmother's features. The tip-tilted nose, green eyes and generous mouth all belonged to his mother. He hasn't seen a photo of her in twenty-five years, and her image has faded in his mind. Carol has the same green eyes as their mother, and he has inherited her blonde hair, but there the resemblance ends.

He thumbs through the photos, looking for one featuring his father. Judging from Ron Reilly's absence from most of the snaps, it seems that he was usually behind the camera. Eventually Noel finds a picture of the two of them together. This one predates Carol's arrival. Noel is seated inside a plastic toddler swing. His father has one hand on the chain, the other on his little boy's shoulder. There is pride in the young man's smile as he gazes towards the camera. Noel understands why Eileen Baxter did a double take when he opened the door to her three afternoons ago. As a grown man, he looks very like his father, although he is short and slight where his father was tall and broad.

'You'll be here all day if you start going through those old pictures.'

His sister's sharp voice recalls him abruptly to the present. He springs up from the bed, scattering the photos across the floor.

'For goodness' sake.' She makes no effort to hide her exasperation, nor does she offer to help when Noel stoops and begins to gather up the photos. His cheeks are damp, and he realises that he has been crying. He takes the prints over to the desk, keeping his back to her as he shuffles them about, taking longer than he needs while he composes himself. Then he stuffs them back inside the packet. When he trusts himself to speak, he says, 'Shall I get some copies, so that we can both have some?'

'If you like,' she says indifferently. 'I wouldn't have thought you'd want any.'

He squares his shoulders and looks out of the window, gazing across the rows of terraced streets which lead downhill to the town centre. 'They're photos of our mum and dad,' he says quietly. 'Of us as children. Family photos.'

'So?'

Noel rams his hands into the pockets of his bomber jacket, wondering how to broach the past with his sister. A collared dove alights on the roof of the shed in the back yard. It reminds him of Sonia, and he instantly feels calmer. His right hand encounters a cool, hard object. Sonia's wooden cross. He curls his fingers around it before turning towards his sister, fixing his eyes on hers as he searches for the right words.

'What happened later, after Mum died,' he says slowly. 'Dad regretted that. I understood that on Monday. He explained what happened.' He grasps the cross tighter. 'What I'd blanked out, about how she died.'

This time it is Carol who drops her gaze. 'It's a long time ago,' she mutters. 'What's the point of raking it all up? Why can't you let him rest in peace?'

'That's what I want.' He pauses, weighing his next words carefully. 'But I want us to be able to get on better too, be more like a proper brother and sister. Apart from Jade, you're the only family I have.'

Carol's hand flies up to her ponytail and she gathers it up so tightly that Noel flinches, certain that she must be hurting herself. 'Then why did you leave?' she asks, her voice low and furious. 'Why did you leave me, an eleven-year-old girl, alone here with a broken-hearted man? Have you any idea what it was like when you'd gone? He hardly spoke for weeks after you left, took to his bed for two months. I had to fend for myself, do all the things you used to do. Get my own meals, do the washing, sort out the shopping, try to coax him to eat something. Can you imagine what that was like?'

She releases her hair from its band and shakes it out around her shoulders, raking her fingers through it. Her chest is rising and falling rapidly beneath the khaki hoodie, and there are two red spots in her pallid cheeks.

Noel forces himself to maintain eye contact. 'I get that it must have been terrible for you. I didn't want to leave you behind, Carol. Honestly I didn't.'

'Then why did you?'

He hesitates. The truth is brutal, but he feels driven to be frank, in case he doesn't get the chance to explain himself again.

'Because I thought he might kill me.'

Now it is Carol who recoils, then covers her face with her hands. 'He wouldn't have done that,' she says. 'He couldn't have.' Her tone is that of a child pleading that Santa Claus must be real when the magic has been broken. 'It wasn't that bad, surely? I mean, I remember…' Her voice trails off.

'What do you remember?'

She shakes her head. Noel doesn't know whether she is unable or unwilling to dredge up the painful childhood memories.

He hitches a hip on to the edge of the desk. 'It *was* that bad,' he says bleakly. 'He'd come home drunk from the pub. I always made sure that you were in bed, out of the way. So that you never saw what he did.' He swallows. 'But maybe you heard something?' She doesn't respond. Having begun, he feels compelled to carry on. If he doesn't tell her now, she'll never understand. 'Usually it was a few punches, but it was getting worse. I'd thought of going for months before I finally left. I delayed, because of you. On that last night –' He breaks off and gazes around the room, suppressed memories flickering through his mind. Closing his eyes, he grips the edge of the desk tightly in a futile effort to dispel the images. He sees himself cowering beneath the desk, with blood spurting from his nose and filling his mouth. He can almost taste the rusty tang all these years later. For a moment he wonders if he is going to throw up. 'I was so scared,' he says finally, sparing his little sister the details. 'And I couldn't take you with me, because I didn't know where I was going, what I was going to do. I didn't want you to be out on the streets with me. Not

131

that it came to that, but I couldn't be sure when I left. Besides, I didn't want to drag you away from school. You had friends there.'

'But you were my *brother*.' Her voice is a strangled sob.

'I know, and I'm sorry that I left you. But it was for the best. I couldn't cope any more, Carol. I was scared for my life.'

She leans over to scratch a piece of tape left behind on the wall. 'How did you know he wouldn't turn on me when you'd gone?' she asks tightly.

'I honestly didn't think he'd ever hurt you. It was always me he went for. You were the only one who ever managed to make him smile, on his few good days. I felt as though he blamed me for something, but I didn't know what until Monday.' He collapses onto the bed. 'I thought he hated me.'

'But he didn't.' Carol peels away the tape with long nails. The red polish is chipped and growing out. 'He never hated you. He missed you so much. You'd kept us together, getting the meals, doing the chores, making sure I'd done my homework and was ready for school.' She steps back from the wall. '*I* missed you too,' she whispers, sinking on to the bare mattress alongside him, her face turned away.

Noel puts his arm cautiously around her slender shoulders. She tenses, but lets him hold her as she sobs quietly. He remembers his first impression of her when he set eyes on her after his long absence, his kid sister grown up into this scrawny woman with the careworn face. He'd thought she was like an underfed cat. Not only underfed, but neglected, he realises now, semi-feral after having to fend for herself from a young age. Carol needs to learn to trust again. He wonders vaguely what type of man her partner is, whether he has been able to break through her barriers and offer her the consistent kindness which Noel senses she needs after her fractured upbringing.

A shaft of sunlight falls on the packet of photos on the desk. Noel's heart lifts as he sits quietly alongside his sister. There's a long way to go, but he senses this moment offers the hope of a new beginning. Their dark and damaged past has been brought out into the healing light. It occurs to him that they are like survivors of a shipwreck, dazed to find themselves safe on land.

He gives her a gentle squeeze. She wipes her eyes with the heels of her hands and starts to pick at the flaking red polish on her thumbnail.

'I did hear things when he came home from the pub,' she admits quietly. 'But I didn't want to think about it. I used to pull the pillow over my head, so I couldn't hear.'

'That's all right. You were only a kid.' Noel clears his throat. 'I want you to know that I haven't told you this so you'll think badly of Dad. It's just so you understand what it was like for me, why I felt I had to go. I'm telling you so that we have a chance of a fresh start.'

She is silent for a moment, then nods. 'I get that.' She stands and goes across to the window. 'I've been so angry, especially these last few weeks. He started talking about you every day, asking if you'd be coming home. I didn't know what to tell him. And I thought, here I was, dealing with it all, visiting him in hospital, doing his laundry, sorting out things so he could come home to die.'

Her voice catches, and she brushes further tears from her cheeks. 'All he went on about was "our Noel". "Do you think our Noel will come? I need to see him. There's something I've got to tell him." I offered to pass on whatever it was he wanted to say to you, but he wouldn't have it. "I don't think he'll be coming back, Dad," I said, "not after all these years." He begged me to try, and that's when I rang you, though I wasn't sure it was for the best. I was worried it might upset him, seeing you. I wanted him to slip away in peace. I could tell you weren't keen, when you said you'd think about it. Now I know your ex was murdered the day after I rang, wasn't she?' She glances at him over her shoulder. Noel bows his head and she tactfully turns back to the window. 'I'm so sorry about that,' she says gently. 'But I was mad that you didn't come over the weekend. All I could think about was how you'd gone, all those years ago, and left us to it. Then, at the end, Dad was so desperate to see you. It didn't seem fair after everything I'd done for him. I suppose I was jealous.

'After I phoned you, and you didn't say whether or not you'd come, he got even more agitated. He kept clawing at the sheet and moaning. I couldn't tell if it was the physical pain, though the nurses made sure he had morphine whenever he could, or some kind of mental distress. He was like an animal in agony.' She shudders. 'But then you did come, and after you'd talked, he just slipped away, didn't he?' She pivots round, her face wan and tear-stained in the sunlight shining through the window.

Noel studies the backs of his hands, his throat thick with emotion as he thinks again of his final exchange with his father.

'What happened when Mum died?' Carol asks suddenly. 'That's what was bothering him, wasn't it? What did Eileen Baxter have to do with it?'

Noel massages his temples. He has thought several times about how his father seemed to shake his head when Eileen Baxter phoned to say she was on her way that afternoon. He hasn't worked out whether their father didn't want Carol ever to know about his affair with Eileen, or whether he just didn't want her to hear about it during his final hours.

'If we're going to be a family again, we shouldn't have secrets.' Carol's voice cuts into his thoughts with something of its usual stridency.

'There's no easy way of telling you this,' he warns. 'Dad doesn't come out of it well.'

She lifts her chin and makes his dilemma easier by guessing. 'Did they have an affair? Dad and Eileen Baxter?'

He nods. 'Yeah. They were together on the bus that day. I saw them, but I'd forgotten until Dad reminded me. Blocked it out, the doctor thought.' He plunges on in brief staccato sentences. 'Mum had taken the two of us out that afternoon.

You had an appointment at the clinic. I saw Dad on the bus. With Eileen.' He is about to say he saw them kissing, but stops himself. She doesn't need to know that. 'I chased after the bus, excited to see Dad. I ran out into the road without looking. Mum came after me.' He gulps. 'I made it to the pavement just in the nick of time, but the bus knocked her down. Killed her.'

Carol buries her head in her hands. Tears leak through her fingers. 'No,' she whimpers, like the small child she had been in the buggy. 'No.'

Noel scrubs tears from his own cheeks and gets to his feet. 'That's how it happened,' he says softly. He puts his right arm around her and draws her to him. 'It came back to me when Dad explained it. He'd been carrying the guilt all those years, the guilt of his affair with Eileen Baxter. I'm not a psychologist, but I think he turned that guilt against me, for running after him on the bus that day. If I hadn't, Mum might still have been alive.'

He gazes out of the window as Carol sobs quietly on his shoulder. The collared dove is still perched on the shed roof in the yard below. He finds its presence oddly comforting.

'That's why he lashed out at me after she'd gone, the violence getting worse as his guilt grew,' he says. 'I think that's why he wanted to see me before he died.'

'For forgiveness,' murmurs Carol. 'He wanted your forgiveness.'

'Yes.' With his free hand, Noel touches the cross in his pocket. 'That's what I've realised. He wanted my forgiveness.'

Chapter twelve

After the last estate agent has valued the house, Noel accompanies Carol to register their father's death. They eat a late lunch in one of the cafés near the Registry Office. Both of them are quiet after their emotionally charged conversation. Carol nibbles half a cheese sandwich and gulps down her tea before saying she has errands to run, leaving Noel to finish his pea and ham soup alone. He ordered the soup in a fit of nostalgia, asking Carol if she remembered their mother making them a similar thick broth. But his sister is too young to share the memory.

Setting out on the journey home, with the toy box rattling in the back of the van, Noel is in pensive mood. There are things in his past which no one else remembers, now that his father has gone. After spending his adult life trying to draw a shroud over his early years, he finds himself actively retrieving his memories. His route takes him past the municipal park where he used to have a kickabout with his dad when he was small. The playground would be where his mother took the photo of him in the toddler swing, his father leaning in proudly. He remembers trips to the park with his mother and Carol in her pushchair, and how he would beg to stop by the aviary on entry and exit, fascinated by the tweeting, fluttering budgies, finches and cockatiels.

On a whim, Noel takes a detour along the back street where his red-brick Victorian primary school still stands. Groups of parents throng the playground, waiting to collect their offspring. He has a sudden vivid recollection of his mother bending to kiss him, her hand smoothing his hair, of him turning back towards her in tears halfway across the yard. He wonders if it's a memory of his first day as he drives carefully down the busy street lined on both sides with parked vehicles.

He rejoins the main road and winds his way back through the villages towards Trentby. Traffic is heavy along the dual carriageway leading into the town. Behind the cylindrical chimneys of the power station to the west, the sky is a palette of pinks, reds and oranges. Noel gazes absently at the autumn sunset as he brakes behind an HGV, lost in his memories. There's one item he pounced on when he found it beneath a pile of long unused napery in the chest of drawers: his grandmother's black leather Bible.

Carol had looked at him askance when he'd asked if he could take it. 'What would I want with a Bible? It won't be worth anything, will it?'

It had been on the tip of his tongue to say that it was priceless to him, but he had bitten back the words. He judged that after all they had shared about their troubled family history that day, this wasn't the time to tell her about his new-found faith.

In the queue of vehicles crawling towards the lights over the bridge into town, Noel thinks about how much he is looking forward to showing Sonia the Bible. He plans to take it round on Sunday, when he has agreed to go to church with her. She's offered to cook him lunch afterwards, an invitation he accepted eagerly when she rang him the previous day. He shakes his head with a wry smile as he crawls forward a few yards and draws level with the pub. The very idea of going to church would never have crossed his mind a week ago. But then it will be a week tomorrow since he found himself at rock bottom following news of Kylie's murder, a week since his bizarre experience by the river.

Watching the flaming sun sink lower across the fields, Noel realises with a sense of wonder that the Being's words have been partially fulfilled. His conversation with his sister has deepened the peace he has known since Sonia prayed for him two days ago. But the Being spoke of him being an agent of justice too, of righting wrongs. The greatest wrong that continues to haunt him and which means that his new sense of equilibrium is fragile is Kylie's murder. He hasn't heard the news since breakfast, when no mention was made of her murder. The speed with which the media have moved on from the tragedy strikes him as heartless. His hands clench the steering wheel at the thought that her killer is still at large.

The traffic grinds to a halt, signalling that the lights over the other side of the bridge have changed to red. Noel yanks on the handbrake and glances along the riverside path which leads down from the road past the pub. It's impossible not to look, after that peculiar vision, and the coincidence of Mrs Mullins' fixation with the river. That's something else to chew over with Sonia – Florence's strange talk of the Grey One, the Bright Giant and Jesus, and her research into the unusually high number of suicides, accidental and violent deaths in the small town. Kylie's murder, the violent death of Michelle's husband, the drowning of Florence's brother and the suicide of the son of his elderly neighbours' late friend are four such deaths that he has heard of in the past week. Is it possible that there is some malevolent influence at work, named by Mrs Mullins as the Grey One? The question has circled in Noel's mind since his conversation with the old ladies. It seems too fantastic, but so many strange things have happened recently that he finds he can't discount the possibility. He shivers involuntarily at the thought of how close he came to being numbered among the grim statistics. He wonders again whether the peculiar mist and the voice he heard urging him into the water were manifestations of the Grey One.

The sun dips below the horizon as the vehicles in front begin to creep forward. Noel releases the handbrake to move off, then notices a pedestrian coming down the pavement from the bridge. From the skipping gait, he recognises Mrs

Mullins. Closer up, he sees that she is dressed in her usual tweed coat and black fur hat. His eyes fixed on his elderly neighbour, he loses concentration and stalls the van. His heart sinks when Florence canters right along the riverside path, picking up speed on the descent. He restarts the engine and turns left into the pub car park without indicating, earning a beep from the car behind. Ignoring the sign that the car park is reserved for patrons only, he swings into a space and leaps out of the van. By the time he reaches the path, Florence has disappeared from view behind a clump of trees.

Noel tries to tell himself that his worries for Florence's safety are irrational as he sets off along the narrow track at a run. Maureen told him that her neighbour knows the path well, and used to walk her dog down here. But when he rounds the copse and sees only a teenage girl jogging towards him, he isn't sure whether it's exertion or fear for the old lady that is making his heart hammer in his chest.

'Have you seen an old lady?' he gasps out, stepping off the path to make way for the girl.

The teenager doesn't reply. When she draws level, he notices her white ear buds. Her magenta lips move soundlessly along to the music, and she barely glances at him as she nods an acknowledgement for his courtesy in stepping aside.

Noel puffs out his cheeks and looks around in the gathering dusk. There is no chance that Florence could be so far in front of him that she has traversed the stile at the far side of the field. That was the route he took in his drunken despair. Relief that his neighbour can't have made it towards the river along the path is short-lived when he sees that a high hedge forms an unbroken boundary to his left. His stomach churning, he realises that only leaves the river, which lies behind a hedge to his right. He breaks into a run down the slope, slipping and sliding in the mud. 'Mrs Mullins!' he calls. 'Mrs Mullins!' But the only sound is the whoosh of traffic on the road behind him.

Reaching the hedge, Noel sees that brambles have grown over a three-bar wooden fence. He jogs along, scanning for a gap, hoping that Florence won't have forced her way through the prickly bushes. The brown shrivelled blackberries evoke another childhood memory, of blackberry picking with his mother, and the sweet smell of her crumbles and pies percolating through the house. Halfway along the field, the brambles thin out to reveal an old stile. He steps warily onto a rotting plank of wood. It holds his weight and he surveys the riverbank, looking for signs of his elderly neighbour. The bank falls away steeply in front of him towards reeds and bulrushes marking the edge of the river. To the left is an overgrown track rutted with puddles. A notice in flaking paint prohibits fishing without a permit. Noel hears the faint lap of water and shivers.

A final blaze of colour from the dying sun illuminates something dark along the path. Noel jumps down from the stile into long grass and moves towards the object, catching his breath when he recognises Florence's fur hat. He picks it up and jogs along until he almost loses his footing. The track here is lined with reeds, and his trainers squelch in the mud. There is enough light for him to see that the way ahead looks increasingly boggy. Glancing down, he makes out a few dainty footprints among the larger prints of wellington boots. The churning in his stomach intensifies. He shouts as loudly as he can. 'Mrs Mullins! Mrs Mullins!'

A harsh explosive sound pins him to the spot. He swivels round to see a heron rise from the reeds. Its legs trail behind as it flies low towards the river, flapping its wings slowly, a flash of white against the indigo sky. A gust of wind bends the reeds, and carries another noise to his ears. He holds his breath, straining to listen. Then he hears it again, nearer this time, the sound of a woman singing softly.

And here is Florence, picking her way carefully through the reeds. Noel identifies the wartime tune, 'We'll Meet Again'. *Appropriate*, he thinks dryly, and exhales in relief.

Florence cuts a bedraggled figure. Released from the black fur hat, her white shock of hair rises in tufts around her head. Her mid-heeled tan shoes are caked with mud, and there are further splodges below the waist of her tweed coat. She stops singing abruptly when she sees Noel, and comes to a standstill, peering towards him in the twilight. 'Oh!' she exclaims.

Belatedly, Noel realises that he might have frightened her. He summons a smile. 'Hello, Mrs Mullins. Are you looking for this?' He holds out the hat.

Her face lights up and she advances immediately, any apprehension forgotten. 'You found my hat!' She grabs it from him.

'It's covered in mud,' warns Noel.

But the old woman takes no notice. She plonks the hat on her head and stares into his face, mud trickling down her cheeks, before asking the inevitable question. 'Do I know you?'

'Yes.' Noel yawns. 'I live across the road from you. I think we should go home, don't you? It's getting dark.'

Florence glances around but doesn't move. Her voice drops to a stage whisper. 'Did you see him?'

Sweat runs down Noel's spine. 'I've not seen anyone except you and a jogger.' He extends his arm towards her. 'Shall we go?'

She ignores the proffered arm, her head turning towards the reeds. 'Such a glorious sunset, did you see?'

'It was beautiful. But I think we should leave now.'

She takes a few paces down the bank.

'It's very slippery down there, Mrs Mullins.' He manages to speak calmly, though the lapping of the water is getting louder and sounds as if it's coming closer. The river is tidal, with the highest tides in spring and autumn. He looks along the boggy path, but can't see anything apart from the reeds and bulrushes bending in the wind. He steps towards the old lady slowly, careful not to alarm her.

'I thought I'd find him for sure,' she murmurs. 'The Bright Giant. I went down to where the boathouse used to be. Do you remember it?'

'I didn't live round here then.'

'Oh.' She is nonplussed, then brightens. 'But that sunset!' She folds her arms across her chest, hugging herself. 'It seemed just the right time for him to be here, don't you think?'

'Maybe another day,' he suggests gently. 'Let's go home and get some tea now, shall we?'

An eerie sound fills the air, beginning as a low moan, then rising in intensity to a shrill high-pitched whistle, before falling away to a sibilant whisper. Noel breaks out in goosebumps.

Mrs Mullins grabs his arm, her eyes wide with terror. 'Did you hear that?'

'Yes.' His teeth are chattering. 'It must have been the wind,' he says falteringly, conscious that the reeds around them are very still.

She shakes her head. 'That wasn't the wind,' she says, her voice quavering. 'That was the sound of the Grey One. He's getting stronger.'

Noel shudders. 'Let's go, shall we?'

She casts a lingering look over her shoulder. 'If only the Bright Giant would come. But it's much too dark now.'

'Much too dark,' he echoes, clamping her hand more firmly to his arm as he guides her back up the bank. He is chilled to the bone, and is well aware that this has nothing to do with the disappearance of the sun on the autumn evening. He has been so preoccupied with searching for the old lady that he has barely thought about the terrible state he was in when he last stumbled along the riverside path. He finds he is seriously considering Florence's explanation that the sinister sound they have just heard is the noise of the Grey One, not least because he is in the place where he so nearly ended his life last week. He seems to hear again that terrible whisper, *It will all be over soon,* as he yanks the old lady along.

'Do you think the Bright Giant will come tomorrow?' asks Florence, as he helps her over the crumbling stile.

'Umm...' Catching her hopeful expression, he refrains from making the sceptical response which has risen to his lips. 'Maybe.'

A girlish smile lights up her face as they set out across the field. 'He will! I'm sure of it!' She lowers her voice to a conspiratorial whisper. 'You've seen him, haven't you?'

Noel pretends he hasn't heard. The wind is beginning to rise now, soughing through the belt of trees ahead. Florence seems to be tiring, dragging her feet in the ruined shoes. He links his arm through hers as they emerge from the spinney.

The lights of the pub are inviting with their promise of company and normality. It's on the tip of Noel's tongue to suggest they go in for a drink, but the old lady is sagging against him, and seems to have little energy left. He decides that the best course of action is to get her home as soon as possible. Besides, her dishevelled appearance might draw unwelcome attention. The last thing he needs after a long and draining day is to fend off questions from strangers.

Back at the van, Florence is so tired that he has to lift her inside. She lolls back against the headrest while he buckles the seat belt over her. He is shocked to see that it's almost seven o'clock. By the time he has got in and turned on the engine, she is asleep. Just like a child, thinks Noel, as he turns left on to the bridge, wistfully remembering the number of times Jade would fall asleep after a family outing when she was small. He wonders again when he might next see his daughter.

Florence stirs and yawns when Noel pulls up behind a black BMW parked below her house. He sees that the 1930s semi is ablaze with light as he jumps out of the van and goes round to help her out.

'Where am I?' asks the old lady.

Noel leans over and unfastens the seat belt. 'Home, Mrs Mullins. Safely home.' He helps her out onto the pavement and slips his arm through hers to guide her up the steep steps.

They are only halfway up when the porch door is flung open and they hear Maureen's voice, hoarse with relief. 'There you are, Florence! Geraldine and I have been worried out of our minds. Has Noel had to rescue you again?'

Another harried voice calls, 'Wherever have you been, Mum? I was about to call the police.'

A slight figure steps out on to the patio and waits for them to climb the final steps. Evidently this is Geraldine, Florence's daughter. She takes Florence's free arm when they reach the patio, and Noel lets go on the other side.

Geraldine guides her mother into the porch. 'Oh, Mum, look at your coat!' she scolds. 'And for goodness' sake, let me take your shoes or you'll tread mud everywhere. They're ruined!'

Florence allows Geraldine to help her out of her coat and shoes, but squawks in protest when her daughter removes her filthy hat and drops it on to the tiled floor of the porch alongside the shoes. 'My hat! I want my hat!'

Geraldine gives her mother a little push into the hall. 'Don't be ridiculous. It's disgusting! Now go and sit down.' Geraldine points into the sitting room, then looks down at her dirty hands and screws up her nose. 'I'll go and wash my hands upstairs.'

Moaning about her hat, Florence follows her daughter's instructions. Geraldine sprints up the stairs.

'I'll go and put the kettle on,' offers Maureen. 'Where did you find her, Noel? She wasn't by the river again, was she?' She heads towards the small kitchen.

'Yes.' Noel steps into the porch, smothering a yawn. 'I spotted her when I was driving over the bridge. Don't worry about making me a drink. I should be getting home.'

'Nonsense!' says Maureen briskly. 'We want to hear about how you found Florence. Besides, you look frozen. A hot drink will be good for you.'

Noel can't summon the energy to say he could make himself a hot drink at home, or even better, fix himself a whisky. Maureen is beckoning him to join her in the kitchen and he traipses reluctantly after her, leaving his muddy trainers in the porch.

Maureen runs water into the kettle, sets it on its base and flicks the switch. 'I want you to help me persuade Geraldine that her mother isn't safe on her own any more,' she says. 'That's two days this week you've fetched her home from the river. What was she doing down there at this time? She's never wandered off so late before.' She takes four china mugs from the cupboard above the kettle. 'Or not that I know of.'

Noel runs his hand across his head. 'I think it was the sunset that attracted her.'

Maureen grunts and drops two teabags into a large teapot. She gives him a sharp look. 'She didn't start on about them things again, did she? The Bright Giant and the Grey One?'

He looks down at his socks, soiled where the mud has soaked through his trainers. 'I'm afraid she did.'

Maureen scowls and pours boiled water into the teapot. 'That reminds me.' She nods towards the microwave on the counter on Noel's left. 'I found that file yesterday in Flo's bookcase. She said I could lend it to you, though she'll have forgotten that now, poor thing.'

'Oh?' Noel picks up the battered buff folder from the top of the microwave.

'Flo's notes and newspaper cuttings are in it.' Maureen pours milk into a jug. 'All her research that I was telling you about.'

'Right. Thanks.' Noel contemplates the bulging folder uneasily. From what Maureen told him earlier in the week, it contains information of tragic deaths. He wonders if it will help him to understand more about the root of Mrs Mullins' fixation with the river and the phenomena she claims to see. If so, what will that mean about his own experience? Is it possible that his vision was real, and that he has been chosen, as the Being said? He is finding it easier to believe in the Grey One after the eerie sound he heard by the river with Florence

145

tonight. Rationally, he wonders if the Being he met and Florence's Bright Giant are the product of some kind of wishful thinking to counteract the disturbing associations of the river for both of them. But the similarity of Florence's description of the Bright Giant with the Being of Noel's vision is so striking that he is open to the idea, incredible as it is, that he and Florence have encountered the same other-worldly phenomena by the river. He is even wondering if the Being is some kind of representation of Jesus, however incredible that seems, after Florence suggested it was Jesus who rescued her from drowning like her brother all those years ago.

Maureen is still rattling on, remarking how fortunate it is that he happened to be driving over the bridge at the very time Florence was there. 'You're turning into her guardian angel!' She gives him a broad smile which softens the lines on her face. 'Why don't you put the folder on the hall table to make sure you don't leave it behind? Then you can take the tray through for me, and we'll have our tea.'

He follows the old woman's instructions, his mind racing. Could this be part of what it means to be chosen? The Being's words echo around his head. *You have been chosen to right the wrongs in this place, to shine as light in the darkness. First, you will find your own healing.*

He is in no doubt that he has begun to find his own healing. Is it possible that 'righting the wrongs' in the town includes looking after an old lady whose mind is wandering, and learning about the grim record of untimely deaths contained in the file she compiled?

And could it be that this dark history is somehow connected with Kylie's murder?

Chapter thirteen

In the sitting room, Noel finds Florence in her armchair, staring vacantly at her daughter. Geraldine is pacing the room, berating her mother. She is a slim, wiry woman in her mid-forties, dressed in an expensive-looking black logo jersey sweatshirt and matching leggings. Her highlighted blonde hair is styled into a pixie cut which shows off her heart-shaped face. Noel can see that some men would find her attractive, but he detects an off-putting hardness in her blue eyes. She pays no attention to him as he sets down the tray on the coffee table.

'I was so worried when Maureen phoned, Mum. I was just about to go to the gym. What were you thinking, going down to the river at this hour?'

'She wasn't,' mutters Maureen, who has followed Noel into the room. She plumps up the cushion in the armchair next to Florence.

Geraldine frowns and stops pacing. She places her hands on the back of the leather buttoned sofa and stares at Maureen. 'Wasn't what?'

'Wasn't thinking.' Maureen sinks down into the chair. 'Will you pour, Noel?'

Noel obligingly lifts the heavy teapot and begins to pour.

'None for me, thanks.' Geraldine doesn't look at him. She has evidently chosen to overlook Maureen's comment and turns her attention back to her mother.

Florence has picked up a tangled ball of yellow wool lying beside her, and is plucking away at it with her long white fingers. 'Can't find the end,' she mutters. 'I wish I could find the end.'

'Do put that wool down, Mum!' chides Geraldine. 'Why do you always insist on messing about with it when I'm here? You know I don't like it.'

Florence ignores her daughter and continues to tug at the yarn.

Maureen reaches forward and takes a steaming mug off the tray. 'It's what they do,' she says, *sotto voce*.

Geraldine taps her fingers against the top of the sofa. 'What who do?'

'People suffering with your mother's problem.'

Geraldine gives an exasperated sigh. 'Mum wouldn't have a problem if she would only stay at home. Look at the state she's in! Her hair's like a bird's nest, and her stockings torn to shreds. Whatever happened, Mum?'

'I don't remember,' Florence looks up from the wool for a moment. 'Never mind. Here we are, safe and sound.' She smiles round at them, then bows her head and resumes her task. One strand of wool has split into three threads.

'That's thanks to Noel.' Maureen looks pointedly at Geraldine.

The younger woman nods reluctantly towards Noel, who is standing by the door, nursing his mug between his hands.

'Yes. Thank you for your help,' she says curtly. 'Do you know what my mother was doing? Where did you find her?'

Noel blows on his tea. 'She was wandering along the riverbank. I found her down by the reeds.'

Maureen clears her throat. Noel takes it as a signal for him to say more following their conversation in the kitchen. He musters the courage to meet Geraldine's icy blue stare. 'It wasn't safe,' he says quietly. 'It was getting dark and I could hear the river rising.'

Geraldine drops her eyes and examines her manicured violet nails under the ceiling light. 'Maureen told me that you found my mother on Tuesday as well. We're very grateful, aren't we, Mum?'

Florence doesn't reply. Maureen leans over and taps her arm, and her head jerks up.

'Geraldine was saying how grateful you are that Noel rescued you,' says Maureen.

Noel's cheeks burn. He drinks deeply, hiding his face behind his mug.

'Noel rescued me?' Florence glances around. Her bewildered gaze alights on the only man in the room. 'Are you Noel?'

He lowers the mug and smiles at her. 'That's right.'

'You see?' says Maureen to Geraldine. 'Your poor mum can't remember things for ten seconds. She isn't safe here any more. She's obsessed with that river. What if Noel hadn't been there at just the right time?' Her voice wavers.

Geraldine begins to pace again. 'It's very fortunate he was there,' she agrees coolly. 'But I'm sure she would have come home safely. She's walked along the riverbank all her life, haven't you, Mum?'

Florence continues to pick at the yarn without looking up. Nor does she pay any attention when Geraldine says again, her voice fraying like the mauled ball of wool, 'Mum?'

'She doesn't know you,' murmurs Maureen.

'Of course she does!' But Geraldine's voice wobbles, like a frightened child. For the first time, Noel feels a spark of sympathy for her.

Maureen also hears the panic in the younger woman's voice. Her face softens. 'Look, duck, I've known you since you were tiny and playing with my Barry. And I know it's hard to face this, but your mum really shouldn't be on her own.' She casts a glance at Florence, who continues to tug at the wool. 'It breaks my heart to say it, after she's been my neighbour and best friend for so long, but it's time to think about her moving somewhere she can be looked after.'

Geraldine picks up a slender blue and white vase from the wooden mantelpiece and traces the swirls on it with her forefinger. 'But I promised her she could stay here,' she says miserably. 'After Dad died, she made me promise.'

'She was well then,' says Maureen gently. 'Neither of you could know she'd get like this. It would be for her own safety, wouldn't it, Noel?'

Noel isn't at all sure that Geraldine will be interested in his opinion, but he is compelled to agree. 'I've only just got to know your mother, but I'm afraid Maureen's right. She's very confused.'

Geraldine replaces the vase on the mantelpiece with a sigh. 'I'll think about it.'

Relief spreads across Maureen's face. 'Just make sure you don't think about it for too long. That place up the hill has a good reputation. Freshfields. My friend Brenda settled in very well last year. She's all right up here' – Maureen taps the side of her forehead – 'but kept falling at home, so it was safer for her to move in. And they have a special unit for people in Flo's... situation.'

Noel stiffens at the mention of the residential home where Kylie worked.

'I've heard something about that recently.' Geraldine knits her plucked eyebrows. 'I know, it's the place where that woman worked, isn't it? The one who was murdered?'

Maureen nods. 'That's it. Terrible business. They haven't found anyone for it yet. Brenda knows the girl's mother, and she told me that the police took her ex in for questioning the day it happened. He wasn't charged, though.'

Blood thrums in Noel's ears. He buries his head in his mug again and gulps down the rest of his tea.

'Them poor kiddies,' continues Maureen. 'She left behind two little boys, Brenda said.'

Noel's chest tightens as he thinks of Bradley and Liam. Both good kids, for all their squabbling. It breaks his heart to think what they must be going through, knowing only too well the unbearable nature of losing his mother as a small boy himself. He wonders how they will be getting on with their grandma, and how Susan Weatherall is coping with them. She isn't in the best of health, and it won't be easy for her, bringing them up. However hostile she was towards him in the convenience store, and however much she might have been bad-mouthing him, he feels desperately sorry for her and her grandsons.

'So sad,' murmurs Geraldine. But her mind has already moved on to other things. She glances at her watch. 'I need to get home to my two soon, check they're getting on with their homework. Harry needs to knuckle down, with his A levels coming up. No chance of the gym tonight!' She glances with distaste at her mother's bent head, with its mussed thatch of muddy hair. 'I suppose I should wash Mum's hair before I go.'

Noel exhales now that the conversation has moved on. He looks at Florence. Judging from the speed with which her fingers are plucking at the wool, she is becoming increasingly frustrated at being unable to find an end. Or perhaps that isn't what she's agitating over, because she suddenly raises her head, fixes him with one of her intent gazes and says clearly, 'It's the Grey One's doing.'

Noel's scalp prickles.

Geraldine rolls her eyes at Maureen. 'You're not on about that again, are you, Mum? It was all she would talk about when I dropped her shopping in on Saturday. The Grey One and that other thing.'

Maureen levers herself out of her armchair. 'That'll be the Bright Giant. That's what she goes looking for down at the river, isn't it, Noel?'

Noel is speechless, and can only manage a nod. Florence's words, spoken directly to him, reverberate in his mind. *'It's the Grey One's doing.'* The old woman is still staring at him. He shudders. *Is it just coincidence that she mentioned the Grey One when Kylie's murder was being discussed? And why is she looking at him as if he is the only person in the room who will understand?*

'All part of her condition, I expect,' observes Maureen complacently. 'Now, shall I do the washing up while you wash your mum's hair, Geraldine?'

'Thanks.' Geraldine is watching Noel, her brow puckered. 'Are you all right? You're not disturbed by my mother's talk of these ghost things she's invented, are you?'

'Course he's not!' Maureen peers towards him, the light reflecting off her bifocals. 'Though you do look very pale, duck.' She clicks her tongue against her teeth. 'You won't have had chance to get anything to eat, will you? You'd best get off home.'

'Home,' echoes Florence unexpectedly. Three heads swivel towards her. 'I love my home,' she announces, with one of her beatific smiles.

Maureen bends over the tray, shuffling the mugs around. Watching her, a lump rises in Noel's throat. It must be difficult for this doughty woman to face the fact that her best friend and neighbour is no longer safe in the home she loves, and that the time has come for them to part company.

'We know you love your home, Mum.' Geraldine's voice catches and she bites her lip before continuing briskly, 'Come on, let's go and wash your hair, and then I can go.' She strides across to Florence.

Noel moves forward to take the tray back to the kitchen for Maureen, who gives him a wan smile of thanks. He deposits it by the kitchen sink and makes his farewells, picking up the buff folder from the kidney-shaped table in the hall on his way out. On the patio, he takes a few deep breaths of the crisp evening air, and turns his face up to the sky. The tension that has filled the last moments begins to melt away as he gazes at the starry expanse above him.

The steps to the street are slippery with frost, and he picks his way down them carefully in his muddy trainers. The van windscreen is already icing over. He decides to leave it outside Florence's house for the night, remembering first to retrieve the carrier bag of canned food salvaged from his father's house.

Walking up the street, Noel finds himself thinking about the homes he has lived in, beginning with the terraced house in Oldford which has brought back so many memories that day. After various shared rentals, he saved up to buy the little cottage on the edge of town which Gemma moved into when they married. She made it very clear that she viewed it as no more than a starter home. He'd been forced to sell it when they divorced. It was the only means by which he could afford to pay her the lump sum the court ordered was due to her under the financial settlement. After another tenancy in a street known locally as 'Drug Alley', there had been the three months in the local authority housing with Kylie and her sons which had ended so badly. Now here he is, at forty-one, living alone in a rented terrace in the wrong end of town, on a street where he doesn't know anyone apart from two old ladies.

Noel shakes his head as he clasps Florence's folder to his chest with one hand and fishes for the house key in his jacket pocket with the other. He's never had a life plan, drifting along after fleeing his father's violence. He'd been fortunate to secure regular employment with a local builder in Trentby, and it was a job he enjoyed until the builder retired. When he bought his cottage and married Gemma, he thought he was settling down. He'd expected Jade's birth would bring them closer together, but it was soon after Jade was born that Gemma's dissatisfaction with their modest standard of living emerged. He feels the familiar pang as he thinks of his daughter. His fingers close over the wooden cross in his pocket, nestling alongside his key. He surprises himself by whispering a quick prayer, 'Let me see Jade soon, God, please.'

He isn't at all sure that God will answer the simple prayer of an ordinary man. But as he extracts the key and turns it in the lock, Noel reckons there's no harm in asking. He makes a mental note to ask Sonia more about prayer when he sees her on Sunday. He wonders how believers deal with unanswered prayer. Sonia must have experience of that. No doubt she would have prayed for her husband's recovery from cancer, and for those involved in her son-in-law's death to be brought to justice. He wonders fleetingly if Michelle shares her mother's faith, or if she has lost it following the difficulties she has encountered in her life. Stepping into the cold, dark house, Noel finds himself uttering a further simple prayer for Sonia and Michelle, Bradley, Liam and Susan Weatherall, 'Help them, God. Let those who killed Sonia's son-in-law and Kylie be found.'

Warmth fills him as he says the words. Inside the cold house, he switches on the light and turns up the thermostat on the wall. The boiler roars into life in the airing cupboard on the upstairs landing. It occurs to him that perhaps prayer is part of the task assigned to him by the mysterious Master, a step towards righting the wrongs in the town.

It's a dizzying thought. Noel is too hungry and tired to dwell on it, and pushes it from his mind as he goes through to the kitchen. He sets Florence's folder and bag down on the small functional beech table and slings his jacket over the back of a matching chair. The prospect of cooking after a long day is even less inviting than usual, and he is grateful for the tinned pork and beans that he brought back from his father's house.

He discovers that he doesn't enjoy the cooked pork as much as he did when he was a boy, but he still feels better for the basic meal. He turns on the TV and flicks through the channels, settling on a football match. In theory, it should be a one-sided FA Cup tie, with a Premiership club pitched against a non-league team. The Premiership club are fielding a second team. Not many of their supporters have bothered to make the cross-country journey on a midweek night to the ground of their lowly opponents. But the locals are out in force, cheering on their team.

Noel takes a can of beer from the fridge and settles back in the chair. A few minutes before half-time, the unbelievable happens. The Premiership goalkeeper fumbles a tame strike from the non-league captain. The keeper watches, disconsolate, as the ball trickles into the back of the net. The captain launches into a victory dance, then disappears from view under a sea of blue and mauve striped shirts as his exultant teammates swamp him. The home supporters go wild, and Noel cheers along with them. The cameras focus briefly on the strained faces of the manager and supporters from the Premiership team, before showing countless replays of the goal from different angles. After another two minutes of play, the referee blows the half-time whistle.

The commercial break follows. Noel completes the meagre amount of washing up, then resumes his seat for the review of the first half. The commentators excitedly trot out the usual statements about the magic of the FA Cup making possible these David and Goliath contests. Noel grins to himself and sips his beer, legs outstretched. The odds might be stacked against the non-league team holding on to their lead, but the slim chance of them achieving the feat makes compelling viewing.

After more adverts, the second half begins. There is a new confidence about the minor club's players as they run out onto the pitch, heads high. In contrast, the Premiership team jog out dejectedly. The home crowd sound more vocal than ever, especially as thirty minutes go by and their players continue to hold their own. 'Can the team from the minor league hold on and slay the Premiership giants?' asks the commentator breathlessly.

The reference to 'giants' causes Noel to glance instinctively at the buff folder lying on the table. It looks innocuous enough, but he has a sense of misgiving as he reaches across for it. Then his mobile rings, its usual jaunty tone muffled inside the pocket of his jacket. He pulls it out and looks at the screen. He doesn't recognise the number, so he answers with his trade name after muting the TV. 'Reilly's Repairs.'

A woman giggles. 'Seriously? Is that the best you could come up with?'

Noel's hackles rise, even as his heart begins to beat more quickly. 'Gemma. Is Jade OK?' *Because why else would his ex-wife ring after months of avoiding his calls? But if anything has happened to Jade, she wouldn't be giggling, would she?* The questions race through his mind in the few seconds before she answers.

'Jade's fine.'

'That's good.' He closes his eyes. *She isn't ringing for more money, surely?* He conscientiously pays what was agreed when they split, but he can't think of any other reason why Gemma would suddenly contact him.

Switching his attention back to the TV, he sees that one of the Premiership club's strikers is preparing to take a penalty. The cameras show the anxious faces of the home crowd as the man in the maroon shirt eyes up the net. Noel holds his breath.

'Yeah, she's doing good at school. Proper little swot, she is. Don't know where she gets it from!'

'That's great.' He isn't only commenting on their daughter's progress at school. The striker has run forward to take the kick. The minor club goalkeeper has guessed correctly, diving to his left and gathering the ball to his chest. Noel finds himself grinning along with the delighted supporters at the chance that has gone begging for the Premiership team to equalise.

'Yeah.' Gemma falls silent.

Noel sighs. *Must be money.* 'How can I help, Gemma? It's been a long time. I didn't recognise the number. Have you changed your phone?'

'Changed it a while ago. Didn't I give you the new number?'

He bites his lip. *All those times he's phoned her old number, hearing it go to the robotic answer service.* He's certain that she knows full well she hadn't passed on her new number. Nor would he put it past her to change it deliberately so he couldn't call her. Still, he doesn't want to antagonise her. She's phoned, and this gives him a chance. He draws himself up in his chair.

'No, you didn't. Since you've called, I should mention I'm planning to go and see my solicitor about contact.'

'No need,' Gemma jumps in. 'That's why I'm ringing. I've been thinking, and it'd be good if we can sort out regular access.'

Noel feels his eyes widen. *Seriously? Is this an answer to prayer already?* 'That would be great,' he says cautiously. 'Every other weekend, like we agreed at the start?'

'Sure. Shall we start a week tomorrow? Could you pick Jade up from school?'

'No problem.' His heart lifts. 'Instead of Saturday morning?'

'Yeah. Why not? Thing is, Damian and me are going to a wedding in Wales. Kids aren't invited. I didn't realise until today. Mum's in Tenerife.'

Noel can't help smiling to himself. 'Sounds like I'm the last resort.'

'It's not like that,' Gemma insists, her voice unusually serious. 'I'd been thinking we should get something sorted.'

He senses her hesitation and stares unseeingly at the TV, wondering what's coming next.

'Look, I'm sorry,' she says unexpectedly. 'About your ex. I couldn't believe it when I heard.'

'Thanks,' he says thickly. 'I appreciate it.'

'Yeah... well... Those poor kids. Their dads aren't around, are they?'

'No. Cleared off years ago.' Noel remembers Kylie's bitterness towards her ex for leaving soon after Liam was born. Her older son's father lived in Scotland and rarely made contact with Bradley. No wonder she had jumped to the conclusion that Noel wouldn't stick around to support their baby after her experiences, especially after his lukewarm response to her revelation that April evening.

He screws up his face as he ponders again the question that has haunted him since the police told him about her murder: *If he had stayed, would she and their baby still be alive?*

'It's awful,' says Gemma. 'Anyway, it made me think. I should let you see Jade.'

'Right.' Noel tilts back his head and surveys the ceiling. He wonders if he would be having this conversation with his ex-wife if Kylie hadn't died. But the fact is, he's going to see his daughter for the first time in nine months. Never mind how it's come about. It feels like a minor miracle.

'I'll text you next week, just to confirm. And I'll make sure Jade takes her overnight bag to school.'

'Right. Thanks. Tell her I'm looking forward to it.'

'Sure. Bye.'

'Bye.'

Noel ends the call and flicks the sound back on the TV. Only two minutes of the match remain. The minor league team supporters are singing more quietly, though no less tunelessly, tension etched in their faces as the seconds tick away. The Premiership club manager patrols the touchline, barking orders at his dejected team.

The final whistle blows. The commentators are hoarse with excitement. 'Who would have thought it? Who would have predicted that this little team would be capable of delivering the biggest shock of the FA Cup so far this season?'

A grin splits Noel's face from ear to ear. The football result and the prospect of seeing his daughter have made this a good night. He takes another beer from the fridge.

Turning back towards the table, his eyes alight on the buff folder. He covers it with some junk mail he hasn't got round to recycling. Then he settles back in his chair for the post-match analysis.

'Out of sight, out of mind,' he mutters. Florence's research will wait.

The policeman who interviewed the staff at Freshfields last weekend came to the house yesterday afternoon. 'Just a few routine enquiries,' he said at the door, after explaining that he was investigating the carer's murder.

I'd been expecting him ever since the manager said he wanted to question everyone who works at Freshfields, including those of us who weren't on shift when he visited. I took it that every day that passed was a sign that I was low on the list of suspects. Even so, I was a bit rattled to see him on my doorstep, especially with Nosy Crow next door stepping out to clear a few leaves from her front patio. Coincidence that she appeared just after the policeman arrived, it was not! 'Everything all right, duck?' she called.

'Yes, thank you,' I said coldly. Then, thinking I'd better look friendly in front of the policeman, I added, 'And don't forget, June, if there's anything I can get you when I go shopping tomorrow, just drop me a text.' Her jaw dropped open, showing all her black fillings. Oh, you would have laughed to see her looking so gobsmacked, Mum!

I invited the policeman inside with my most charming smile and offered him a cup of tea. His questions were straightforward enough, and nothing I hadn't anticipated. I told him I didn't know Kylie well, although we'd been colleagues at Freshfields for the last couple of years. I'd already worked out that although I didn't have an alibi for the time of the murder, the police can't suspect everyone who doesn't have someone to vouch for them. I must admit that I took the precaution of slipping out the back door last Friday morning. Although I know Nosy Crow's bedroom is at the front of her house and she gets up late, it would have been just my luck if that morning she was up early and saw me.

I kept my answers brief and to the point, and was particularly careful to remain composed when the policeman asked me about access to medication. I told him that I did have access to morphine and outlined the procedure for preparation, administration and disposal of drugs at Freshfields. He's probably checked the procedure already, and seemed satisfied with my answer.

I promised I would be in contact if I remembered anything at all that might help with the investigation, and made some appropriate comments about what a terrible tragedy it was for the two little boys Kylie left behind.

But it would be even more of a tragedy if I was stopped from trying to help these poor old folk and their families, wouldn't it, Mum?

Chapter fourteen

Noel catches up with some minor client work on Friday, clearing the odd jobs that have arisen during his days off. He begins by installing new fence panels for an elderly couple who have been loyal customers since he set up his business. After a sandwich lunch in his van, he carries out two minor plumbing repairs in houses close to the municipal park. Then he drives over to one of the new estates on the edge of town to fit some blinds and curtain poles for a professional couple who have recently moved in.

His final call of the day is to another of his regulars, a widower in failing health. Mr Craven lives a few doors down from Noel's old cottage, and he has asked Noel to tidy his small front garden before the winter. It doesn't take Noel long to complete the weeding and clear the fallen leaves. Inside the cottage, he changes two light bulbs for the old man, who is no longer able to climb a stepladder.

Noel is replacing the stepladder in the musty understairs cupboard when Mr Craven asks if he would like a cup of tea. Noel had anticipated the invitation, which is always offered, and which he invariably accepts, knowing his customer has no remaining family and few friends. Their conversation rarely ranges beyond talk of the weather and football. Today is no exception until Mr Craven mentions a late nephew he has never spoken of previously.

'I'll be lucky to see out the winter, according to the doctor,' he says. His tone is matter-of-fact, and he raises his hand when he sees the concern in Noel's face. 'I'm not worried. I've had a good innings at eighty-three, can't complain. Just the old ticker's wearing out.' He pats his chest. 'Thing is, I should make a new will. Never got round to changing it after my nephew died, though it's fifteen years ago.'

Noel grimaces. 'I'm sorry. I didn't know you'd lost your nephew.'

Mr. Craven sips his tea slowly. 'Aye, well, I don't like to talk about it. The shock killed my brother.' He shakes his round head, which is bald, apart from a few white wisps of hair combed across the crown. His blue eyes and ruddy cheeks give him a gnome-like appearance. Noel, grunting sympathetically, wonders if the flush might be symptomatic of the old man's heart condition.

Mr Craven nods towards the window, through which the autumn sun is shining from a blue sky dappled with white clouds. 'It was a day like this when it happened. A beautiful autumn morning, touch of frost on the ground. I remember, because I was out walking the dog early along the river. It's days like this I'll miss.' He smiles regretfully, then looks at Noel. 'Why would you take your life on a morning like that?'

Noel becomes very still in his armchair. 'Your nephew took his own life?'

'Aye. It may sound stupid, but that was something I couldn't understand. Killing himself on a day when you'd think anyone would be glad to be alive. Of course, he was low when his mother died a few years previous. Poor lad was only fifteen at the time. But he seemed to pick up a bit after he left school. Met a nice girl. It didn't last, though there'd have been others in time. He was a good-looking lad, nice-natured too. And he'd nearly finished his electrician's apprenticeship, got a job lined up. He had a lot to live for.' He stares down into his mug, sloshing his tea around. 'The worst thing was him not leaving a note. Just telling his dad he was going for a walk by the river. His dad saw no sign of it coming, then no clue why he did it. Terrible thing for our Phil, finding him strung up in the boathouse. Broke his heart. He was in the ground, too, six months later.'

'I'm sorry.' Noel is uncomfortably aware how inadequate the words sound. But that isn't the only reason for the sudden chill he feels despite the warm glow cast by the coal-effect electric fire in the beamed living room. He is struck by the similarities between this young man's death and the suicide of Maureen and Florence's friend's son. Sudden, no note, in the boathouse, and the surviving parent dying soon after. Once more, he pushes aside the thought that he himself could have been another suicide in the river. He shivers.

Mr Craven doesn't notice, looking towards the window as a delivery van rumbles along the quiet lane, momentarily blocking out the sun. 'Ah, well. It'll all be forgotten when I go. No one to remember.'

'I'll remember,' Noel responds instantly, and he means it. 'And Mr Craven, if there's anything I can do to help…'

The old man smiles at him. 'You're a kind lad, Noel. I'll phone if I need anything. Now, you've spent long enough listening to me.' He yawns and leans back in his chair, his breathing noticeably heavier.

Noel takes the old man's weariness as his cue to leave and sees himself out of the heavy oak front door. Across the fields, the sun is sinking. The blaze of colour is less spectacular than on the previous evening, but it's still beautiful.

Driving home across the town, Noel decides to stop off for fish and chips. He eats on a bench overlooking the river, enjoying the sunset. He only has a few chips left when he hears the chug of a barge above the noise of the traffic on the road behind him. He gets up and wanders over to the wall to watch the barge approaching from the south. Few boats make their way along the wide, sludgy river these days, although less than 200 years ago the town was a busy port. Noel licks salt from his fingers and looks over at the opposite bank, hoping that Mrs Mullins hasn't ventured out again. He suspects that

Maureen will have kept a close eye on her neighbour after yesterday.

Noel drops the tray and bag in a litter bin and crosses the road to his van. Thinking of his elderly neighbours after listening to Mr Craven's sad tale of his nephew's death, he resolves that his first task when he gets home is to look through Florence's folder. He has an obscure sense of responsibility that he needs to read it. It seems uncanny that in the space of a week he has met Florence and Maureen and learned of the suicides of their friend's son, Mr Craven's nephew, and the childhood drowning of Florence's brother. Considering these tragic events along with the violent deaths of Sonia's son-in-law and Kylie, he finds himself inclined to agree with Maureen's report of Florence's research, that the town has an unusually high rate of untimely fatalities.

He's also unable to shake off a suspicion that the contents of the folder will somehow make sense of the Being's words to him: *'You have been chosen to right the wrongs in this place, to shine as light in the darkness.'*

Thirsty after the fish and chips, he brews up again at home, then settles down at the kitchen table. He pulls Florence's dog-eared buff folder towards him and mutters a quick prayer before he opens it, 'Show me what to see.' Then he lifts the flap and gasps when he sees what is lying on the stack of papers inside. He closes his eyes in disbelief.

But when he looks again, it's still there. A glossy black tress, identical to the one he found in his bathroom sink the morning after that strange experience by the river. Remembering how the previous lock of hair scalded his hand, Noel touches it warily with his fingertips. It's warm, but doesn't burn. He draws the papers out carefully, then fetches a saucer from the cupboard. He tips the tress onto the saucer and contemplates it reverently. He is more certain than ever that the radiant Being of his vision is both real and identical to Florence's Bright Giant. 'Thank you, God,' he murmurs, sensing that the coil of hair is at least a partial answer to his prayer.

He examines the contents of the file. There is an assortment of yellowing newspaper cuttings and a few pages of notepaper covered in a beautiful rounded hand which presumably belongs to Florence. He leafs through the newspaper articles first. From a cursory glance, he notes that they have been arranged in date order, with the most recent at the top. They are extracts from the weekly local newspaper ten summers ago, mainly from the correspondence page. Florence's contributions are circled with a red highlighter. As Maureen said, her friend's letters refer to accidents, suicides and murders. Some took place close to the old boathouse, others elsewhere in the town.

Next, he considers the handwritten notes and sees that these record similar incidents. Florence has carefully noted her sources, including versions of the local newspaper dating back a century, and a book of the town's history, written by a John Marshall. The notes are written in blue ink. Alongside some are dates from 2010, written in red. He checks them against the newspaper cuttings and finds that Florence has cross-referenced her accounts with the date when *The Tribune* published her letters. He feels a pang of sadness as he contrasts the meticulous researcher of a decade ago with the confused old woman he has recently become acquainted with.

He begins by reading the notes taken from the local history book. Florence has printed out the title alongside the publication date of 1902. Her first reference is to the Battle of Trentby in 1643. Noel's historical knowledge is sketchy, and he was unaware that the town had been the site of a battle in the English Civil War. From Florence's brief outline, he gleans that the town was in Royalist hands before the Parliamentarians attacked. The Parliamentarians forced Royalist cavalry downhill to the flat marshy land by the river where 300 Royalists perished. Florence has copied out some sentences from the old history book and underlined them heavily:

> Legend has it that these unfortunate men died not only because of Colonel Cromwell's superior military tactics, but that they were lured to their deaths by a strange phenomenon rising from the river and sucking them down into the marshes. It is said that the phenomenon was peculiarly formless and grey. When it appeared, it was accompanied by an unseasonal mist which confused the Royalist forces.

Noel rereads the sentences and leans back in his chair. Closing his eyes, he visualises the peculiar fog that enveloped him when he wandered in drunken distress by the river. He had wondered if the miasma was a product of his disturbed and alcohol-fuelled state, until Florence first mentioned the Grey One to him. He was also forced to re-examine his scepticism when he heard the terrifying noise by the river the previous night, which Florence had insisted was the sound of the Grey One. This information from the local history book is further evidence that Florence's Grey One exists, and corroborates his own experiences.

He turns back to Florence's notes. She has copied out further paragraphs from John Marshall's book. In one passage, the local historian offered some of his personal insights:

> Even today, there is much superstition among the townsfolk. Readers will recall mention of the sinister phenomenon which was believed to have contributed to the demise of the ill-fated Royalist cavalry in the marshes by the river. Misfortune, violent and untimely deaths are frequently associated with this creature even in our scientific age.
>
> Eschewing the superstitious approach on this occasion is one of the town's oldest and most respected residents, Mrs Josephine Bartlett. Mrs Bartlett is the

widow of the esteemed vicar who spent thirty-five fruitful years ministering at the parish church. She urges the faithful to hold fast to the Christian hope that this creature will be, and has been, definitively defeated by the cross of Christ. 'Jesus has the victory,' she tells me earnestly, 'and we must trust that the grey one who would wreak destruction will finally be vanquished.'

The writer will say no more on this subject, other than to observe that in his humble opinion, humankind seems to take perverse pleasure in dwelling more on tales of ghosts and phantoms than reading the words of Holy Scripture and learning of Christ and His angels.

Noel stares down at the page. Florence has underlined 'Jesus' and 'grey one' three times with her red pen. The historian's words seem to provide further evidence that the manifestations that preoccupy Florence have a long history in the town. Unless, of course, they have lodged in her imagination from this book, which is more than a century old, and she has somehow tangled the references to the sinister creature with the tragic death of her little brother.

But Noel is convinced that the coincidence of his own experience is too remarkable to be dismissed. He is struck, too, by the writer's comments. Only a few days ago he would barely have comprehended what the historian meant. He may be no more than a 'babe in Christ', as Sonia had said when he left her house on that momentous afternoon just three days ago, but he has already realised that the spiritual dimension of his new-found faith is overlooked by people who speak dismissively of religion. Any conversations he has ever had regarding the supernatural have been principally concerned with poltergeists and ghosts and the like. His ex-wife, Gemma, had dabbled with a belief in guardian angels, but not in a relationship with Jesus. He makes a mental note that this is something else to discuss with Sonia over Sunday lunch.

The next section of Florence's notes is a list of untimely deaths taken from editions of *The Tribune* over the last century.

Noel glances through them. With a deep sense of sadness, he sees that the small market town has suffered more than its fair share of tragedy. One name jumps out at him, the entry circled several times by Florence's red pen: *William Roberts, aged 4, drowned 5 August 1948.'* Although he doesn't know Florence's maiden name, he remembers her brother was called William, so this must refer to his drowning. The latest date listed is 8 June 2010. Noel rifles through the newspaper cuttings and finds the first letter she submitted at the start of her campaign to have the old boathouse pulled down.

Last week this newspaper recorded the death of Peter Simpson in Family Announcements. I had known Peter throughout his twenty short years. He was a fine young man taken from us too soon. Rumours circulate that Peter took his own life, hanging himself from the roof of the old boathouse. But he left no note for his mother, Alma. Alma is a good friend of mine, and her grief has been exacerbated by these rumours. In my opinion, it is possible that he was lured to his death by a dark force in that gloomy place where another young man hanged himself five years ago.

Noel pauses at the mention of the earlier suicide, guessing the anonymous young man is Mr Craven's nephew. The old man had said his nephew took his life at the boathouse fifteen years ago. Noel paces the kitchen, then pours himself a whisky. He settles back down to continue his perusal of Florence's notes with a deepening sense of foreboding.

I suggest that Peter was supernaturally lured to his death because of the circumstances surrounding my young brother William's drowning close to the boathouse more than sixty years ago. I have rarely spoken of this family catastrophe, but I believe it is right that I should do so now. I hope that this might help Alma in some small way. I also hope to raise awareness of the dangerous phenomenon which I believe is responsible for these catastrophes.

Florence's outline of the details surrounding her brother's drowning accords with the account Noel heard from Maureen. She described the riverside picnic on a hot August day in 1948 when she and William went off to play hide-and-seek, leaving their mother reading. She explained how she had begun to count to fifty, until she heard her brother's screams.

I ran as fast as I could. I could hear my brother shouting, 'Leave me alone! Leave me alone!' as I rounded the corner of the boathouse. To my horror, William was entangled in the reeds. Only his head and arms were visible as he desperately tried to extricate himself. It seemed that the more he struggled, the deeper he sank. Instinctively, I ran into the reeds towards him, but immediately felt myself being sucked down into the bog. I could see that my brother was tired and giving up his battle against the marshes. I tried desperately to free myself.

All of a sudden, despite the bright sun, a strange vapour seemed to overshadow my brother. I screamed his name, 'William!' over and over, but I could no longer see him. The grey mist hung over the reeds where he had vanished, and was accompanied by an awful stench. There was a terrible moment where I wished that the river would take me too. But in the same instant that I wished it, I thought of my parents, and how dreadful it would be for them to lose us both.

Our family went to church, so it was natural for me to pray desperately, 'Save me, Lord!' At once the grey mist dissolved as suddenly as it had appeared, and was substituted by a multicoloured iridescent haze. A beautiful fragrance replaced the horrible smell. I saw some kind of colossal bright creature with a flowing black mane of hair and the most piercing gaze. Like a man, but of gigantic proportions. He reached towards me with a bronze arm and said gently, 'Do not fear.' Suddenly I was free of the reeds and there was solid ground beneath my feet. The Bright Giant had vanished. My mother was running towards me, shouting William's name. I collapsed on the bank.

Naturally, my parents and a policeman questioned me about the catastrophe. I tried to tell them about the peculiar vapour that enfolded William, and that I had been rescued by a bright giant, but no one believed me. In my childish way I was convinced the Bright Giant was Jesus answering my fervent prayer. I recounted how William had shouted, 'Leave me alone!' But the grown-ups said he was crying out against the reeds and the bog. Our doctor suggested the phenomena I claimed to have seen could be accounted for by my near-death experience. I quickly learned to speak no further of what I had witnessed when the doctor subsequently suggested that the balance of my mind might have been disturbed by the calamity.

But I know what I saw that fateful day, and I am persuaded that the excessive untimely and violent deaths in this town are somehow perpetrated by the peculiar mist which I privately named as the Grey One.

The only hope for us all is Jesus who I summoned by my childish prayer.

Chapter fifteen

The only hope for us all is Jesus who I summoned by my childish prayer.
Florence's words echo in Noel's mind as he places the notes
alongside the newspaper cuttings on the table. He stands and
stretches, rotating his injured shoulder. It's much better, but
has stiffened after his first day of work since he fell down
Sonia's stairs. His mind is spinning. Any doubts he had that
Florence's Grey One and Bright Giant are not only real but
also identical to the phenomena of his vision have been
comprehensively dispelled by Florence's account of her
brother's drowning. He finds himself sharing his neighbour's
belief that the unusually high number of early and violent
deaths in the small market town are somehow connected with
the malevolent Grey One.

Glancing down at the black tress of hair on the saucer,
Noel realises that he can no longer ignore the commission that
the Being told him the Master has entrusted to him. Florence's
narrative proves that his experience by the river wasn't the
result of his drunken, distressed state after he was questioned
by the police in connection with Kylie's murder. His vision
was real, just as real as Florence's sighting of the Bright Giant
and the Grey One more than seventy years ago. The
connection between their experiences is too similar to be
discounted as the product of psychological disturbance as
Florence's doctor suggested. However much he has wondered
if mental disorder was the source of his own encounter, he is
now persuaded otherwise by Florence's account.

But while the revelation is reassuring, Noel remains puzzled about why the Master has chosen him. Resuming his seat, he picks up the papers again and discovers that the remainder of her notes and correspondence with the local newspaper comprise other tragic accidents, suicides and violent deaths. One letter referred to the loss of a rowing team on the river in 1925. No adequate explanation of how the crew got into difficulties was ever given, and the inquest recorded a verdict of accidental death. Florence observed that the weather conditions had been good:

> It was a fine, sunny Saturday afternoon. No evidence of damage to the boat. An unexplained mystery.

In another letter, she mentioned a spate of burglaries and murders in the late 1960s in a desirable area to the south of the town. All the victims were well-off elderly people who lived alone. Florence recorded that no one was ever charged with the murders.

> Perhaps the murderer died or moved away. I hope the former, since it is horrible to contemplate the perpetrator carrying out similar terrible crimes elsewhere. I believe the perpetrator is in the grip of the dark force that permeates this town.

In her final letter to the newspaper, she posed the suggestion that the boathouse had been built on the site where many of the Royalist cavalry had drowned in the Civil War battle of 1643.

> There are those who talk of past events leaving some kind of trace on a place. I find myself wondering if the reason for the catastrophes close to the boathouse is that other unfortunates have encountered the strange grey indefinable creature there, and have been destroyed like those 300 Royalists so long ago. I would

urge that the boathouse is pulled down, in the hope that fewer people will be drawn to this gloomy place with its tragic associations and evil happenings.

In this letter, Florence also alluded to her contact with the local clergy, which Maureen had mentioned:

Anyone who grew up in church, as I did, will be familiar with the stories of Jesus exorcising demons. I have entreated all the local clergy to consider whether an exorcism might be necessary in this instance, explaining to them my own terrifying experience on the day my dear brother drowned. All listened sceptically to my story and advised me that exorcism belongs to the past. They told me that today's scientific and medical advances mean that there are rational explanations for the manifestations named as demons in the Gospels, and they supported the doctor's view that my own sighting of the sinister grey phenomenon and the Bright Giant who saved me are explained by my traumatised state. I remain unconvinced that these mysteries have a rational explanation, and am disappointed by the response of our clergy. The scriptures tell us, 'Our struggle is not against enemies of blood and flesh, but against the rulers, against the authorities, against the cosmic powers of this present darkness, against the spiritual forces of evil in the heavenly places' (Ephesians 6:12). The writer of the epistle to the Ephesians goes on to urge us to clothe ourselves with spiritual armour to play our part in this cosmic battle.

If our churches pursue this rational approach, I fear that our spiritual lives will be greatly impoverished. It will become increasingly difficult to persuade people that the invisible Christian God exists, if our supernatural experiences are so quickly dismissed. I know what I saw in 1948, and, as I have mulled over my own terrible memories and researched the other tragic deaths in our town over the years, I am certain that the rulers of darkness described in Ephesians 6:12 are at work in this very place. Perhaps the Grey One is such a manifestation. And maybe, just maybe, the creature I refer to as the Bright Giant really was Jesus who came to save me that day. I certainly believe my desperate prayer, 'Save me, Lord!' was answered in a miraculous way.

Noel pulls out a final cutting from *The Tribune* dated a week after Florence's last letter. The article is headed, 'Local historian greets Town Council's decision to pull down boathouse with cautious relief'. It recounts Florence's campaign and records the landlord of the riverside pub complaining of a fall in trade since *The Tribune* featured her letters. The council seemed anxious to distance themselves from any suggestion that Florence's revelations had influenced their decision. One councillor stated that since the rowing club was no longer in existence and the boathouse was falling into disrepair, the monthly Town Council meeting had deemed it prudent to demolish this 'obsolete structure'. The reporter attributed Florence's caution to her conviction that the 'supernatural phenomena she claimed to have seen might not disappear with the boathouse'. Nevertheless, she welcomed the destruction of the building, expressing the hope that this would mean no one else would die in the vicinity like her brother and Alma's son.

Noel replaces Florence's notes and the newspaper cuttings carefully in the file. He rests his chin in his hands, thinking over what he has read. Florence's concern that the supernatural phenomena would continue to exist after the boathouse was destroyed has been justified. He himself has witnessed them. According to Florence and the superstitious townsfolk a century ago, including Rev Bartlett's widow, the Grey One is a malevolent force somehow responsible for the tragic accidents and violent deaths within the town. Florence attested to the benevolence of the Bright Giant. Noel's experience by the river on that terrible evening of Kylie's death bears out the women's assumptions. He understands dimly that these creatures are not ghosts. Florence's quotation from the Scriptures makes clear her belief that the mysterious entities are in some way connected with a cosmic battle in the spiritual realm.

A few days ago, Noel would have rejected outright Florence's concluding suggestion that the Grey One might be a manifestation of the 'rulers of darkness' and that the Bright Giant might be Jesus Himself. Now, sitting in the quiet kitchen at the end of a week that has transformed his life, he finds himself seriously considering the possibility. His own conversion has taken him across a threshold into another dimension of life, a spiritual dimension, which he hadn't known existed. And however extraordinary, it seems that he has a role to play in ensuring that the light spoken of by the bright Being in his vision should prevail against the darkness of the formless grey creature who has wreaked such havoc in the town. He suspects both Michelle's late husband and Kylie have been victims of this destructive force, in addition to those identified by Florence in her research.

He reaches towards the glossy black tress lying on the saucer beside the file and touches it. It is warm beneath his fingers. 'I'm ready,' he whispers. 'Ready to do what the Master wants.'

Immediately the words are out of his mouth, the warmth from the lock of hair seems to spread through his body. He is filled with a deep peace, similar to what he felt in Sonia's sitting room a few days ago. Sonia, he realises, is the person with whom he can share Florence's findings and his own experience. If anyone can offer insight into the mysterious events, it is his new friend with her deep Christian faith. Alongside the peace suffusing him is a firm resolve, a new sensation for a man who has spent so much of his life uncertain of his purpose. He rises from the table and goes to bed secure in the knowledge that he is, at last, treading the right path. On impulse, he carries the saucer with the coil of hair upstairs and sets it down on the bedside table.

As Noel sleeps, he dreams. He finds himself on a street of terraced council housing. Wreaths of mist hang in the air beneath a leaden sky. It's a street he knows only too well, and he is standing on the pavement adjacent to a familiar house, Kylie's house. Three magpies stand in a row along the rooftop. Red and pink geraniums planted in terracotta pots on either side of the front door have faded, and their leaves are brown and shrivelled.

A figure with cropped blonde hair materialises outside the house, dressed in a grey suit and mid-heeled charcoal shoes. Noel watches as she raises a hand and raps on the door.

The door is flung open by a plump young woman in a grubby cream dressing gown, soiled with unidentifiable stains and cigarette ash. She calls over her shoulder, 'Shut up, Bradley! You too, Liam!'

'Yeah?' Kylie challenges her caller. She takes a gulp from a chipped, chunky red mug. Noel knows it will contain strong, sweet tea.

The suited figure doesn't reply.

Kylie shakes back shoulder-length chestnut curls, damp and tangled from the shower. 'What are you doing here? What d'you want?' She tightens the dressing-gown cord over her bulging belly, glancing past her visitor to the very spot where Noel is standing outside the wooden gate of the neighbouring property. Her expression doesn't change. He is invisible to her.

Next, Noel finds himself in the kitchen with Kylie and her visitor. The sink is stacked high with dirty pots, the work surfaces are grimy, and the window is misted with condensation. There is a jumble of laundry on the greasy floor in front of the washing machine, which is working up to spin a load already on.

Both women have their backs to Noel. A cloud of steam rises from the cream plastic kettle. Kylie is taking a mug off the tree beside it. She drops a teabag into the mug from a box next to the kettle. Behind her, the woman is reaching into her pewter shoulder bag.

Noel watches the woman step up behind Kylie as Kylie pours water on the teabag and stirs it round. He tries to move forward but is frozen to the spot in front of the closed door. He opens his mouth to shout, 'Get out, Kylie! Get out now!' But his words are inaudible.

Turning with the steaming mug, Kylie jumps to find the woman inches away. Brown drops of the scalding liquid spray the laundry heaped on the floor. The woman grabs Kylie's free arm and roughly pushes back the sleeve of her dressing gown. The mug falls from Kylie's other hand.

The woman plunges a syringe loaded with a thick clear liquid into Kylie's forearm.

Kylie opens her mouth to call out, but there's no chance that anyone will hear her above the white noise. She's staring at the spot where Noel stands beside the cooker as she sinks to the floor, shrouded among the dirty clothes. She opens her mouth again. Noel is sure her lips are shaping his name.

The washing machine continues to spin as the woman slips out of the back door.

Footsteps clatter down the staircase. A boy's voice shouts, 'Mum! We're going to be late!'

'No. Please, no,' groans Noel, as the door bursts open and two small boys hurtle into the kitchen. They stop dead when they see Kylie slumped in front of the washing machine. The older boy advances slowly. 'Mum?' he asks, his voice uncertain. 'Did you fall?'

'Mummy? Are you playing?' asks his little brother. He darts past the older boy and shakes the motionless form, scattering muddy football strips, socks and underwear across the floor. Kylie's eyes are open and glassy, and still seem to be fixed on Noel.

'Wake up, Mummy!' the young boy sobs. 'Please, wake up!'

'Take me away!' begs Noel. 'Please, take me away! I don't want to see! I don't want to hear!'

He is aware of someone grasping his shoulder in a vice-like grip. A mellifluous voice whispers in his ear, 'Now you know how this terrible thing happened. You must trust the Master's call.'

Then the kitchen containing the murdered woman and the two heartbroken boys dissolves in front of Noel. He is spinning through pitch darkness, plunging on and on, until he lands on something soft.

His eyes snap open. He gasps for air. He is drenched in sweat and his heart is thudding so hard that he is certain it will burst through his chest. Disorientated, it takes a moment for him to realise that the softness beneath him is the mattress of his double bed. He is pressing his hands into it as if trying to break his fall. His duvet is askew, lying diagonally across his body. He wipes saliva from the corner of his mouth, drooled as he shouted out in his dream.

Noel waits for his breathing to slow, then hauls himself out of bed and runs downstairs barefoot. He finds a pen and an envelope on the kitchen table and scribbles down as much as he can remember from his dream about Kylie's visitor before it fades from his consciousness. It isn't much, as he only had a rear view of her and never saw her face. 'Short blonde hair. Grey suit. Mid-heeled charcoal court shoes.'

It's only then that he realises the significance of what he saw. The woman in his dream is surely a manifestation of the Grey One.

He chews the end of the pen and screws up his eyes, trying to recall as much as he can of the scenes that flashed before him. Then he writes, 'Did Kylie know her???' It strikes him as a possibility, given Kylie's question, 'What are you doing here?' and the fact that she invited the woman in and made her a drink.

The basic scene corroborates the scant information passed on to him by the police and included in the news bulletins: Kylie was found by her sons in the kitchen around 7.40am, approximately ten minutes after she had answered the door to an unseen visitor. But the idea that the murder has been shown to Noel in a dream is so outside anything he has ever experienced that he struggles to accept it. He wonders if there might be some other explanation. Has he been so obsessed with picturing Kylie's death that his subconscious has filled in the gaps while he slept?

Noel dismisses this rational explanation as he runs water into the kettle. The routine action is soothing after the intense dream, reconnecting him with the day-to-day. It occurs to him that perhaps he asked inadvertently for this revelation when he fingered the tress of black hair last night and said he was ready to do what the Master wants. *Could the dream be another answer to prayer?*

He remembers what the Being said during that otherworldly encounter by the river. 'Then you must trust.' Similar to the words that returned him to reality from the dream: 'You must trust the Master's call.'

Noel flicks on the kettle and raises the blind. Two collared doves are sitting on top of the low wall that separates his back yard from his neighbour's. They stare back at him. He senses a challenge in their unblinking red gaze. 'All right,' he says aloud. 'I will trust the Master.'

They swivel their heads in unison towards the bird table. He grins as he retrieves the bag of bird food from the windowsill. *What is he thinking, talking to the birds about the Master? They're just telling him they're hungry.* He slips his feet into his battered trainers and unlocks the back door. The birds don't fly away as he expects, but continue to perch on the wall, watching as he shakes nuts and seeds onto the bird table. It's another crisp, sunny morning, and Noel shivers in his nightwear of T-shirt and boxers. He thinks of Mr Craven and the old man's bewilderment that his nephew should take his life on a beautiful autumn day like this.

'I'm ready,' he says, as he had said the previous evening. He retraces his steps across the yard. 'Ready to right the wrongs in this place, to shine as light in the darkness.'

He eyes the doves from the doorway. They still have their red eyes fixed on him. Then they flap their wings, totally in sync with one another, and cover the short distance to the bird table where they coo contentedly over their breakfast.

Chapter sixteen

Noel spends Saturday quietly. His only outing is to an out-of-town retail park where he buys a suit for his father's funeral. He sleeps well, waking on Sunday in a state of nervous anticipation about accompanying Sonia to church. He had been taken aback when she told him that her congregation meets in a community centre. His experience of worship has been limited to the Anglican tradition, and the last service he attended was his daughter's baptism. Gemma and her mother were keen that Jade should be christened in the parish church where they were married, and where Gemma herself had been christened as a baby. Noel had been willing to go along with the suggestion to keep them happy, although he had long since lost any vestiges of the faith his grandmother had attempted to instil in him.

The community centre has recently benefited from local authority funding. Its recently decorated daffodil-yellow walls and large picture windows overlooking the river are far removed from the crumbling stone and dim interior of St John's Parish Church in Oldford where his grandmother dragged him when he was small. In these unlikely surroundings, where he finds himself sneezing because of paint fumes rather than dust, Noel discovers that the worship service is also completely different. Instead of traditional hymns played on the organ, a male and female singer lead modern songs accompanied by guitar and keyboard. One change he welcomes is the digital projection of the service. He had never managed to navigate *The Book of Common Prayer* without his grandmother's help.

When the worship leader announces a time of open prayer after three songs, he is amazed to hear voices rising spontaneously around the room. Only the vicar ever intoned set prayers at St John's. As a little boy, Noel had imagined God's voice would be the same as the clergyman's resonant bass. Amid the cacophony of prayer, the hairs rise on the back of his neck when he tunes into a woman calling out in an unknown language which sounds very similar to the cadences of the Being's strange speech.

After the prayers, a youth reads two passages from the Bible. Noel vaguely knows one, the Parable of the Good Samaritan. Then the preacher steps forward, a casually dressed man in an open-necked shirt and jeans, most unlike the black-cassocked vicar at St John's. The brief homily of Noel's memory is replaced by a half-hour address, during which he finds himself distracted by cries of 'Amen' and 'Praise the Lord!' from some of the worshippers. One of those shouting out is Sonia, sitting beside him. She chuckles when he jumps in his comfortable cushioned chair the first time she exclaims, 'Praise the Lord!'

More songs and prayers follow the address, before the service draws to a close ninety minutes after it began. Sonia introduces him to some of her friends and fetches them both tea and biscuits. Noel knows he won't remember the names of all those he has met, but he is touched by their sincere welcome.

It's 12.30 by the time they leave. Overwhelmed by the new experience, Noel is quiet as he drives Sonia back to her house for lunch. She displays the sensitivity he is becoming used to and doesn't make small talk. He drops her off by her gate before parking the van in the usual place in front of the garage, and then walks back down the street carrying Florence's file together with a bouquet from his local corner shop.

Sonia has left her front door ajar for him. The mouth-watering aroma of roast chicken wafts towards him in the hall. She calls him through to the kitchen, where she is basting the chicken with gravy in a battered roasting tin. Her smile of welcome widens further when she sees the spray of white carnations and pink roses. 'Thank you. I love flowers.' She points a wooden spatula towards the buff folder. 'Have you brought me work to do?'

Noel smiles back. 'I'm hoping you can help me, give me some advice.' He becomes serious, thinking of the folder's contents. 'It's a record of accidental and violent deaths in the town, compiled by my neighbour, the old lady who wanders by the river. There seem to be an unusually high number of these deaths, just as you said.'

Sonia's smile fades.

'I'm sorry,' says Noel, kicking himself. 'I know this is difficult because of what happened to your son-in-law.'

She ducks her head. 'Thank you.' She opens the oven door and slips her hands inside blue and red-checked oven gloves, then lifts the roasting tin back into the oven. 'Please, go on.'

He hesitates. The revelations seem outlandish in the cosy domesticity of Sonia's shabby kitchen with the autumn sun streaming through the window. But he is certain that if anyone is able to shed any light on the strange events that have overtaken him, it will be his new friend. So he continues, 'I'm struggling to understand it all, but there seems to be a spiritual dimension to it, and somehow...' He runs his hand over his head, unsure how to explain about his encounter with Florence's Bright Giant. 'Somehow I seem to have become involved in it.'

She glances at him, then removes her glasses, steamed up from the heat of the oven, and wipes them on the hem of her flowery apron. 'Please, sit down and tell me all about it.' She gestures towards the chair by the table and he sits, running his hands over the folder on his lap. Sonia stretches up into a corner cupboard for a vase, fills it with water and sets about trimming the stems of the flowers with a knife.

Noel begins by telling her how he left the pub on the night after he was questioned by the police about Kylie's murder, and about the unusually dense patch of mist by the river which seemed almost to acquire human shape. He describes his uncanny sensation of hearing a voice goading him to end his life, his desperate prayer for help, and his vision of the radiant Being. Then he explains how the Being matches Florence's description of the Bright Giant, and that the swirling vaporous form he encountered seems identical to the phenomenon Florence calls the Grey One.

Sonia peels and chops vegetables and places them in a steamer without interrupting his narrative. He is grateful she has her back to him as he stutters over the idea that the Bright Giant is Jesus Himself. He goes on to outline how Florence's young brother died, and recounts the suicides of Mr Craven's nephew and the son of Florence and Maureen's friend, along with some of the other tragic deaths uncovered in Florence's research. He explains that these seem to date back to the heavy losses suffered by the Royalist army in the marshes during the English Civil War. He tells her how Florence wrote that she was in agreement with the opinion of the vicar's widow a century earlier, that spiritual intervention is required to put an end to the litany of destruction. Then he opens Florence's folder and fishes out her last letter to the local newspaper where she included the Bible verse from Ephesians 6:12.

Sonia removes the roasting tin from the oven as he reads the letter. She joins in the quotation as she jabs a knife into the chicken: 'Our struggle is not against enemies of blood and flesh, but against the rulers, against the authorities, against the cosmic powers of this present darkness, against the spiritual forces of evil in the heavenly places.'

Finally, Noel describes his dream of Kylie's murder the previous night. Then he falls silent. His friend doesn't speak immediately, concentrating on pouring boiled water over the cooked rice. She sets the sieve of drained rice over the saucepan, then turns her attention to the gravy.

Noel drums his fingers on the table, worried that she might not believe his bizarre tale. What if she thinks that his experience is the result of psychological distress after all? What if he is deluded, maybe even mentally unwell? He tips his head back and studies the damp patch on the ceiling, jiggling his leg beneath the table. The movement jangles the cutlery which Sonia has laid.

She turns at the sound, continuing to stir the gravy, and reads something of Noel's apprehension in his face. 'I'm sorry,' she says. 'You have told me so much. It's astonishing. The Lord has much in store for you!' She beams at him.

He smiles back uncertainly.

'Now, before we talk further, let's eat. In the fridge you will find a bottle of grape juice. Please pour some into the glasses.' Sonia nods towards the tumblers on the table. Inside are pink linen napkins folded into star shapes. She watches as Noel follows her instructions, then says, 'I would be grateful if you would carve the meat. I haven't had roast chicken since my husband passed, and he always used to carve.'

She takes two plates from the oven where they have been warming. Noel is unsurprised to see that they bear the image of Prince Charles and Lady Diana Spencer. The recollection of his mother's prized dinner service doesn't disturb him as it did a few days ago, and he views this as an encouraging sign of his healing promised by the Being. He carves the chicken carefully while Sonia doles out rice and assorted vegetables and pours the gravy into a ceramic jug.

There is a substantial amount of food left over. Noel is thinking that his hostess will be eating leftovers for days, when she remarks that her daughter and grandson will call in for dinner after Michelle's shift at the home ends at four o'clock. He glances at his watch and sees that it's barely 1.30. There is plenty of time for him to help with the washing-up after they have eaten and so avoid another awkward meeting with

Michelle. He wonders uneasily whether Sonia has told her daughter that she has invited him for lunch, but doesn't ask. He suspects that Michelle would disapprove.

Sonia motions to Noel to resume his seat at the table and brings over their loaded plates. The fragrance of the food is delicious. A lump rises in Noel's throat as he realises how much he has missed a proper home-cooked meal since he left Kylie's house six months earlier. The roast chicken, rice and vegetables make a welcome change to his usual diet of convenience food and takeaways. He is also overcome by deep gratitude, that this kind woman has so quickly offered him her friendship and hospitality. He swallows and bows his head, and is taken aback when Sonia takes this as a signal to offer a prayer of thanks for their food and friendship. He has never previously been present at a meal where grace was spoken, and thinks again how much his life has changed in such a short time. Dashing away a tear that leaks from his right eye, he meets Sonia's solicitous gaze over the steaming plates.

'This is a whole new start for me,' he says.

She raises her glass. 'Then we toast new beginnings.' They clink glasses before eating in companionable silence.

Noel savours each mouthful. 'That was delicious,' he says eventually, lining up his knife and fork on his empty plate. 'Thank you so much.'

She beams widely, revealing her crooked teeth. 'Would you like any more?'

Noel shakes his head. 'No, thanks. I'm stuffed!'

'I hope you have room for dessert.' Sonia rises and takes their plates across to the sink. 'I made mango cheesecake.' She produces the dessert triumphantly from the fridge and cuts two generous slices, serving them in bowls that match the plates.

Noel declines cream. He can't remember the last time he ate such a sumptuous dessert, and tells Sonia so. She is delighted and begins to prepare coffee in a percolator on the gas hob. At her request, Noel wheels the trolley laden with the familiar royal wedding cups and saucers, milk jug and sugar bowl through to the sitting room. Presently she follows with a coffee pot and pours for them. Before she sits down in her armchair, she takes her Bible from the mahogany bureau, adjusts her bifocals and begins to flick through it.

Noel sips the strong coffee and waits, guessing his hostess is looking up the passage in Ephesians 6 which Florence had written down. But a moment later, Sonia emits a yelp of triumph and reads aloud verses Noel has never heard before, although the familiarity of their subject makes him catch his breath.

> I was standing on the bank of the great river … I looked up and saw a man clothed in linen, with a belt of gold from Uphaz around his waist. His body was like beryl, his face like lightning, his eyes like flaming torches, his arms and legs like the gleam of burnished bronze, and the sound of his words like the roar of a multitude … My strength left me, and my complexion grew deathly pale, and I retained no strength. Then I heard the sound of his words; and when I heard the sound of his words, I fell into a trance, face to the ground.

Sonia stops reading. Noel is shaking so much that he is in danger of dropping his cup and saucer. He sets them down on the trolley with great care. 'That's what He was like,' he whispers, when he trusts himself to speak. 'I don't understand everything you read, but that sounds very much like the Being I met by the river that night. That's Florence's Bright Giant. I'm sure of it. But how…?' And how can it be written down in there, in that ancient book?' He nods towards the Bible.

Sonia strokes the gilt-edged pages reverently. 'The Bible contains God's word for us today,' she says. 'Some of it was written thousands of years ago, but it still speaks to us now. I was reading from chapter 10 of the book of Daniel, in the Old

Testament. It seems to me that you have had a similar encounter to Daniel.'

He gulps. 'But why?' he asks. 'What does He want with me? I mean, I didn't even believe in God until the other afternoon.'

Sonia closes her Bible. 'Your reaction is typical of those called by the Lord in Scripture,' she says. 'Moses, Gideon, Isaiah, Jeremiah...' Seeing Noel's puzzled expression, she explains. 'They were leaders and prophets in the Old Testament. All of them resisted God's call in the beginning. The Lord had to reassure them, give them signs.' She smiles. 'It seems to me that God sees us differently to how we see ourselves. We focus on our shortcomings and limitations. God knows our hearts, and if He sees potential, He will provide what we lack. Tell me, how did you respond?'

Noel chews his lower lip, struggling with the idea that he has been 'called by the Lord' as Sonia says. He recognises how resistant he was too, like the biblical characters she has mentioned. He hasn't heard of any of them except Moses. 'I asked why I had been chosen,' he admits sheepishly, 'and who this Master was that the Being was talking about.'

'Then you reacted in typical fashion,' observes Sonia, with one of her throaty chuckles. 'And what was the answer?'

He shuffles around in his chair and looks towards the window, remembering the Being's rebuke. A cloud passes over the sun above the houses across the street. 'He said that it wasn't for me or Him to question the ways of the Master, that the Master's ways are perfect.'

'Mm-hm,' Sonia nods. She hesitates, her dark eyes large and serious behind her glasses. 'You understand now that the Master is God, don't you, and the Being, Florence's Bright Giant, is Jesus?'

'Are you sure?' Noel stares at her, his pulse racing. Even though he had entertained the thought, to hear it confirmed by Sonia overwhelms him.

'Of course,' she says serenely, as if it is the most natural thing in the world that Noel should have been commissioned by Jesus. 'Jesus is charging you with the task of stemming the tide of evil in this town. There is only so much we humans can perceive of in the battle between good and evil. Our perception is limited. Only God knows the full perspective, and there are powers at work that we barely notice. The writer of the letter to the early believers in Ephesus understood this when he wrote that our battleground isn't in the human sphere, but in the heavenlies, "against the spiritual forces of evil".'

Noel frowns. '"Spiritual forces of evil" – you mean like demons, the devil, that kind of thing?'

Sonia nods gravely. 'Many people dismiss this dimension today, even in the churches. We think we have become so clever that talk of the devil is superstitious nonsense from a bygone age. But that is very dangerous. Think of an iceberg. Did you know only around 10 per cent is visible above the water?'

'Yes.' He wonders where Sonia is going with this analogy.

'As I understand it, it's the same in the spiritual realm.' Sonia taps the Bible on her lap. 'We operate in this material world, unaware of what is going on most of the time in the spiritual world. Sometimes the Lord breaks in – as you now know from your own experience.' She smiles tenderly at him. 'Your encounter by the riverbank came about because you prayed so desperately for help. You were at the end of your human resources, and received this commission from the Lord: to bring light to the darkness of this town. He said you would first experience healing. From what you have told me, this is happening. Your relationship with your father was restored on his deathbed, helping to heal those wounds you have borne for many years. Then the greatest healing of all took place in this very room just five days ago when you came to Christ. During this time, the Lord has used you to help your neighbour, the poor, confused lady, and He has shown you the murder of your ex-partner in your dream. Does this make sense?'

Noel's head is spinning, but he recognises the truth of what his friend is saying, however incredible. He nods his head. 'Yes,' he says slowly. 'I think so. But what do I do with this information about Kylie's killer? I mean, the police aren't going to believe me, are they? They'll probably think I'm mad, or maybe –' He breaks off and clears his throat, then continues haltingly, 'Maybe they'll think that I did do it after all, and am trying to point the finger somewhere else. I mean, it's not as if I saw the person's face. I had the impression that it was a woman, maybe someone Kylie knew, but other than her being such a grey figure, I've got nothing to go on.'

'I see that,' agrees Sonia. 'We will pray that the Lord will provide an opportunity for you. Then all you need to do is trust that your prayer will be answered. How does that sound?'

Noel rubs his temple. The dream has never been far from his mind since he woke yesterday morning, and he has been puzzling over how he could share his knowledge with the police. What Sonia says makes sense. After all, how many women who might have known Kylie would be covered by his description? And could it be that the grey suit, shoes and bag were symbolic, so that he would understand that the Grey One was behind Kylie's murder?

'I guess you're right. I'm going to have to trust God.' He shakes his head. 'It still seems so strange. I didn't even believe in Him a week ago, and now here I am somehow involved in working on His behalf.'

'You are accepting His will,' says Sonia gently. 'That is all He asks. No matter what our doubts and fears, our concerns that we're not good enough or don't have the abilities to do what He asks, if the Lord finds a willing servant, He will use that person. Now, let me pray for you.'

Noel bows his head and Sonia prays that God will show him how to use the knowledge that came to him in the dream.

'It's over to the Lord now,' she says, when he raises his head. 'Only trust, and God will do the rest. I will keep praying for you, until you have the opportunity to share your knowledge, so that Kylie's killer can be brought to justice. How does that sound?'

'Good.' Noel leans forward and reaches for his coffee. Sonia's advice seems practical, and it's a relief to hear her say that the situation is now in God's hands.

Chapter seventeen

Sonia and Noel sip their coffee in silence for a few moments. Noel ponders all that he has learned from Sonia, and then remembers something else he wanted to ask her, about how he heard a woman praying during the worship service in a language that sounded similar to the one spoken by the Being. He asks her to explain this.

Sonia lays her hand reverently on her Bible. She briefly explains that the New Testament contains a number of letters, known as epistles. She tells him that these were sent by Church leaders including the apostle Paul, to groups of early believers in different places. One of these letters is Ephesians, which Noel has heard of from the text quoted by Florence in her research notes. Sonia says that two letters were written to the church in Corinth, Greece. She turns to chapters 12, 13 and 14 of the first letter to the Corinthians, and reads out scriptures about gifts given by the Holy Spirit to believers. One of these is the gift of knowledge, which she suggests accounts for Noel's dream of Kylie's murderer. She tells him that dreams are often a means of divine revelation in Scripture. Another gift conferred by the Holy Spirit is the gift of tongues.

'The gift of tongues allows us to speak a language other than our mother tongue,' explains Sonia. 'From what you say, it could be that the language used by the Being you encountered by the river was the same as that of the person praying at church. The gift must be used carefully, because we read in 1 Corinthians 13:1, "If I speak in the tongues of mortals and of angels, but do not have love, I am a noisy gong or a clanging cymbal." Love, you see, is the most important quality or characteristic of the believer.'

'Right. I understand that, that love is the most important thing. This gift of tongues sounds strange, but it makes sense of what I heard.' Noel whistles through his teeth. 'I have so much to learn!'

'I will help you as much as I can,' she assures him. 'If you come to church again, I will introduce you properly to the pastor. He is a good man, and walks very closely with the Lord.'

'I'd like that,' says Noel hesitantly, not quite sure what 'walking very closely with the Lord' might involve. With the clock showing that it is already quarter past three, he decides to postpone further questions until another time. Mindful that he wants to leave before Michelle arrives, he drains his cup and stands. 'You won't object to me washing the dishes after that wonderful meal, will you, Sonia?'

She waves her hands dismissively, but doesn't demur when Noel wheels the trolley with their used crockery back into the kitchen. She follows him and ignores his suggestion that she should relax in the sitting room, insisting that she will dry the pots. They have almost finished when the front door bursts open.

A shout of 'Grandma!' is accompanied by the sound of running footsteps. A sturdy small boy wearing an Arsenal football T-shirt and jeans tears into the kitchen. He stops in his tracks when he finds a stranger washing up.

Noel's heart sinks. *Too late to avoid another encounter with Michelle.* The boy stares at him, and Noel forces a smile.

'This is my friend Noel,' says Sonia. 'Noel, my grandson Joshua.'

'Hi, Joshua.' Noel keeps his eyes on the boy's face, aware of Michelle approaching through the hall. She pauses on the kitchen threshold.

'Hi,' mutters Joshua. 'What are you doing here?'

'Joshua!' chides his grandmother. 'Where are your manners?'

'It's OK,' says Noel quickly. 'Your grandma very kindly invited me for lunch. I'm leaving now.' He swivels back to the sink and squeezes out the dishcloth.

'Please don't rush off,' says Michelle unexpectedly. 'If you have a minute, I'd like to speak to you.'

Noel glances at her. She is wearing the burgundy carers' uniform of Freshfields, the same uniform Kylie wore. He swallows and looks away.

'Sure,' he mutters. He hopes she isn't going to warn him off spending time with her mother. At least she doesn't look as hostile as she did the other afternoon.

'Come, Joshua,' says Sonia. 'I'm having issues with my iPad and I'm sure you will be able to help me.'

'Not again!' groans Joshua, rolling his eyes. But he is grinning as he trots behind his grandmother towards the sitting room.

Michelle steps forward and lifts the tea towel from the rail at the side of the sink unit. She picks up a tumbler and begins to dry it. Noel shifts slightly to his right. The kitchen seems smaller with her alongside him. Unlike her slight mother, Michelle has a rounded figure. Noel's cheeks flush as he catches himself noticing her curves. With exaggerated care, he folds the dishcloth and places it on the tiled windowsill.

Michelle seems to be in no hurry to tell him whatever it is she wants to say. To avoid an uneasy silence, Noel fiddles with one of the broken splashback tiles and says, 'I'll be fixing these for your mum this week.'

Michelle tips the tumbler back and forth in her hand, apparently checking there are no drips left inside. 'Ah, yes. Mum said.' She moves behind him towards the corner cupboard where Sonia keeps her glasses, her left hip brushing against Noel in the narrow space.

He jerks back against the sink. 'Sorry.'

'No, I'm sorry.' Michelle replaces the glass in the cupboard. 'I caught you.' She smiles at him over her shoulder.

It's the first time Noel has seen her smile. He is struck by the transformation in her careworn expression and finds himself grinning back. 'There was something you wanted to say?'

Michelle drops her gaze, balling up the striped tea towel in her hand. 'I wanted to apologise,' she says, 'about the other afternoon, what I said. Mum was right. I should have been prepared to listen to you, instead of believing the gossip.' She looks at him, her dark eyes wide and appealing.

'No problem. You wanted to protect your mum. I get that.'

She shakes her head. 'That's not an excuse. I judged you, and that was wrong.'

Noel feels lighter as he smiles at her. He wouldn't be able to articulate why it is so important to him that Michelle shouldn't hold a negative opinion of him. But he is conscious that her words bolster the hope that has replaced his recent despair.

'It's OK. Thank you.'

'No. I should thank you.' She reaches for the other glass and dries it. 'Mum has been happier this week than she has been for ages. That's because she has got to know you. I haven't been able to see her as much as I would like since Dad died.' She twists her generous mouth. 'I'm always too busy working and looking after Joshua.'

Noel ducks his head, embarrassed. 'She's a lovely lady,' he says. 'It's no trouble. Besides, I'm going to be getting on with these jobs for her this week.' He sweeps his hand towards the ceiling, and finds himself prattling on about the leak from the bath, and how he should be able to fix that, along with the handles that are falling off the kitchen cupboards and drawers, and repair the broken tiles.

'You sound as though you enjoy what you do.' She squeezes past him again to return the glass to the cupboard.

He catches the yearning in her tone, and remembers Sonia telling him that Michelle held teaching ambitions before her teenage pregnancy. He recalls how tired Kylie used to be after her shifts at Freshfields.

'How about you?' He settles into one of the dining chairs to give her space. 'I know it's a difficult job, being a carer.'

Michelle rubs the bridge of her nose. 'It can be hard.' She reaches for a saucepan, the final item in the draining basket. 'Especially when we lose residents we're close to. We know it will happen, but it's still sad.' Her back to him, she dries the pan vigorously. 'When I got to work this morning, Priscilla, the manager, told me that one of my favourite residents had passed early yesterday. No real warning, though he had been suffering from a water infection this last week. He was in his late nineties, so of course I knew he might go any time. But he was a fixture of the place, an old man who had lived there for eight years. Unlike many of the other residents, Reg didn't suffer from dementia, although he was a bit confused towards the end. I used to enjoy chatting to him. He would tell me about his service in the army during the war.'

'He sounds great. I love listening to people reminiscing about the war.'

'Yeah.' Michelle smiles, then her brow puckers. 'I say there was no warning. He had been agitated lately. I thought it was because an old lady, Elsie, died about three weeks ago. They'd struck up a great friendship since she moved in. They always sat together at meal times, played cards and dominoes together. It was sweet. She died very suddenly too.'

'Must have been a shock for Reg.'

She nods and twists a gold ring on the third finger of her right hand. Noel presumes it's the wedding ring given to her by her late husband, and then finds himself wondering if there is a man in Michelle's life now. She is attractive, especially when she smiles… She is talking again, and he forces himself to concentrate.

'He said something strange the other day, the last time I saw him. I didn't take any notice of it. I thought that he was muddled, upset by Elsie's death, or that his mind was wandering because of the water infection.' She breaks off, her attention caught by a movement outside.

Noel follows the direction of her gaze. A collared dove has flown down onto the apex of the bird table roof. It bows its head then raises it again, cooing loudly enough for them to hear through the kitchen window.

Michelle smiles. 'Those doves… Mum loves them. Reg did too. He would watch them for hours.'

She seems to have lost the thread of her tale. 'You were saying he said something strange?' prompts Noel.

'Oh yes.' She nods. 'He said, "That woman's dangerous. I saw what she did."'

Noel flinches and rotates his shoulder which has suddenly begun to ache. The pain still flares up intermittently. 'What woman was he talking about?'

'I don't know. He was sitting up in bed, looking towards the door. I wondered if someone passing by had upset him. But when I went to look on the corridor, there was no one there. I'd forgotten all about it, until this morning when Priscilla told me he had died. Then it came back to me. I don't know why.' She gives herself a little shake. 'Maybe it was because it was our last conversation. Anyway, I'd picked up a bag of mint balls for him, the old-fashioned sweets, you know?' She flicks a glance at him, and he nods. 'They were his favourites.' Michelle stoops to open the cupboard alongside the oven. 'Reg had no family nearby, so I used to buy them for him at the weekend. That's when most of the other residents have visitors.' She sets the pan down with a clatter, then turns and looks at Noel, her eyes glittering with tears. 'All I could think when Priscilla told me that he had passed was, "What will I do with these sweets?" How foolish is that?' She dashes the backs of her hands over her cheeks and tries to smile.

Noel shakes his head, moved by her kindness. 'Not foolish at all. Practical.' He pauses for effect. 'By the way, I like mint balls.'

He is delighted when she chuckles. 'Then you can have them. They're still in my bag.' She tilts her head on one side and surveys him in an unconscious imitation of her mother's gesture. 'Do you have time for any other odd jobs this week? There are a few things need fixing at Freshfields. The manager is struggling to find someone. The bigger contractors don't seem interested in odd jobs.'

Noel sobers. His instinct is to refuse, thinking that he doesn't want to go anywhere near the home where Kylie worked. But he's hardly in a position to turn down work, with the debt from the fateful Caribbean holiday still to be repaid. And there will always be minor repairs at a residential home. If the manager is satisfied with him, it could provide an ongoing source of income, maybe even be a breakthrough for his business. 'I could make time,' he says eventually. 'Shall I come over and see what needs doing, before or after I finish here one day? Any day but Tuesday,' he adds, without specifying why.

But Sonia has filled her daughter in. 'Is that the day of your father's funeral?' When he nods, she says softly, 'Mum mentioned it. I'm sorry for your loss.'

'Thank you.' Noel looks down at his hands. The funeral is hanging over him, and the reconciliation with his sister still feels very new. He expects to meet her partner, Jack, on Tuesday. He wonders whether the man will resent him for leaving Carol to look after their father, despite the troubled past. He has been wondering too what Eileen Baxter wanted to tell their father on his deathbed, and whether she will divulge this at the funeral.

Dragging his thoughts away from the funeral, and mindful that he is intruding on Sonia's time with her family, Noel stands and picks up his jacket from the back of the chair.

'Shall I take your number?' asks Michelle. 'I'll check with the manager when I get in tomorrow and give you a call.' She takes her mobile out of the pocket of her burgundy trousers.

Michelle has just punched Noel's number into her phone when Joshua bounds into the kitchen, clutching a football to his chest. 'Grandma says to ask if you'll have a kickabout with me,' he says, gazing eagerly into Noel's face.

'I should be going.'

'*Please*,' begs Joshua.

Noel glances uncertainly towards Michelle, who nods, smiling. 'OK,' he says to the boy. 'Just for ten minutes. Then I'll go, leave you all in peace. Your grandma will want to give you your dinner.'

'I can prepare it for half past four if you are able to stay a little longer, Noel?' suggests Sonia, who has followed her grandson into the kitchen. 'I think Joshua could do with the exercise after spending all day on his gadgets with his big brother at home. Isn't that right, Joshua?'

Her grandson nods enthusiastically.

Noel grins at the little boy. 'Go on, then.'

'Thank you,' say Michelle and Sonia in unison.

'Great!' Joshua pulls open the back door and darts out to the overgrown lawn.

The sun is beginning to set, its blaze putting Noel in mind of his return to town on Thursday evening when he found Mrs Mullins by the river. Despite the autumn chill, he has an unexpected insight that he is inwardly reflecting the warm colours of the sky as he kicks the ball to and fro with Joshua. During this brief time with Sonia and her family, he has had a rare sense of belonging, something he hasn't known since he lived with Kylie and the boys. Not that he had ever felt completely secure there, he realises, as he applauds Joshua's prowess in heading the ball to his feet and then kicking it back to his head. The constant disapproval of Kylie's mother had meant that he was often on edge, striving to prove that he was better than Kylie's ex who had left her when her second son was born.

But the knowledge that Kylie believed that he had failed her when he had reacted unenthusiastically to the revelation of her pregnancy has become less painful. Noel has a new assurance that he did what he could at the time, something Sonia helped him to see with her generous words the other afternoon. Kylie had chosen to cut him out of her life. He glances towards the kitchen window as he hears water gurgling down the drain. Sonia raises a hand to him with a smile. He waves back, then leaps up to catch a high kick from Joshua and save the ball from sailing over the fence into the neighbouring garden.

Forty minutes later, Noel parks up outside his house. He has just locked the van when he hears a voice shouting, 'Excuse me! Hello!' from across the street.

Turning, he recognises the trim figure of Geraldine jogging towards him along the opposite pavement. She is again dressed in designer sports gear, although today's outfit is purple. Instinctively he looks towards her mother's house. Dusk is beginning to fall, and the sitting-room curtains are drawn. Somewhere a dog barks.

'Is your mother OK?' he calls, as Geraldine waits for a cyclist to whizz by before crossing the road. 'She's not gone wandering again, has she?'

'No, she's fine. Safely indoors. I just wanted to let you know – Maureen asked me to tell you when she saw your van just as I was leaving – that a room has come up at Freshfields. Mother can move in on Wednesday.'

'I see.' It occurs to Noel that the room might have belonged to Reg, the elderly man whose death has saddened Michelle. He touches the pocket holding the bag of mints she had bought for the late resident of the residential home. 'That's happened quickly, hasn't it?'

'Yes. It will be good to get her in there now that the decision's made,' says Geraldine briskly. Evidently any doubts she had about moving her mother into care have evaporated. 'I've told her she can try it for a couple of weeks, see how she likes it, but of course she'll forget. She'll soon settle in. Maureen's convinced it's for the best.'

'I'm sure that's right,' agrees Noel. 'Thanks for letting me know,' he adds, as Geraldine hovers. 'I might be doing some work up there soon, so I'll pop in and see how she's settling in.'

'That's kind.' Geraldine's tone is indifferent.

It occurs to Noel that she is probably thinking that her mother won't remember him. This may be true, but he suspects that if his mother had survived to old age and ended her days in a residential home, he would have been grateful to anyone who offered to visit her. 'I hope the move goes well,' he says curtly, and takes a step towards his house.

'Er… I wondered if you might be able to help with that.'

'Oh?' He turns back towards her.

'Yes. With moving a few items of furniture.' Geraldine nods towards the van. 'Her armchair, the TV, a chest of drawers. There should be space in her room. I went up today. Apparently, it helps if they have some of their familiar items with them.'

Noel notes the dispassionate use of 'they' and is tempted to refuse.

Geraldine registers his hesitation. 'I'd pay, of course,' she says, looking down her nose. 'I suppose you have an hourly rate, do you, or perhaps a set charge for removals?' She casts a disparaging glance over the battered van. 'Or perhaps you don't often get involved in removals?'

Noel looks down at the pavement and scratches his head. There is a turd of dog poo close to Geraldine's foot. He chooses not to point it out. He would be reluctant to take money from Florence, but her daughter is a different matter, and business is business.

'£40,' he says. 'I can move the things on Wednesday.'

'That will be fine. In fact, if you could take them up there first thing, that would be very helpful. You could arrange them before my mother arrives.'

'I'll check with the customer I'm working for that day,' says Noel smoothly. He is confident that Sylvia won't object, but he isn't going to fall in with this woman's assumptions. He is gratified to see surprise flash across Geraldine's carefully made-up face.

'Oh. OK.' She spins round, the expensive-looking trainer on her left foot scraping the dog poo. 'Ugh! How disgusting!'

Noel pretends he hasn't heard. He is smirking as he makes his way down the path and unlocks his front door. He has a rare sense of having got the upper hand with someone who would usually intimidate him, and it's very gratifying. Hadn't the Being told him, 'Be strong and courageous'? This might not be the kind of situation the Being had in mind, but Noel is quite exhilarated to have departed from his usual meek manner in dealing with Geraldine, a woman he finds intimidating.

He only hopes and prays that he can find similar courage in the coming days, as he prepares for his father's funeral and trusts that God will help him to find Kylie's killer.

I went for a walk by the river this morning. I needed time to think. I was tired after night duty, but I was rattled after work and knew it would take me a while to get to sleep if I went straight home. I was on my way out of Freshfields when I overheard sobbing in the manager's office. The door was ajar. I stopped on the corridor to listen and opened my folder, so that it would look as though I was checking my notes if anyone came by.

I recognised the carer's voice between sobs. It was Michelle, telling Priscilla how surprised she was that the old man hadn't got better. She said he seemed to be responding well to the antibiotics when she was last on duty and even suggested there should be a postmortem. As you might imagine, I came over a bit shaky then, and nearly dropped the folder, but Priscilla pointed out that people often rally just before the end. Michelle said, 'I guess so.' Then Priscilla's phone rang and I heard Michelle's footsteps coming towards the door, so I sprinted off.

The walk by the river calmed me. It always has, ever since you took me down there when I was little. There were a few joggers and dog walkers around and I wanted to be on my own, so I took the path that led to the site of the old boathouse. I've always liked it there. It's a lonely spot, and that suits me well enough.

Remember how you used to tell me those tales about people who died down there, that it was a well-known suicide spot? They obviously got to the point of realising their lives weren't worth living. Some of the Freshfields residents would understand that if they were still compos mentis. Luckily, they've got me to help them.

I'd parked outside the community centre. The car park had filled up when I got back from the river, and there was a banner over the entrance which hadn't been there when I arrived, advertising 'Riverside Church'. It looked like one of those happy clappy churches from what I could see through the window. There was a girl singing, eyes closed and hands in the air. She looked well out of it. One lad was playing the guitar and another was on the keyboard.

There was a youngish man by the entrance wearing ripped jeans and a T-shirt with a bearded face printed on it, presumably supposed to be Jesus. The man was one of those bright-eyed, bushy-tailed types who looks like life is one long party. The kind of person I can't stand.

'Are you coming in?' he called. 'You'd be very welcome.'

I pretended I hadn't heard and unlocked the car. I'd just thrown my fleece in the back when I realised he was right beside me. 'You're a nurse,' he said, nodding at my uniform and smiling. His teeth were so white that he could have been on a toothpaste advert. 'You do such valuable work. We often pray for those who care for others.'

'Who to? Who do you pray to?' I asked. That wiped the smile off his face, I can tell you!

'Well, God, of course,' he said. 'I know you might not believe in God, but we believe He answers our prayers.'

'Do you? I don't see any sign of it,' I snapped. The tiredness from my night shift had caught up with me. 'Not in my work, with old people failing in body and mind. Don't you think your god would want to put them out of their misery if He existed?'

You'd have laughed if you'd seen how horrified he looked, his eyes wide and a tic starting in his cheek. 'But life is sacred,' he muttered. 'It's not for us to decide when life isn't worth living.'

I raised my eyebrows, slammed the door and drove off. I could see him gawping after me in the rear-view mirror.

How can anyone believe in God in this miserable world?

Chapter eighteen

Noel arrives at the crematorium fifteen minutes before his father's funeral on Tuesday morning. Carol had texted him to say that she had decided against a funeral car on the basis of cost. Noel hadn't objected. He feels he has no right to interfere with her arrangements following his lengthy estrangement from his family. It also occurs to him that a funeral car wouldn't be the best place for his first meeting with Carol's partner.

The crematorium opened three years ago, and is set back from the road two miles west of Oldford. Approaching slowly along the drive, Noel sees a modern brick structure with large picture windows overlooking the countryside. There are no more than a dozen vehicles in the car park. He chooses a space in the row furthest from the entrance, wanting to give himself time before he joins those who have come to pay their last respects to Ron Reilly.

Climbing out of the van, he glances towards the crematorium. People are gathering under the wooden canopy. The key is slippery in his damp hand and he fumbles to lock the vehicle. He tries to slow his breathing by casting an eye over the van, which he washed the previous evening after returning from Sonia's. He made a good start on her house repairs, fixing the bath leak and the handles on the kitchen fittings in between the inevitable cups of tea. Weather permitting, he will return mid-morning tomorrow to tidy the garden. Before that, he will move Mrs Mullins' items over to Freshfields and inspect the maintenance jobs at the residential home. Michelle had phoned during her shift yesterday to confirm the manager would like him to quote for the work. She'd also thanked him for spending time playing football with Joshua on Sunday, saying how much the boy had enjoyed it.

'No problem,' said Noel.

'It meant a lot to Joshua,' she replied. Noel wondered if she was thinking about her late husband, about how he would have played with their son. But when she spoke again, she said, 'Thank you for listening to me, too, about Reg.'

'No trouble.' He wished he could think of something else to say, but found himself tongue-tied. It didn't help that he was in her mother's kitchen, with Sonia stirring broth from the carcass of Sunday's chicken on the gas hob.

Michelle cleared her throat. 'I hope your father's funeral goes OK.' A buzzer sounded in the background and someone called her name. 'Got to go.'

'Thanks,' he said, but she had already ended the call.

He realised during his drive to Oldford that he had forgotten to ask if she would be on duty at Freshfields on Wednesday. He was surprised how much he hoped so.

Pushing aside thoughts of Michelle, he walks around the van. However clean it might be, it is undeniably old and battered. Since he moved to his present rundown neighbourhood, Noel has given up on repairs to the bodywork. There are numerous key scratches on both sides and a dent in the rear door, bumped when he backed into a concrete post outside the social club where Kylie's sister and brother-in-law held their wedding reception. Scraping the bollard had been a fitting end to a trying evening.

Noel straightens his tie in the wing mirror. He doesn't remember having worn a tie since Jade's baptism nine years ago. The thought of seeing his daughter in just three days' time gives him the lift he needs to make his way across the car park. Traffic whooshes by on the road below. White clouds are massing, and the strong wind bends the trees in the field fringing the grounds to his right. A murmuration of starlings wheels above the copse.

Aware that he is still breathing rapidly, Noel remembers the Being's words, 'Be strong and courageous.' He reaches for the wooden cross in his jacket pocket. The black suit is new, purchased from a department store at the out-of-town retail park on Saturday. There were none in his size, so he bought the next size up, and it hangs off his slight frame. He fastens the buttons on the jacket as he approaches the crematorium entrance.

Noel spots his sister chatting with an elderly couple. She is wearing a black dress suit and high heels, the smart outfit a contrast to the casual attire she was wearing at their father's house last week. The tailored suit emphasises her skinniness. At her side is a slim man with receding hair and freckles, also dressed in a black suit. His eyes are fixed on Noel, who guesses that this is Carol's partner, Jack.

Noel inhales deeply and looks past the man to survey the group who are making their way through the glass doors. He spots Eileen Baxter's cherry anorak. She is followed by a broad-shouldered man with a shaved blond head and a tattoo snaking above the collar of his navy fleece. From the rear, Noel observes that the man is too young to be Eileen's husband, and wonders if she has a son. He realises that he knows nothing about her personal life, whether she is married, widowed or divorced. Before the affair with his father, he knew her only as his mother's friend, and doesn't remember hearing any man's name linked with hers. From the recesses of his memory, he dredges up the names of couples his parents socialised with on occasional nights out, when they would leave Noel and Carol in their maternal grandmother's care. *Pete and Jan. Mike and Sylvia. Marjorie and Graham.* Noel wonders whether any of them are here this morning, if maybe the couple speaking with Carol is one of them.

'You'll be Noel.' The man beside Carol steps forward. Close up, Noel sees that he appears to be a few years older than Carol. His forehead is lined, and his sandy hair is threaded with white.

'Hi. Jack, isn't it?' Noel extends his right hand. 'Good to meet you.'

Jack's handshake is limp. He raises a salt and pepper eyebrow. 'Finally.'

Noel's heart sinks. The man's attitude doesn't surprise him, but he had hoped that Carol might have explained enough of their family's history for Jack to understand why Noel has kept away. Perhaps, despite their heart-to-heart last week, she wants to protect their father's memory, and hasn't told her partner what happened in their benighted household.

She turns towards them now. The couple she has been talking with move inside after casting a curious glance at Noel.

'You made it, then.'

Noel bites back the "Course I did' which springs to his lips. Instead, he says, 'I said I would,' regretting the words as soon as they are out of his mouth, thinking they sound equally churlish.

He turns towards the drive to hide his disappointment at his sister's lukewarm greeting. He'd thought that they had moved beyond these barbed comments. Then he reminds himself that it's early days, that it's going to take time for her to trust him. It's possible that Jack has warned Carol to be cautious too. Noel appreciates that might have been his own advice if he were in Jack's position, and an estranged brother reappeared after an absence of twenty-five years.

'Mr Reilly?'

Noel spins round to face a woman of medium height. Her grey hair is piled into a bun at the nape of her neck. Some wisps have escaped and blow around her gaunt face. She is dressed in a black robe which billows around her ankles. 'I'm Reverend Hill. Frances.' She extends a hand. Noel takes it. Unlike Jack's, her grip is firm. 'I'm sorry to meet you under these sad circumstances.'

'Thank you.'

'I explained to your sister that the family usually sit on the front row. You could go inside now, or follow behind your father's coffin as you wish.'

'I said Jack and me will follow.' Carol tosses back her hair, hanging loose around her shoulders.

She is staring down the drive as if Noel's decision is of no consequence. He sees Jack reach for her hand. Noel swallows, feeling very alone and out of place. He wonders if he should have stayed away.

The vicar gives him a small smile. Her eyes are kind and shrewd behind round, rose-gold, wire-frame glasses. 'Would you like to join Carol and Jack, Mr Reilly? The car's here now.' She nods towards the road where a row of vehicles trails behind a long black car. The vehicles speed away as the hearse turns up the drive.

Noel watches the hearse progress slowly towards them and licks his dry lips. He thinks of his last meeting with his father, and of how his childhood room was almost untouched for all those years. He is suddenly certain that his father would have wanted him to take his place behind the coffin, whatever Carol's thoughts on the matter. He squares his shoulders inside the loose-fitting jacket and clears his throat. 'Yes. I'll walk behind too.'

The vicar nods approvingly. 'Good.'

Noel stands a little apart from his sister and her partner as the undertaker and bearers alight from the car, solemn and immaculate in black suits. Two wreaths adorn the heavy oak coffin, and he kicks himself for forgetting to ask his sister about flowers. *Too late now.* The funeral director exchanges a few quiet remarks with Rev Hill, and then steps towards the small family group. His eyes flicker over Noel, then settle on Carol. 'Ready to go in?'

Carol blinks hard and gives the slightest nod. Noel feels a rush of sympathy for her. He resists an impulse to cover the few yards between them and hug her, or at least place a reassuring hand on her arm. That would be normal between brothers and sisters, but there is nothing normal about his relationship with Carol. He is miserably aware that her attitude towards him today suggests that whatever progress they made last Thursday, she is keeping him at a distance once again.

They enter the chapel to a Barry White song. Noel remembers his parents dancing to the song in the living room behind their lock-up newsagents. Carol is too young to remember, and he speculates that their father must have told her that it was one of their parents' favourites. The thought that his father was able to talk about their mother to his sister is bittersweet: during the years when Noel was living at home after her death, they never mentioned her for fear that their father might sink deeper into despair.

The vicar confirms Noel's supposition when she refers to the song in the eulogy: 'Ron often enjoyed dancing with his beloved late wife, Ann. They met at the dance hall in Oldford. The Barry White song we heard as we entered was a particular favourite.'

Noel glances at Carol out of the corner of his eye. She is sitting ramrod straight, attention fixed on the vicar.

'Ron never married again,' Rev Hill continues. 'He brought up Carol and Noel on his own after Ann's tragic death in a road accident. Carol describes him as a devoted husband and father.' Rev Hill seems to be looking directly at Noel. Is it his imagination, or did she emphasise 'Carol describes him as…?' He breaks the eye contact and rubs moist hands along the thighs of his new trousers. He wonders what Eileen Baxter is thinking, sitting somewhere behind him in the chapel. He hadn't looked round when he processed in, eyes glued to the coffin wheeled in by the four bearers.

Rev Hill concludes her address with some words about the Christian hope of eternal life, and speaks of the forgiveness of sins through the cross of Jesus. Noel realises that the words would have washed over him until a week ago, the day when he had that extraordinary experience in Sonia's sitting room.

After some prayers, the vicar invites the small congregation to join her in the Lord's Prayer. Noel raises his head to look towards the coffin on the catafalque when they reach, 'Forgive us our trespasses as we forgive those who trespass against us.' The words have never held so much meaning for him.

Rev Hill commits Ron Reilly's body to the elements and presses the button that closes the thick blue curtains around the catafalque. Noel doesn't want to think about what is going to happen next to the coffin. It seems impossible that the man who has had such an influence in his life will soon be a pile of ashes. His throat contracts, and he loosens the knot of his tie. The vicar offers a blessing, and then the exit music begins.

Carol has chosen Barry White's song for the recessional too. If Noel never hears it again, it will be too soon. Sweat prickles between his shoulder blades. It's a relief when the undertaker nods to the three of them on the front row to leave the chapel immediately behind Rev Hill. Noel rushes out, gulping in the fresh air. The sky has darkened to an ominous leaden grey.

The vicar is standing at a discreet distance from the double doors, on the edge of the patio where the floral tributes are laid. Noel shakes her hand and mutters some conventional thanks for a lovely service, avoiding meeting her astute gaze. He considers making a dash for the van, to drive home as fast as he can, but he knows that this will do nothing to help rebuild his relationship with his sister. Instead, he wanders over to where Carol and Jack are standing by the flowers.

Jack is bending over the smaller wreath of red and cream roses. 'Who's Eileen?'

Carol twiddles a fabric button on her black jacket. 'An old friend of my parents'.' She darts a warning glance at Noel. He interprets this to mean that she hasn't confided in her partner about their father's affair.

Jack straightens up. 'I thought you asked for donations to the local hospice, family flowers only?' He looks sideways at Noel.

'Sorry about the flowers, Carol,' says Noel quickly. 'I forgot to ask. I'll send a donation instead.'

Carol purses her lips. 'Right.'

'But this Eileen sent flowers,' observes Jack. 'You'd expect her to have sent a donation, wouldn't you, when that's what you asked for?'

Carol shrugs. 'It doesn't matter. Perhaps she missed the notice in the paper.' She turns to two women who have joined them. Noel notices the resemblance between them, and guesses they are mother and daughter. Both look vaguely familiar.

'Beautiful service.' The older woman angles her curly white head towards Noel. 'How are you, Noel? It's been a long time.'

He detects sympathy in her smile, and is abruptly transported back to the town library one Saturday morning many years ago. He clears his throat. 'Mrs Mercer? Jessica?'

Jessica nods curtly without making eye contact. She takes a few paces to stand on the other side of her old school friend, Carol. Noel is left in no doubt that Jessica has a poor opinion of him, influenced by whatever his sister has told her.

Mrs Mercer is still smiling at him. 'It's good you came today,' she says quietly. She hesitates, weighing her next words carefully. 'I know it was very hard for you after what happened.' She glances towards Carol and Jessica, chatting with Jack. 'I'm sure Carol will come round. You're the only family she has left now.'

Noel looks down at his polished black shoes. 'Maybe.'

Mrs Mercer touches his arm, then says in a brighter tone, 'Do you remember Margaret and Graham Anderson? They knew your parents well, back in the day. Come and have a word.'

A little unwillingly, Noel allows her to steer him towards the elderly couple whom Carol was speaking with earlier. *Marjorie and Graham.* One of the couples whose names he had remembered. They have aged well. Both are lean and wiry, with the weather-beaten faces of those who enjoy the outdoors.

'Noel.' To Noel's consternation, Marjorie wipes tears from her tanned cheek. 'I'm sorry,' she sniffs. 'I'm just so pleased to see you. We felt terrible when you disappeared, didn't we, Graham?'

Her husband shifts his weight from one foot to the other. 'It's good to see you, lad,' he says gruffly.

'Your dad cut himself off from us all after your mum was killed, you know.' Marjorie reaches into a black handbag for a tissue. 'We wanted to keep in touch, but he never answered the phone. If we tried to chat in the shop, he always said he was too busy, didn't he, Graham? We gave up after a while.'

Graham adjusts his square metal glasses. 'Lot of water under the bridge. Poor man's gone now.' He glances briefly towards the crematorium. 'What are you doing with yourself these days then, Noel?'

Noel is grateful that Graham is keen to change the subject, and gives a brief outline of his repairs business. The older man starts describing a DIY project he's working on at home, creating a sewing room for Marjorie. Noel is only half-listening. He's never given much thought to what happened to his parents' friends after his mother died. When he has considered it, he's assumed that they hadn't known how to cope with a depressed widower and found it easier to avoid contact. From what Marjorie has just told him, it seems that she and Graham at least had tried, and that it was his father who rejected their overtures. It makes sense, given how morose and withdrawn his father became. How sad, though, that support was available and his father was unable to accept it.

'Anyway, keeps me busy,' winds up Graham.

'Sounds like it does,' smiles Noel. 'What —?' He is about to ask Graham about his next project, happy enough to remain chatting with the older people rather than to try to join Carol's trio, but breaks off when he hears Mrs Mercer gasp.

Marjorie begins, 'Surely they're not coming over. What can she –?' Graham elbows her sharply in the ribs and she bites back the rest of her question.

Noel turns to see who has caused such consternation. Eileen Baxter is approaching, tottering in unaccustomed heels. A tremulous smile plays around her lips. She is followed by the blond man whom Noel had assumed to be her son from his rear view on the way into the crematorium. The man is staring down at the concrete, his broad shoulders hunched inside his fleece.

'Hello, Noel,' Eileen sounds breathless, her voice thready. 'I'd like you to meet my son, Eddie. Eddie, this is Noel.'

Eddie raises his head and smiles sheepishly. Noel begins to tremble as he looks from mother to son. He opens his mouth but no words come. He blinks hard in case his eyes are deceiving him.

But there is no mistaking the resemblance between Eddie and Ron Reilly.

Chapter nineteen

'Eileen,' says Noel hollowly. 'Eddie.' He takes the hand proffered by the younger man, who appears to be in his mid-thirties. Maths was never Noel's strong point, but it doesn't take much to work out that this matches the date of his father's affair with Eileen.

'Hi. Sorry about... your dad.' Eddie doesn't meet Noel's gaze as they shake hands. Eddie's grip is firm and muscular.

Just like Dad's, thinks Noel, clocking Eddie's hesitation before 'your'.

'Thanks.' Noel is aware of a lull in the conversation among his sister's group. He takes a step to his left, intent on blocking Carol's view of Eddie. Her ignorance of Eileen's significance before their conversation last Thursday means that she will be unaware of Eddie's existence. He guesses that she didn't notice him when he arrived, because there is no way she could have missed the man's likeness to their father. Whatever resentment Carol may continue to harbour against him for leaving her with their father all those years ago, Noel is determined to do his best to protect her from further upheaval on this emotional day. Perhaps Mrs Mercer has the same idea, because she moves behind Noel to join her daughter, who is still chatting with Carol and Jack. Noel hears the older woman saying something inconsequential about the rain holding off so far.

'Graham and Marjorie, isn't it?' Eileen's mouth twitches towards a smile, but falters when Graham places a hand in the small of Marjorie's back and turns pointedly away.

Marjorie throws Noel an apologetic glance as her husband marches her towards the car park. It's clear to him that the two of them and Mrs Mercer all knew about Eddie.

'Lovely service. Nice that the vicar mentioned your mum and dad meeting at the Palais.' Eileen pats her hair. The pink tint is brighter, presumably freshened up for the funeral. 'Ann and I were there together the night your dad first asked her for a dance. He danced with me too, that night. But it was Ann he danced with the most.' She runs her tongue over her cerise lips and there is a touch of defiance in her expression as she looks at Noel. 'Ann he married. Then you came along, and later Carol. I used to visit when you were little, do you remember?'

'Vaguely.' Noel's heart is banging against his ribs, but he relaxes slightly as Eddie goes over to study the two floral tributes, his back to Carol.

'Carol was a difficult baby,' Eileen goes on. 'Tired your mum out.' She leans her head towards his sister. 'That's when me and your dad... you know... And then, well...' She waves a veined hand towards Eddie.

'Right,' says Noel flatly. The first drops of rain begin to fall and he seizes his chance. 'Did Eddie drive you, Mrs Baxter?' He places a hand below her elbow and guides her towards her son.

'It's not Mrs Baxter,' says Eileen. 'I never married. There was no one for me besides your dad, you see.'

Noel keeps his head averted, pretending he hasn't heard. Eddie turns from the flowers. 'All right, Mum?'

'I was just explaining,' says Eileen.

'Nothing to explain. Shall I walk you back to your car?' Noel tightens his hold on Eileen's arm and picks up pace as they round the front of the crematorium. Rain bounces heavily on the tarmac. Any concern he has for the old woman getting wet is outweighed by his determination to prevent a meeting between Eddie and Carol.

'I thought I'd have a word with your sister.' Eileen's tone is mulish.

'I'll pass on your regards. Which car is it?'

'The Polo.' Eddie nods in the direction of an old burgundy Polo in the second row of spaces. Other cars are pulling in for the next funeral, which has attracted many more mourners than Ron Reilly's. 'I'd have liked to meet Carol too,' he adds unexpectedly, as he flicks the remote to unlock the car.

'I'll let her know you were here,' says Noel.

They reach the car. Eddie shoots his mother a glance over the roof of the vehicle and raises his blond eyebrows enquiringly. Noel opens the passenger door for her, wondering what else they want to say to him.

Eileen sinks down sideways on the seat. She drops a black clutch bag into the footwell, then looks up at him before levering her legs round. 'I expect you're wondering why I brought Eddie today, aren't you?' Rain is beating down on the car roof, and Noel has to crouch at the side of the car to hear her. Eddie is settling into the driver's seat. 'The thing is, I never told him – your dad – about Eddie. That's what I came to tell him last week, the day he died.'

Noel doesn't pretend that he doesn't know what she means. Eddie's profile, as he stares ahead through the spattered windscreen, bears such a strong resemblance to Ron Reilly's thirty years ago that Noel has an unsettling sense of being a small boy again.

'I see,' he says, when he finds his voice. He glances back towards the crematorium. Carol and Jack are chatting beneath the canopy with Jessica and Mrs Mercer. Some of those attending the next funeral begin to trickle inside. He decides to be direct. 'So if you don't mind me asking, why *are* you both here today?'

Eileen twists a diamond and sapphire ring round on the second finger of her right hand. 'Ron gave me this,' she says. 'All those years ago. It's an eternity ring.'

Noel massages his temple.

'I'm sorry,' she says. 'We're not here to cause any trouble.' She takes a deep breath. 'The thing is, I never claimed anything for Eddie when he was born. Any money, I mean. It didn't feel right. Not after what happened to your mum.' The old woman's voice quivers. She scrabbles in the pocket of her anorak, withdraws a crumpled tissue and dabs her eyes before she continues. 'I brought him up on my own. My parents helped out a bit, but they didn't have much. They didn't approve of me being an unmarried mother, either. It was a struggle at times, wasn't it, duck?' She lays a hand on her son's arm.

Eddie doesn't respond, continuing to stare through the windscreen, which is misting up on the inside. His hands clamp the steering wheel, knuckles white with the pressure.

'You can understand how difficult it was, can't you, Noel?'

'I guess so.'

'I wanted to let your dad know. I'd always intended that he should meet Eddie one day. But I kept putting it off. Then I bumped into Sylvia Mercer in town a few weeks ago. She told me how ill Ron was. In the end I was too late.' Her voice breaks and she bends her head. After she has gathered herself, she says, 'So I thought, now that he's gone, it's only fair if Eddie gets a share.'

Noel blinks. 'A share?'

'Of your dad's – and Eddie's dad's – money.' Eileen chews her lip. 'Will you explain to Carol, or shall we?'

Noel raises a hand to his hair, plastered to his head in the rain. He hadn't given any thought to an inheritance from his father. It occurs to him that maybe this is another reason for the hostility he has sensed from Carol and Jack this morning. Perhaps they suspect he turned up at his father's deathbed planning to make a claim. The thought sickens him, but he understands how his sister might have reached that conclusion. He finds himself making some rapid calculations. The house can't be worth much. It's in a deprived area of town and in dire need of updating. It's possible his father had savings. If he left a will, that won't include Eddie, since his existence was unknown to his father.

Through the slanting rain, Noel sees that Jessica and her mother are taking their leave of Carol and Jack. He turns to meet Eileen's expectant gaze.

'Dad might have made a will,' he says carefully. 'I don't know anything about that. It could be he left everything to Carol, since she's the one who looked after him.' He pauses, and finds himself hoping that this is the case. There's no denying that an inheritance would be useful to him, not least in paying off the debt from the fateful Caribbean holiday and helping with his repairs business. Morally, though, he feels that the majority of any money should go to Carol, even if he understands that life has been hard for Eileen as a single parent. Eddie is old enough to stand on his own two feet.

Noel glances across at his half-brother, who is studying a CD cover with great concentration. The shock of the encounter hasn't sunk in yet for Noel. He isn't sure how he feels about it, but he is aware of an overriding sense of loyalty to his younger sister, however negative her view of him.

'It's probably best if I tell Carol about Eddie.' He observes Eddie's shoulders relax, and finds himself warming slightly towards the younger man. It occurs to him that Eddie may have been nervous about this meeting and has perhaps been pushed into it by his mother. 'Maybe we could meet up, mate?' he suggests impulsively.

Eddie slides the CD into the storage compartment of the driver's door. 'That'd be good,' he mutters, still avoiding eye contact.

'Would you like to come over to Trentby? Do you know the pub by the bridge? How about tomorrow at eight?'

Eddie drums his fingers on the steering wheel. Noel wonders if the invitation is too soon, and is about to withdraw it, when Eileen interjects, 'You'd like that, wouldn't you?' There's no doubt she's keen to press the family connection.

Her son nods. 'Sure. See you then.'

'It's been very hard, Noel,' sniffs Eileen. 'We never meant no harm, your dad and me. Truly. What happened to Ann has haunted me all these years. I'm just so sorry, duck.' Her voice falters. 'Every day of my life I've regretted it. But never' – she reaches towards her son with a trembling hand – 'never have I regretted that it brought me my Eddie. I've not been able to make any sense of it, how something could bring so much sadness and so much happiness at the same time. All that sadness for your dad and you and Carol, the sadness that I never saw your dad all those years, then the happiness of having Eddie.' She is sobbing now, the years of pent-up emotion spilling out of her.

Eddie reaches across and places an arm awkwardly around her shaking shoulders. 'It's all right, Mum,' he mumbles. 'It's all right.'

Noel swallows as the old woman rocks back and forth.

'How can something bring that much sadness and happiness?' she asks again.

Words about unfaithfulness and adultery spring to Noel's mind, condemnatory words which he has suppressed since his dying father resurrected his memory of his mother's fatal accident. But he has an instinctive sense that those words have no place here. He grasps dimly that what is happening between the three of them is bringing more of that healing which the Being promised him in that vision by the river. Healing to an old woman who has been lonely for much of her life; healing to a man who never knew his father; and healing to him, Noel, as he learns that forgiveness can bring freedom.

'I don't know,' he says quietly. He glances again towards the front of the crematorium and sees that Carol is looking towards them. She says something to Jack, who follows her gaze. Then they turn and begin to hurry across the car park in the other direction.

Noel places a hand on Eileen's arm, damp from the rain. 'I need to catch Carol. See you tomorrow, Eddie.'

His newly discovered half-brother nods and turns the key in the ignition.

Noel rises and closes Eileen's door, then hastens across the car park in pursuit of his sister. The hearse for the next funeral is processing slowly along the drive, and he pauses to allow it to pass. Through the raindrops trickling down the rear windows, he sees a mahogany coffin decorated with an elegant display of lilies. He wonders fleetingly what secrets the deceased person lying within has left behind, whether they have any unknown children who might turn up at the funeral. *It's the kind of thing you come across in films and books,* he thinks, *not in real life,* and now he has the unenviable task of breaking the news about Eddie to Carol.

He breaks into a run after the hearse has passed. Carol and Jack are climbing into a grey Volvo. Noel draws alongside just as Jack starts the engine. Noel raps on the passenger window. On one level he's shocked that they would have driven off without speaking to him; on another he is unsurprised.

Carol jumps and jerks her head towards him. Recovering his breath, Noel registers a pause before she lowers the window.

'What is it?' Her eyes are swollen in her pale, pinched face. Jack leaves the engine running.

'Could we go for a drink or something?' He knows that Carol hadn't planned a reception after the funeral, but he had vaguely expected that the three of them would go on somewhere together.

'I don't think so. I'm shattered. Jack's working this afternoon.'

Jack places a hand on Carol's knee. 'Need to get off now, mate,' he says. 'Maybe another time.' He rams the gear lever into first.

Noel bites his lip and looks towards the belt of trees fringing the grounds of the crematorium. Rooks circle above them. He remembers how his grandmother hated the birds, calling them harbingers of death. She would have thought they were in the right place, here by the crematorium. He shivers.

221

In his preoccupation with Eileen and Eddie, he'd barely noticed how cold and wet he is in his ill-fitting black suit.

Jack revs the engine. Noel lowers his head to Carol, and registers mingled impatience and animosity in her expression. He suddenly feels very tired. 'There's something I need to tell you. It's not easy. I could take you for coffee, Carol, if you like, then give you a lift home if Jack needs to go?'

'Whatever you need to tell me, Jack can hear it too.' His sister narrows her almond-shaped green eyes. 'Is it something to do with Eileen Baxter? I saw you talking to her and that man. Is he her son? I didn't notice them when they arrived.'

Noel pauses. It's not an ideal way to tell her, outside the crematorium immediately after their father's funeral. But he calculates that it's better coming from him than risking Eileen or Eddie contacting Carol directly.

'What is it?' she presses.

'Yeah, spit it out.' Jack revs the engine again. 'We need to go.'

'Eileen's son,' says Noel. 'His name's Eddie.' He swallows and closes his eyes a moment, then looks at his sister. 'The thing is… the thing is, Eileen says that Dad's his father.'

Carol's jaw drops. 'You've got to be kidding.'

'I wouldn't joke about something like this,' says Noel, more sharply than he intended. 'Sorry. I didn't mean to snap.' He rubs the top of his back where rain is dripping uncomfortably down the gap between his shirt collar and skin. 'We'll need to do checks, but he's the spitting image of Dad.'

Carol's wan face whitens further before she lowers it into her hands.

Beside her, Jack snorts, then slips the gear stick back into neutral and turns off the engine. 'Another long-lost brother coming out of the woodwork. Turned up for a share of the money too, has he? Like vultures, aren't you?' He gestures through the windscreen towards the circling rooks, then gazes at Noel, his face set.

Noel's chest tightens. 'I didn't turn up for a share of the money,' he says, struggling to keep his voice level. 'I had no agenda, except to see Dad before he died. I thought you understood that, Carol, after we spoke the other day?' He looks down at his sister's bowed ginger head.

'I don't know what to think.' Her voice is muffled behind her hands. 'Is that why Eileen visited Dad at the end, to tell him about this other son?' She begins to cry.

Noel reaches through the car window and places a hand on her arm. She shakes it off as if it burns. Jack glowers at him. Noel rams his hand into his jacket pocket where it encounters something cool and solid. The wooden cross. His heart rate slows.

'Yes. Eileen wanted to tell Dad about Eddie.' He allows a beat to fall. 'It's been difficult for her, bringing him up on her own.'

'So they're after something now, are they?' sneers Jack. 'Just like you?'

Noel grips the cross tightly and makes up his mind about the half-formed decision he had reached standing by Eileen a few minutes earlier. 'I'm not claiming anything.'

Startled, Carol looks up at him. Mascara tracks stain her cheeks.

Jack gives a mocking laugh. 'You're named in the will,' he says. 'What Carol hasn't told you, because she only found out from the solicitor yesterday, is that the miserable so-and-so left you three-quarters of everything. After all she did for him.'

'What?' Noel stares at his sister. 'Why would he do that?'

'The will said it was because I'd benefited during his life,' she replies dully.

'Whatever that means,' Jack says. 'He was an old curmudgeon, your dad. Bet you won't want to go against his wishes now that you've heard that, will you?'

The rain is easing. Noel looks up at the grey sky. A milky disc beyond the trees shows where the sun is trying to break through. 'I'll be able to do what I want with the money when the solicitors pay it over, won't I?' he says slowly. 'Or maybe I can ask the solicitor to vary the will. Eileen is looking for something for Eddie, and I can kind of understand that. But it seems to me that you deserve far more than me, Carol. I'll see you right, I promise. I don't want a penny.' He gazes at her, hoping she'll believe him.

She stares back at him, her red-rimmed eyes searching his face. His heart lifts a fraction when he sees her expression soften.

Jack still looks sceptical as he turns the key in the ignition. 'Got to go,' he says curtly. 'See you around.'

'I'll call you, Carol,' says Noel. 'We'll arrange to meet up soon, OK?'

She gives him the slightest nod before Jack slips the car into gear and moves off, splashing Noel's new black trousers with standing water.

Chapter twenty

Noel is up early on Wednesday morning so that he can move Florence's items into Freshfields before Geraldine drives her mother to the residential home at ten o'clock. He has a quick breakfast of tea and toast, then tops up the bird table and feeders before going across the street.

Florence's front door is unlocked. Noel steps into the porch and knocks on the inner glass door. He can hear Maureen's voice. She'd told him she intended to be round early to ensure Florence was ready in good time for her move. He casts an eye over the chest of drawers which someone has brought down from the bedroom and left in the porch. It's made of oak, and looks heavy. He suspects that he will need to take out the drawers to get it down the steps to the street.

Maureen opens the door, leaning heavily on her stick. 'Always slow in the morning,' she puffs. 'Come in, Noel. Flo's in the dining room if you want to say hello before you move her things. I'm just getting us both some breakfast.'

He follows her inside and goes into the dining room. Florence is sitting at the table, peering through the window which looks out over the tiered back garden. She is wearing a red and white Fair Isle jumper over a black, pleated skirt. As usual, her fur pill box hat is jammed on to her white head. The hat has clearly been cleaned since she dropped it by the river.

'Morning, Mrs Mullins.'

The old lady jumps and swings round. 'Good morning,' she replies formally. 'Who are you?'

'Now, you know Noel.' Maureen enters, pushing a trolley. 'He's our neighbour from across the street, and he's been very good to you lately, fetching you back you from the river.'

Florence brightens. 'The river. I must go down there! Such a lovely sunny day. He'll be there, won't he? The Bright Giant?'

Maureen grunts and begins to unload the trolley. Noel is touched to see the care she has taken over the preparation of their breakfast, the last meal the friends will share in Florence's house. The table is laid with a white linen tablecloth embroidered with red, pink and yellow roses. He vaguely recalls his grandmother owned a similar tablecloth, and wonders whether anyone still spends their time on embroidery as he moves forward to help Maureen.

He lifts the heavy china teapot onto the table and Maureen arranges the matching milk jug and sugar bowl alongside. Then she sets out cups, saucers and two bowls of cornflakes. Settling her stout frame into the dining chair opposite Florence, she sighs. 'Spoons. I forgot the spoons. Would you mind, Noel?'

'Course not.' He goes to fetch them from the kitchen drawer.

When he returns, Maureen is pouring the tea. Florence peers at the items on the table, then over at her friend. 'What's all this?' she asks. 'Why are you having breakfast with me, Maureen?'

'Thanks, Noel.' Maureen adds milk to the tea and both bowls of cornflakes. 'I thought it would be nice, Flo, that's why.' She flashes Noel a warning glance.

Noel interprets this to mean he shouldn't say anything about Florence's imminent move. Remembering Florence talking about her love of her home the other evening, he understands Maureen's sensitivity.

Florence swivels her head and gives him one of her disconcerting, piercing blue stares. 'Are you coming with me?'

Perhaps she does realise that she is moving after all. Noel exchanges a look with Maureen, who shrugs her rounded shoulders inside her knitted royal blue cardigan before tucking in to her cornflakes.

'Not exactly,' he says. 'I'm going to move some furniture for you.'

Florence frowns. 'Furniture? What do you mean? I don't want furniture by the river!'

Maureen rolls her eyes. 'You're not moving to the river, Flo. Now, eat your cornflakes.'

Florence digs into her bowl with her spoon, scattering cornflakes and milk over the tablecloth. Maureen tuts but carries on eating.

'Shall I get a cloth?' offers Noel.

Maureen shakes her head. 'There'll be more mess before we've finished. Do you want to make a start loading the van? You've seen the chest of drawers Geraldine's sons brought down to the porch last night, and there's some boxes and a suitcase in the sitting room.'

Florence pauses in the action of lifting her spoon to her mouth. 'Suitcase? Are we going on holiday? Is that why we're having breakfast together, Maureen?'

Her friend dabs milk from her chin with a white napkin and smiles wistfully. 'No. I wish we were, though. We've had some lovely holidays, haven't we?' She turns to Noel. 'We've been on a few coach trips since our husbands died.'

'Devon,' says Florence unexpectedly. 'That place by the river. Where the crime writer lived.'

'Well, I never,' Maureen shakes her head. 'It's amazing what you *do* remember, Florence. Yes, that was a wonderful holiday. We stayed at Dartmouth and visited Agatha Christie's house,' she explains to Noel.

Florence slurps the last of her cornflakes and drops the spoon into the bowl with a clatter. 'Rivers are dangerous,' she announces. She gazes at Noel again. 'I lost my brother in the river. Did you ever meet him?'

'Noel's far too young to have known William,' interjects Maureen. 'But he knows all about the accident.'

Florence runs her forefinger over a red rose stitched on to the tablecloth. 'It wasn't an accident. He was taken.'

'That's right.' Maureen sips her tea. 'He was taken by the river. Drowned.'

Florence shakes her head impatiently. 'Not taken by the river. By the Grey One.'

Noel shivers.

Maureen blows out through her teeth. 'Now, don't start all that. Won't you drink your tea, Flo?'

Florence, however, is looking through the window again. She stands abruptly, knocking her thigh against the table. Tea splashes over the edge of her cup into the saucer. 'He'll be there this morning. Why don't you come with me, Maureen?'

'Sit down and drink your tea,' says Maureen wearily. 'We're not going to the river today.'

Florence plonks herself down like a sulky child, but she does take a gulp of tea, still staring into the sunlit garden. 'Why?' she asks querulously. 'Why can't we go to the river?'

'Because Geraldine's coming soon,' says Maureen.

'Oh.' Florence drains her cup. 'Maybe later, then.'

Maureen doesn't reply, leaning over to pour them both more tea.

Noel sidles out of the room, not wanting to distract the confused old lady. As he foresaw, the chest of drawers requires disassembling to take down to the van. He carries out the armchair and TV next, then the eight boxes and suitcases which Geraldine has packed. It occurs to him that this is rather more than he had agreed to transport for his £40 fee, but he decides that it would be petty to raise this with Geraldine. If she plans to take the money from her mother rather than pay herself, he would feel he was taking advantage of Florence by increasing his charge.

After he has loaded the van, he says goodbye to the two old ladies, and drives off to Freshfields. He's in sombre mood, saddened by the knowledge that he won't visit Florence again in her own home. Inevitably her remarks about the river lead him to mull over the mystery of the Bright Giant and the Grey One once more. Sonia's interpretation that they are some kind of spiritual beings is persuasive, although his conviction has wavered since they spoke on Sunday. The possibility that the Bright Giant might be Jesus Himself seems far-fetched when he is away from Sonia; Noel struggles to imagine himself ever having such a strong faith as she has, even though he recognises that she has been a follower for many years while his faith is very new. He still finds it extraordinary to think that he himself has been charged with fighting the evil within the town, even if he has accepted the call.

Discomfited by his inability to dislodge Florence's words, 'Taken ... by the Grey One,' from his head, he switches on the radio. As usual, it's tuned to the local station. The nine o'clock news bulletin is just starting.

Noel makes slow progress behind a dustbin lorry as he drives along the road where Kylie lived. He can't resist glancing towards her house as he waits for the two refuse collectors to empty the bins of the neighbouring properties. His stomach lurches when he sees the yellow crime scene tape covering the house. There is no reference to the police investigation on the news, so he assumes no progress has been made. The fact that the murderer is still at large is a frightening prospect.

Noel has found himself mentally running through Kylie's family members and friends since his dream that led him to wonder whether she knew her killer. He can't imagine that any of them is capable of murder, and has felt guilty for even contemplating the idea. Another disquieting question worries him. What if the killer is some kind of psychopath with a grudge against pregnant women? The prospect that another man might experience anything of his anguish over the loss of an unborn child and partner is intolerable. Even if he and Kylie did separate months ago, he knows that the loss of her and their baby will weigh heavily upon him for the rest of his life.

Preoccupied with his gloomy thoughts, Noel turns into the driveway of the residential home. He parks up and goes across to the double glass-door entrance. Freshfields is a single-storey modern brick building with well-tended flowerbeds along its frontage, and has a reputation for being the best home in town. He presses the intercom. There is a crackle before a woman says, 'Hello?'

Noel identifies the speaker as Michelle, and his heart lifts. Then he feels guilty, having just been thinking of his ex-partner who worked here too, whose life has been so cruelly cut off. He strives for an impersonal tone, as though he doesn't recognise her voice. 'Hello. My name is Mr Noel Reilly. I've brought some items for a new resident, Mrs Mullins.'

There is a pause, during which he feels colour flood his face at both his dissimulation and the ridiculous stiffness of his words.

When Michelle answers, she sounds equally formal, although he is sure he hears a stifled giggle. 'Good morning, Mr Noel Reilly. I will buzz you in and show you to Mrs Mullins' room.'

The locking mechanism clicks and he pushes open the heavy glass door. Michelle emerges from an office to the left of the small foyer. 'Mr Noel Reilly, I believe?' she asks, her dark eyes dancing.

Noel's flush deepens. 'I wasn't sure it was you,' he says defensively.

She raises an eyebrow sceptically, then spins on her heel and sets off down the corridor. He follows, trying not to stare at her hips swaying inside the burgundy skirt of her carers' uniform. They pass through a dining room where the smell of toast lingers in the air from breakfast, and then along another corridor. Most of the doors of the residents' rooms are ajar, pouring out sounds of old songs and daytime TV. A vacuum cleaner hums faintly in the distance.

A large young woman with a clipboard backs out of one room, impeding their progress. 'Cottage pie and jelly for lunch, cheese sandwich and a banana for tea. See you later, Sheila.'

She grins at Michelle and Noel as she squeezes past them. 'All right, Michelle?'

Michelle smiles back. 'Hi, Becky.' She tips her head towards Noel. 'This is Noel… Mr Reilly,' she amends, casting him a sly glance from the corner of her eye. 'He's brought some items for our new resident, Mrs Mullins, and may be doing some odd jobs around the place.'

Becky's grin disappears. 'Noel Reilly? You're Kylie's ex, aren't you?'

Noel studies his grubby trainers. 'That's right.'

'She told us about you.' Her tone and shuttered expression leave them in no doubt about the negative nature of Kylie's tales about Noel. 'Catch you later, Michelle.' Becky plods away in the direction of the dining room.

They continue silently down the corridor and up a ramp leading to a door where Michelle halts. She glances over her shoulder. 'The secure unit. I'll give you a slip of paper with the number for when you come back with Mrs Mullins' furniture.' She presses four numbers into the keypad to the right of the door. They go through and pass a day room where several residents are nodding off in front of an old episode of *A Touch of Frost.* A bald man in a wheelchair with a knitted blanket of squares over his knees waves to Michelle and Noel. The white-haired woman next to him calls, 'Nurse! Nurse!'

'I'll be back in a minute, Sophie,' says Michelle.

Michelle draws to a halt four doors along from the day room. She pushes the door open and he follows her inside.

'This is the room. Mrs Mullins is lucky. Her daughter wanted her to have a double, and this has a view of the courtyard garden too.' She glances at him. 'Costs more,' she adds succinctly.

'Right.' He looks round. Having glimpsed the interior of a single room on the way, he can see that this room is more spacious.

Michelle goes across to the single bed and bends to smooth the lilac duvet cover. 'I hope your neighbour will be as happy here as Reg was.'

'Reg was the old man who used to tell you stories about his experiences in the war, wasn't he? The one who died suddenly?'

'That's right. I know I shouldn't have favourites, but it's difficult not to. I miss him.' She straightens up and crosses to the window.

Two doves are feeding off a bird table in the courtyard garden, which contains an assortment of colourful concrete planters. Noel recognises Michaelmas daisies and some late dahlias among the autumn flowers in the pots.

'Like Mum, Reg loved doves. I've been putting out seed for them whenever I see the container is empty. He used to ask me to do that. Every day I would top up their seeds, knowing he would watch them for hours when he was alone.' She smiles sadly. 'Do you think it foolish that I'm still doing that, when he isn't here any more?'

Noel shakes his head. 'It sounds like the best way you could remember him.'

She blinks hard, then says, 'I'm sorry about Becky.'

He shrugs and rams his hands in the pockets of his bomber jacket. 'I guess it's to be expected.'

'Maybe. But unpleasant all the same. I hope that if you work here, it will help you and be good for your business. People like Becky will get to know you, and realise that they only heard Kylie's side of the story.'

She looks at him intently with her liquid caramel gaze, reassuring him, if he still had any doubts, that she has changed her poor opinion of him since hearing his version of events.

After what feels like a long moment, she breaks the eye contact and adjusts a seascape painting to the right of the bed.

It looked straight enough to Noel, and he thinks she has skewed it, but refrains from saying so.

'Thank you for helping my mother,' she says. 'She's very pleased with the work you did for her on Monday.'

'No trouble,' he says awkwardly, the phrase putting him in mind of their stilted phone call.

Perhaps Michelle is thinking of it too, because she replies, her voice amused, 'So you keep saying.' She steps away from the painting and glances at her watch. 'I'd better go and see what Sophie wants. If she can remember.'

Noel wonders if she ever gets frustrated with her job. He remembers Sonia telling him that Michelle had ambitions to train as a teacher before her unplanned teen pregnancy.

'Do you see yourself working here long term?' he asks, then immediately regrets the directness of the question when he observes the animation drain from her face. 'Sorry. It's none of my business.'

She shrugs. 'It's OK. What can I say? It's a job. It pays the bills. Do I want to be here the rest of my life? No. But as a single mum of two sons, I have no choice other than to keep going.'

It's the first time in their meetings that she has referred to her status as a single mother.

'I'm sorry,' he says cautiously. 'About your late husband. Your mum told me how it happened.'

Michelle looks down at the simple gold wedding ring she still wears and twists it round her finger. 'Thank you,' she says quietly. 'Now, I must get on.' She moves towards the door. 'I'll introduce you to the manager when you're done here. She'll show you the repairs that need doing. And here is today's key code.' She fishes a slip of white paper from the pocket of her tunic.

'Thanks.' Noel takes the paper, his fingers brushing hers.

'You'll find me in the day room, Mr Noel Reilly.' Michelle grins at him before sashaying out of the room.

He gawps after her retreating figure for a moment, then straightens the picture before attempting to find his way out along the maze of corridors. He replays their conversation in his mind, hearing again the inflections of Michelle's voice, watching the expressions flit across her face. He is so preoccupied that he takes a wrong turning after the dining room, where four residents are now playing dominoes, watched by a slim young female carer with rainbow-coloured hair.

A smell of frying mince grows stronger as he makes his way along another corridor, which looks identical to the others. This one, however, leads to the kitchen. A short, wiry man wearing navy and white checked chefs' trousers beneath a white shirt is standing over two large frying pans on a stainless-steel hob. Evidently the cottage pie ordered by Sheila is underway. The meaty odour is unpleasant in Noel's nostrils, and he feels a little nauseous. He hastily retraces his steps.

Back in the dining room, he considers the other three corner exits. The rainbow-haired carer flashes him a smile. 'First visit? Everyone gets lost to begin with. If you're trying to find your way out, it's over there.' She points to the door directly opposite him, then turns her attention back to the dominoes.

The four residents are so immersed in their game that they don't look up. 'Your turn, Dorothy,' croaks an old man.

Heading back towards the entrance, Noel wonders how many thousands of games of dominoes and cards are played in the home, and whether Florence still has the mental capacity to play. It's a depressing thought, and he cheers himself by recalling Michelle's words. 'People will get to know you, and realise they only heard Kylie's side of the story.' It sounds as though she has formed a good impression of him during their brief acquaintance. Noel is surprised how much he wants her to think well of him. He tries to tell himself that it's because of his developing friendship with her mother. At a deeper level, he knows that this isn't the only reason. But he shies away from considering why Michelle's approval is so important to him.

Nor does he examine why his heart beats faster when he sees her in the day room as he passes with the last of Florence's items half an hour later. He has got into the habit of waving to the old man in the wheelchair each time he trundles by with his loaded platform trolley. The man seems to be less entertained by the vintage ITV3 crime shows than by Noel passing. As he pauses to give the obligatory wave, Noel sees that the urban landscape of *A Touch of Frost* has been superseded by the Yorkshire moors of *Heartbeat*. He used to watch the police drama series with Carol on Sunday evenings; sometimes, if he hadn't gone to the pub, their father might even join them. Looking back, Noel reckons that this was the closest they ever got to something resembling a normal family life after his mother's death. He wonders how Carol is getting on, and thinks he might ring her later to find out how she is coping with the revelation of their new brother. He has considered inviting her to the pub that evening, but rejected the idea in view of her initial hostility. Better for him to get to know Eddie on his own first.

'Are you nearly done?' Michelle's voice breaks into his thoughts.

'Last load.' Noel waves back at the old man.

'I'll wait for you,' she says.

Noel's smile freezes on his lips. The phrase reminds him of lyrics from one of Kylie's favourite songs which she used to sing endlessly. He turns abruptly and lurches down the corridor, nearly dislodging the three boxes from the trolley. His hands shake as he unloads them in Florence's room. He goes across to the window, wanting to collect himself before Michelle introduces him to the manager.

Three sparrows are pecking the seeds on the bird table. They fly away and are replaced by others which duck and dive around the table. He watches for a while, centring himself, even as his thoughts flutter like the birds.

He thinks of Florence, who will soon arrive in this room, her final home, and wonders how the confused old lady will cope in this unfamiliar place surrounded by strangers.

He pictures Michelle, still grieving for her husband who was so cruelly taken from her, faithfully refilling the bird food in memory of the old man who died in this room.

He sees his father on his deathbed, and the oak coffin that contained his wasted body.

He visualises Eddie, staring through the windscreen, knuckles white on the steering wheel, as his mother sobs, 'How can something bring that much sadness and happiness?'

Finally, his inner eye settles on Kylie, dressed in her burgundy carer's uniform – the same uniform Michelle wears – singing in her kitchen. The kitchen where she was killed.

He suddenly remembers her singing on their last evening together, when he made spaghetti Bolognese for her and the boys. Maybe that's why the smell of frying mince in the Freshfields kitchen made him gag.

Once again, he reaches for the smooth wooden cross nestling in the pocket of his bomber jacket. As his fingers close over it, he understands with sudden clarity that until Kylie's killer is found, the peace he briefly experienced on that startling afternoon in Sonia's sitting room the previous week will elude him.

He bows his head. 'Help me, Jesus,' he prays. 'Help me right these wrongs.'

When he looks up, a collared dove has replaced the sparrows. The dove is perched on the edge of the bird table, head on one side, and seems to be contemplating Noel intently. Then with a single graceful movement, it unfurls its wings and soars into the cloudless sky.

Chapter twenty-one

A familiar voice breaks into Noel's reverie. 'Why have we come here? It's such a lovely sunny day. We should be going to the river.'

He swings round from the window. He'd intended to be gone before Geraldine arrived with her mother. The sudden movement jars his injured shoulder. He rotates it as Michelle enters the room, followed by Florence and Geraldine.

'It's far too hot in this place.' Florence tugs at the top button of her tweed coat with the fur trim. 'What are we doing here?'

'This is your new home, Mrs Mullins,' smiles Michelle.

'New home?' Florence advances and surveys the room. Her gaze rests on her armchair and chest of drawers. She frowns. 'Those are my things. How did they get here?'

'We thought it would be nice for you to have some of your own furniture in your room, Mum,' says Geraldine brightly from the threshold. She nods towards Noel. 'Your neighbour brought it up.'

Florence scrutinises Noel. 'Neighbour?'

Former neighbour, thinks Noel sadly. 'That's right.'

'Well, you need to take my things back home,' says Florence firmly. 'They don't belong here.'

'They do now, Mum,' says Geraldine in the same cheery tone. 'You're going to be very happy here, once you've settled in.'

Like persuading a child they'll enjoy their first day at school. Noel suppresses a smirk when Michelle, knowing she is shielded from Geraldine by the open door between them, rolls her eyes at him.

'Oh no. I can't stay here.' Florence fastens her gaze on Noel. 'You'll take me back, won't you?'

He shifts uncomfortably and looks at the floor.

'Now, don't be difficult, Mum.' Geraldine rolls back the sleeve of her tailored fuchsia jacket and glances at her watch. 'I've only got half an hour before I need to get back to the office. Shall we start unpacking?' She steps towards the boxes which Noel has stacked in the far corner of the room. Taking some scissors from a smart grey cross-body bag, she snips through the brown parcel tape of the top box.

Florence covers her ears with her hands at the harsh sound of the tape being peeled back. She joins Noel by the window and looks up at the sky. 'He'll be there today, won't He, the Bright Giant? Down by the river?' She claps her hands and clasps them in front of her chest. 'There's not a moment to lose! Why don't you all come with me?' She pivots round, eyes darting between them.

Geraldine groans. 'Mum, you're not going anywhere! Certainly not to the river.' She holds out a black and white photograph in a brass frame. 'Shall I put your wedding photo on the bedside table, or the chest of drawers?'

'What's that doing here?' demands her mother. 'It should be at home.'

Geraldine doesn't reply and sets the photo down on the chest of drawers.

'Would you like a cup of tea, Mrs Mullins?' suggests Michelle.

Florence raises a finger to her lips, considering. 'That would be nice,' she declares. 'There'll be time for a cup of tea, won't there, before we go home?'

'I'm sure there will. Now, why don't you take off your coat and sit down? This is a lovely armchair.' Michelle pats the back of Florence's claret armchair.

The old lady blinks. 'Do you know, that's just like my chair at home.' She fumbles again with the top button of her coat. Michelle helps her out of it, then takes the coat across to the wardrobe and places it on a wire hanger inside. Noel watches, admiring her dexterity in handling the confused woman.

'Are you happy with the chair there?' He addresses the question to Florence, but isn't surprised when Geraldine answers.

'It will do,' she says ungraciously. 'It gives Mum a view of the corridor. You'll be able to see your visitors, won't you, Mum?'

'What visitors?' Florence frowns as she settles into her armchair. Her gaze fastens on Noel. 'Are you a visitor?'

He smiles. 'That's right.'

'What about you, in the uniform? Are you a visitor too?'

'I work here,' says Michelle. 'Now, shall I take your hat? As you said, it's very warm in here.'

'No, thank you.' Florence reaches up and clamps the fur hat lower on her white head.

Geraldine takes more pictures from the box and sets them alongside her parents' wedding photograph. There is a faded picture of a little girl with a boyish haircut in a flowery dress, whom Noel assumes is Geraldine. Another pair of photos in matching wooden frames feature two boys in school uniform at different stages of development, presumably Florence's grandsons.

Geraldine taps the picture of the older boy. 'Did I tell you that Harry is taking his driving test today, Mum? Can you believe it?'

'Driving test? Fancy!' Florence smiles vaguely. 'I don't think I ever learned to drive. I like walking, you see. Especially to the river. In fact, I must be going.' Florence makes to get up.

Her daughter emits an exasperated sigh.

Michelle raises a forefinger. 'First, a cup of tea. Remember?' She moves towards the door. 'Shall I introduce you to the manager now, Mr Reilly?'

Noel knows that she is still teasing him about his earlier formality, and feels his cheeks redden. 'Sure.' He lays a hand over his former neighbour's as he passes her armchair. 'I'll see you soon, Mrs Mullins.'

The colour suddenly drains from her face and her hand tenses beneath his. Noel pulls his hand away, worried that the physical contact has alarmed her. Florence gasps, and crosses her hands over her chest. She begins to rock to and fro.

'Mrs Mullins? Are you OK?' Michelle drops to her knees, seizing the old lady's thin wrist to check her pulse.

'What is it, Mum?' Geraldine drops another photo with a clatter back into the box.

'The Grey One,' croaks Florence. 'Didn't you see? The Grey One is here. Why have you brought me to this place?' Her eyes are fixed on Noel.

His flesh prickles. He turns towards the doorway. There is no one there.

Aware that he wants to reassure himself as much as the old lady, Noel crosses the room and pokes his head out into the corridor. No one is in sight apart from a slim blonde-haired woman whisking round the corner towards the dining-room. She is dressed in a navy uniform, a contrast to the burgundy worn by the carers. Noel guesses she is a nurse.

He turns back to Florence, who is still rocking herself in the armchair. 'The Grey One isn't here, Mrs Mullins,' he says gently.

'Of course that thing isn't here,' snaps Geraldine, glaring at him. 'It's all in Mum's mind. You shouldn't indulge her, checking the corridor as if it's real.'

Noel bites his lip. Quite apart from his belief in the reality of the Grey One, however it manifests itself, he's heard that sharing the perspective of dementia sufferers can help them.

'Perhaps you could get that cup of tea?' Geraldine looks pointedly at Michelle.

Michelle's lips settle into a sullen line, but all she says is, 'Coming right up.' She turns on her heel. Noel follows her out of the room and along the corridor.

Once they are out of earshot, Michelle mutters over her shoulder, 'That is one patronising woman. You were right, checking to reassure Mrs Mullins that whatever it is she is frightened of isn't around. It's best not to challenge the thinking of people with dementia, but to go along with them, enter their world. So that I can tell my colleagues what to expect, does Mrs Mullins often talk about this thing, the Grey One?'

'She does. And she talks about a Bright Giant too.'

Noel wonders what Michelle would make of the full story, especially if he told her of his own encounters with the phenomena that match those spoken of by Florence, and that she has connected the Bright Giant with Jesus. What would she say if he told her that he believes he has a divine mission to accomplish, to bring Kylie's killer to justice? He has no idea whether Michelle shares her mother's faith; Sonia has never mentioned if Michelle accompanies her to church. He hopes that Michelle hasn't turned away from God since her husband's death, and then asks himself why this should matter to him.

They reach the dining room, where dominoes is still in progress under the supervision of the rainbow-haired carer. Noel smiles at her, but she looks through him, stifling a yawn. 'New resident settling in all right, Michelle?'

Michelle waggles her head, her sleek black ponytail swinging from side to side. 'So-so. I'm just getting her a cup of tea, and introducing Mr Reilly to the manager. He may be doing some odd jobs for us.'

'So Becky said,' the carer says flatly. She turns back to the table where an argument has broken out over who should go first in the next game.

Michelle gives Noel a sympathetic look and leads him back along the now familiar corridor to the entrance. He glances through the glass entrance doors as they pass. There is a police car parked in the bay opposite. He digs his nails into his palms. His recent experience of being questioned by the police in the hours after Kylie's murder is still raw.

Michelle registers something of the agitation in his face as she halts outside a door bearing a plastic plaque, 'Manager's Office'. There is a low murmur of voices inside.

'Are you all right? You look pale.'

'I'm OK. Look, if your manager is busy, I can come back some other time, maybe later today after I've got on with the work at your mum's.'

'Sure, if that suits you better.' She frowns. 'You haven't changed your mind because of Becky and Angela, have you? I hope they didn't put you off. As I said, if you –'

The office door is flung open and a policeman emerges, followed by a small Filipino woman whose broad forehead is furrowed with concern. Noel's heart sinks as he recognises the ruddy face and globular nose of DI Pritchard, the policeman who questioned him on the day of Kylie's murder.

'If you think of anything, anything at all out of the ordinary, let us know. And if you've got that list, we'll make a start by questioning the staff on duty the day Mr Barnes died,' DI Pritchard is saying.

Michelle's shoulders stiffen inside her burgundy uniform. 'What's this about Reg – Mr Barnes? Have you found out that he didn't die naturally?' she asks sharply. 'I said so at the time, didn't I, Priscilla?'

The manager spreads her hands. 'Reg was very old. Old people die suddenly. How could I know there was anything unusual about his death?' Her voice rises. 'I can't believe it, that someone here would deliberately inject him with too much morphine. Who would do such a thing?'

'That's what we're going to find out.' DI Pritchard considers Michelle. 'And you are?'

'Michelle Cowan. Reg wasn't –' Michelle swallows. 'You're not saying he was *murdered*, are you? Here, at Freshfields?' She stares up and down the corridor incredulously, as if the perpetrator will materialise.

'We're pursuing various lines of enquiry,' answers the policeman woodenly. 'You knew Mr Barnes well, did you?'

'As well as anyone.' Michelle brushes tears from her cheeks.

Noel has to stop himself acting on an unexpected impulse to put an arm around her.

'Then I'll ask you a few questions first.' DI Pritchard turns back to the manager. 'Did you say there's a room we could use?'

'Yes. I'll show you.' Priscilla nods to Noel. 'Are you Mr Reilly?'

'Reilly,' repeats the policeman, noticing Noel for the first time. 'That name rings a bell.' He scratches his head, ruffling up tufts of cropped greying hair. 'Wait a minute. I interviewed you on the day Ms Weatherall was found. You're her ex-partner, aren't you?'

Noel's heart hammers against his ribs. He nods.

'Ms Weatherall worked here too, didn't she? Didn't my sergeant come up to question you and your staff last week?' DI Pritchard's enquiries are directed to the manager, but his eyes are pinned on Noel.

'That's right.' Priscilla's right hand flies to her throat. 'You're not saying there could be a connection between the deaths of Kylie and Mr Barnes, are you?'

The policeman's expression is grim. 'It can't be ruled out, can it? Bit of a coincidence, her working here and the old man being a resident. I don't like coincidences.' He glares at Noel. 'You're another connection, aren't you?'

'Well, I... I... haven't been... I mean...'

Michelle interrupts the stammering Noel. 'Mr Reilly brought some furniture up this morning for his neighbour who has just moved in. I don't recall ever seeing you here before, Mr Reilly. Is this your first visit?' Her eyes are warm as they settle on him, and he feels his breathing begin to slow.

'Yes. I mean, I picked up Kylie occasionally, but I never actually came in before today.'

The policeman stares at him stonily before saying, 'Right. And you never met Mr Barnes?'

'No.'

'I was bringing Mr Reilly to see you about the repairs, Priscilla,' adds Michelle, before the policeman can ask Noel any more questions.

'I see.'

In the circumstances, Noel is unsurprised to detect a note of doubt in the manager's voice. After all, who would want to employ a man who has been questioned in connection with his ex-partner's murder? 'It's OK,' he says quickly. 'I'm already late for another customer. I'll come back some other time.'

Relief spreads over Priscilla's face. 'I'll let you out.' She moves swiftly towards the keypad by the entrance and types in a code. There is a click, and she pushes open the door.

'Thanks.'

DI Pritchard places a meaty fist on the door, blocking Noel's exit. 'You're not planning on leaving town any time soon, are you?'

Noel's teeth are chattering. 'No.'

'Good. Because we may need to speak again.' DI Pritchard lowers his arm and Noel hastens outside, where he takes large gulps of the autumn air as he crosses the car park to his van. The crisp chill of the October day is welcome after the clammy atmosphere of the overheated residential home.

Once inside the van, Noel switches on the engine and crunches the gears into reverse. He is heedless of the speed bumps as he drives the short distance to Sonia's house, intent on reaching the sanctuary of her peaceful home as quickly as he can. His insides feel as though they have turned to liquid. However unlikely it is that Mr Barnes' untimely death may be connected with Kylie's murder, he is uneasy about the coincidence that both of them have associations with Freshfields.

And now he has a new sense of urgency in his quest to uncover Kylie's killer: DI Pritchard might have temporarily dismissed him as a suspect for Kylie's murder, presumably after checking out his alibi. But the policeman has made it very clear that Noel is once again a person of interest in the investigation into the murders of both Kylie and Mr Barnes.

Chapter twenty-two

Standing on Sonia's doorstep with his bag of tools ten minutes later, Noel wonders whether he should have brought Michelle with him. While it seems ridiculous to consider that Freshfields could be dangerous, the suspicious death of the old man coming so soon after Kylie's murder is deeply troubling. There is something else niggling him too, something he thinks Michelle said to him about Mr Barnes' death, but he is unable to bring it to mind.

Sonia instantly perceives Noel's disquiet when she opens the door to his knock. 'What is it? Has something happened?' she asks, before adding, characteristically, 'Let me make you a cup of tea and you can tell me all about it.'

Noel dumps his tool bag in the hall and follows her into the kitchen. He paces around as Sonia prepares the tea, telling her that the police are investigating the death of the elderly resident at Freshfields.

Sonia recognises the name immediately. 'Mr Barnes? That was the old man Michelle was fond of, wasn't it? She told me he had died very suddenly.' The kettle begins to whistle and she lifts it off the hob.

'Yes. That's Mr Barnes.' Noel stops pacing and gazes out unseeingly over the small garden. He pinches the bridge of his nose between his thumb and forefinger, trying to summon what Michelle had told him about the old man when they were washing up on Sunday.

'So there *is* something suspicious about how he died?' Sonia pours the boiling water into the Charles and Diana teapot and nods towards his usual chair. 'Please, sit down.'

Noel seats himself and crosses his legs, circling his right foot. Sonia carries the teapot over.

'Apparently, he was injected with too much morphine. The policeman has picked up on the coincidence of Kylie working at Freshfields too.' Noel bites his lip. 'I shouldn't have left Michelle. I should have waited until the policeman had finished questioning her, made sure she was all right.'

Sonia cocks her head in her bird-like pose and studies him. 'Michelle has experience of the police,' she says placidly. 'She will be all right. She knows how to handle herself. She will be alert as she goes about her duties.'

Noel rubs his face. From what Sonia has told him, Michelle must feel let down by the police who failed to discover how her husband died in the drunken brawl in town. But this isn't the only concern he has for Michelle. After recounting the discussion with the policeman at Freshfields to Sonia, he finds himself dwelling on Florence's insistence that she saw the Grey One.

'Is there something else?' asks Sonia with her usual prescience. She pours their tea and slides a cup across the table to Noel.

'It's probably nothing,' he says hesitantly, 'but soon after Mrs Mullins arrived, she started agitating that she had seen the Grey One. I even checked the corridor.'

'Did you see anything?'

Noel shakes his head. 'No. There was no one there.' He remembers the flash of navy uniform. 'Well, no one except for a nurse disappearing round the corner,' he amends.

Sonia frowns and sips her drink. 'A nurse,' she repeats. She wanders over to the window. Noel silently drinks his tea, sensing that his friend is thinking deeply. Presently she turns to face him. 'How did you say Kylie died?' Seeing pain flash across his face, she adds, 'I'm sorry, but it's important.'

Noel sets his cup down on the saucer. 'Her mum said she was injected with something, some kind of drug. That's what the police told her.' He looks down at his hands, recalling Susan Weatherall's anger towards him in the mini-market. His jaw drops as he remembers something else. 'That's what I saw in my dream too, the woman in grey injecting Kylie!'

'Mmm.' Sonia nods slowly and sits down. 'So Kylie was injected, like Mr Barnes. And of course, nurses have access to all kinds of drugs, don't they?'

'I suppose so.' Noel gapes at her as he grasps the implication of her words. 'You're not thinking that the nurse I saw could be responsible for the deaths of Kylie and the old man?'

'I am afraid so.' Sonia's expression is grim. 'I imagine it would have been very easy to kill Mr Barnes without any suspicion being raised. What's fortunate – or perhaps providential – is that the morphine was found in his system. I suspect that postmortems are unusual among deaths of the elderly in residential homes. Perhaps this one was carried out because Mr Barnes was in excellent health for his age. Maybe he hadn't seen the doctor for a while.'

'Michelle certainly thought he was very well, apart from a water infection.' Noel stands and resumes his pacing, surveying the bird table as he considers Sonia's suggestion. A magpie swoops down, and it triggers the memory he has been trying to recover from his conversation with Michelle about Mr Barnes' death. She was distracted by a collared dove, he recalls, before she told him what Mr Barnes had said which had worried her. *That woman's dangerous. I saw what she did.* Michelle had said that Mr Barnes had been mourning the death of his friend Elsie, another Freshfields resident.

Noel knows it's a leap in the dark, but could it be that Elsie didn't die of natural causes either? Is it possible that Mr Barnes saw someone – a female nurse – kill his friend?

He claps his hand to his forehead and turns to face Sonia. 'That's it, isn't it? This nurse killed them, a nurse who worked with Kylie and knew Mr Barnes. But why? And how do I tell the police? They'll never believe me! I mean, I only caught a rear view of this woman in the corridor. How on earth can I explain about Mrs Mullins and the Grey One?' He remembers how Kylie's killer was dressed in grey in his dream. 'Besides, the nurse's uniform was navy, not grey like in my dream.'

Sonia shakes her head. 'I don't think that matters. I believe it's possible that your friend, this poor, bewildered old lady, recognises something, a kind of essence of evil, after the trauma of losing her brother. That is the Grey One she speaks of. Maybe the nurse paused and looked in the room, hearing you all in there, and maybe Mrs Mullins sensed this essence of evil. That's what led to her agitation. She recognised the nurse is in the power of the Grey One. As for the grey clothing in your dream, I think that represents this deadly thing you witnessed by the river, that you associate with Mrs Mullins' creature.'

Noel shudders. On a rational level, what Sonia is saying seems unbelievable. But he is beginning, however dimly, to grasp that there is another dimension to the world. From the spiritual perspective, her words make sense.

'But how do I explain this to the police?' he asks again.

Sonia presses her forefinger to her mouth. 'You said the policeman was asking the staff questions, didn't you, starting with Michelle?' she asks eventually. 'Why don't you phone her and ask if she can check which nurses were on duty the day Mr Barnes died? Then she could suggest to the policeman that it has occurred to her that all the nurses have access to medication. That should be enough to encourage him to focus his attention on them. Michelle has told me that there are only two nurses on duty alongside the carers at any one time.'

'Yep. That could work.' Noel pulls his mobile from his jacket pocket. He scrolls down his contacts list and presses the green phone icon beneath Michelle's name, tapping his right foot up and down impatiently as he waits for her to pick up.

After eight beeps, the impersonal answering service gives the customary announcement that the person called is unavailable.

Noel doesn't bother leaving a message. He ends the call and whips out his van key. 'I'm going up there. I'm worried about Michelle and Florence. If we're right, and this nurse is a murderer, they could be in danger.'

'And everyone else at Freshfields. Dear God, keep them safe.' Sonia is already on her feet. 'I will come with you. If the policeman is suspicious of you, perhaps he will listen to me.'

Sonia prays quietly during the short journey through the estate. Noel bounces over the speed bumps once again. His stomach plummets when he sees an ambulance outside the entrance of the residential home. He adds his own silent prayer to his friend's as he swings into the car park. *Don't let us be too late. Let Mrs Mullins and Michelle be safe.'*

The ambulance blocks the route to the one free parking space. With a screech of brakes, Noel pulls up on the grass and leaps from the van, running round to help Sonia out.

Two paramedics emerge through the entrance bearing a stretcher. Noel recognises the bald resident with whom he exchanged greetings on his trips with Florence's belongings. The man's grey face is creased with pain, but Noel's concern is fleeting. He is preoccupied with the safety of his friends.

The diminutive manager is standing by the glass doors, supervising the old man's departure. Her brow puckers as Noel barges in. 'Mr Reilly?'

'Is Michelle still with the policeman?'

Priscilla's frown deepens. 'Yes.'

'Where are they?'

'In the room up there.' Priscilla gestures to her right.

He exhales. *At least Michelle is safe.* 'What about Mrs Mullins? Where is she?'

'In her room, settling in. I think the nurse is with her, checking her medication.'

Noel whirls round to Sonia, who is panting from the dash across the car park. 'Will you see the policeman and Michelle? I need to check on Florence.'

'Sure.'

'What's the problem?' Priscilla has picked up on their urgency.

Noel leaves Sonia to explain. He hurtles along the corridor into the dining room where a game of snap has replaced dominoes. He is vaguely aware of the rainbow-haired carer spinning round from the table as he darts past. Flying out of the opposite door, which leads to Florence's corridor, he narrowly avoids colliding with an old lady shuffling in with the aid of a Zimmer frame.

'Hey!' calls the carer from the dining room.

Noel ignores her, oblivious to anything other than Michelle and Florence being in the same building as a murderous nurse. He pushes open the final fire safety door before Florence's room. A rancid odour assails his nostrils. He pulls up short. It's unmistakably the same stench he smelled by the river on the night of his vision.

He advances slowly along the passage, the fetid air making him gag. Big band swing music spills out from the room opposite Florence's. Her door is closed. Noel presses his ear to it, but the music drowns out any other sound. He takes a deep breath and remembers the cross in his pocket. Reaching for it, he grips the smooth wood tightly.

The big band track ends. In the silence, Noel hears a whisper. *'You have been chosen to right the wrongs in this place, to shine as light in the darkness.'*

Startled, Noel spins round, half-expecting to see the Being. But there is no one there. There is something else, though: a faint, fresh scent. He sniffs. The scent is growing stronger, gradually overlaying the putrid odour. It's a floral fragrance which transports Noel back to childhood days playing in the small garden his grandmother created in the back yard of her terraced house. He has a sudden vivid image of her amid her roses and lavender, freesias and sweet peas.

The voice, the perfume and the memory of his grandmother fill Noel with an unearthly calmness. Still clasping the cross, he opens the door.

Florence is in her armchair, blue eyes wide and terrified below her black fur hat, mouth agape. She is trembling uncontrollably. The sleeve of her jumper has been rolled up to the elbow. A woman in a blue uniform is bending over her, holding a syringe loaded with clear liquid above the old lady's thin, white arm.

Florence's demeanour transforms from terror to rapture as Noel steps forward and she becomes still. 'You came.' She claps her hands together. 'Jesus is always stronger than the Grey One.' She lifts her head towards the nurse, whose expression is impenetrable.

Noel feels the pressure of a strong hand resting on his left shoulder. He has an overpowering sense of the Being's presence, and a sudden conviction that the Being is Jesus. Taking in Florence's rapt expression and her words, he is certain that she shares his understanding.

'Could you come back in five minutes? As you can see, I'm administering medication.' The nurse's voice is toneless, in keeping with her plain, unremarkable face.

Noel glances at the syringe. 'What medication is that?'

A muscle twitches by the woman's thin mouth. She casts a disparaging glance over his shabby bomber jacket and faded jeans. 'You're not a doctor or nurse, are you? The name of the drug won't mean anything to you.'

Keep her talking. Noel knows that Sonia must be explaining their suspicions to DI Pritchard by now, and that the policeman should be here very soon.

'No, I'm not a medic.' He remembers his dream, pictures Kylie sinking to the kitchen floor amid the dirty laundry. He thinks of Bradley and Liam, bereft of their mother, and of the baby Kylie was carrying. His baby. A bubble of anger threatens to burst through his unnatural composure. The grip on his shoulder tightens and helps him to steady his voice as he asks, 'But it's the same drug that you used to kill the old man who lived here, isn't it? Did you kill his friend Elsie too?'

The nurse's expression remains inscrutable, but he notices a faint flicker in her slate-grey eyes. 'I don't know what you're talking about.'

'No? Then you won't mind if I take that syringe to the police, will you?' He holds out his hand.

It's the wrong thing to say. Instead of passing over the syringe, the nurse lowers it so that it's barely an inch above Mrs Mullins' arm.

'Old people die all the time,' she says dispassionately. 'It's the natural way of things. Kinder for them, when they get to this stage.' She nods down at Mrs Mullins. 'Once they've outlived their usefulness.'

Noel shudders. The heat in the residential home is suffocating, but an icy chill has spread through the room. Evidently Mrs Mullins is affected by it too, because her smile falters and she shivers.

'What do you mean?'

The nurse throws him a scornful glance. 'Have you seen the people in this place? Demented, like this one, or immobile and incontinent? What quality of life do they have? What's the point of it?'

He flinches. 'But it's life,' he says simply. 'It's not for you or me to decide who gets to live.' *Or who gets to die,* he thinks, overwhelmed by the injustice that Kylie died so young. He balls his fists at his sides. 'What about Kylie? She wasn't old, was she?'

'No.' The nurse's expression remains implacable. 'Unfortunately, the old man said something which meant there was a danger she might have worked out that it was me who was helping people. I couldn't afford to take the risk.'

Noel crosses his arms over his chest. He is shaking as violently as Florence was when he entered the room.

'Helping?' he repeats, his voice wavery as a small boy's. 'Helping how?'

She stares at him, a strange smile hovering around her lips. 'Helping the helpless find peace.'

Blood pounds in Noel's ears. In his sensitive nostrils, the foul stink seems to be vying with the beautiful fragrance. He begins to hyperventilate.

Florence moans in her armchair. 'Please don't go. *Please*.' She is looking behind Noel. He is tempted to look over his shoulder, but dare not break eye contact with the nurse, whose thumb is now poised on top of the syringe.

The defenceless old woman's plea reminds Noel that even if it's too late for Mr Barnes and Kylie, there is still a chance for Florence if he can continue to distract the nurse by talking. *Where is DI Pritchard?*

'Who's going to miss this poor, crazy old woman?' demands the nurse. 'It will be a release for her and her family.'

'Help me, Jesus,' whimpers Florence. Her bewildered gaze latches on to Noel's face and her eyes clear. 'Make him stay,' she says.

Noel licks his dry lips. He doesn't know where his next words come from, but he says them with certainty. 'The Master will help us. Jesus is here.'

Immediately the sweet perfume wafts more strongly, overpowering the vile stench.

Noel focuses his eyes on the nurse. It takes every ounce of his strength to meet her steely gaze. 'You can't escape. The policeman will be here any second.'

'What policeman?'

The words are barely out of the nurse's mouth when a commotion on the corridor announces the arrival of DI Pritchard.

The nurse starts, dropping the syringe to the carpet beside Florence's armchair. Noel seizes the opportunity and dives forward as DI Pritchard erupts into the room. Noel grabs the syringe and hands it over to the policeman.

DI Pritchard handcuffs and cautions the nurse and begins to lead her from the room. She pauses on the threshold, and turns back to Noel. 'You fool,' she hisses. 'Think of all the others who need my help, trapped in their useless bodies and minds.'

'Thank You, Jesus. You always save us,' mutters Florence. Her head droops onto her chest. Within seconds she is snoring softly.

Chapter twenty-three

It's just before eight o'clock that evening when Noel parks up outside the riverside pub where he has arranged to meet Eddie. There is enough light spilling from the windows for him to see that Eddie's Polo isn't among the other five vehicles in the car park. He switches off the engine but leaves the radio on. He wonders if his newly discovered brother will show, guiltily aware that he wouldn't mind if he doesn't. It's been a long day, and Noel is regretting the impulsive invitation he gave after their father's funeral.

He contemplates the illuminated radio display as the commercials give way to the hourly local news bulletin. The first story is unchanged since late afternoon, but he is compelled to listen again. 'A nurse has been charged with the murders of Kylie Weatherall and an elderly care home resident. Sharon Cooper, age forty-two, was arrested earlier this afternoon.'

Noel leans over, flicks off the radio and rubs his hand over his face. He'd expected to be relieved once Kylie's murderer had been arrested, but the exhaustion has taken him by surprise.

'When you have confronted evil, been involved in spiritual battle, you are drained,' Sonia told him back at her house after the arrest. 'But praise God, it's over. After a good night's sleep, you will feel stronger, at peace. Mission accomplished.' She smiled. 'How appropriate that you are going back to the pub this evening, where it all began, back to the place where you first encountered Jesus.'

Noel had appreciated Susan Weatherall phoning mid-afternoon. He'd just made a start on painting Sonia's kitchen ceiling when his phone buzzed on the worktop. Following the morning's drama, he'd climbed down the ladder to pick up the call from an unknown number with trepidation.

Kylie's mother launched in. 'It's Susan Weatherall. The police have arrested a nurse who worked with Kylie. She killed an old man at Freshfields too, and probably an old woman. Can you believe it? Didn't think they deserved to live, apparently.' Susan's voice broke. Gathering herself, she went on, 'It seems Kylie overheard something that might have put the police on to her. I thought you should know.'

'Thanks.' Knowing what an effort it must have taken for Susan to contact him, Noel decided not to steal her thunder by telling her about his involvement in the nurse's arrest.

'The nurse had a stash of prescription drugs and syringes in the boot of her car. Could have been more deaths, couldn't there, if the police hadn't caught her? Too late for our Kylie though.' Susan's voice wobbled.

'I'm so sorry.'

There was a beat. 'Yeah, well, I shouldn't have bad-mouthed you like I did,' she said gruffly. 'I'll let you know the funeral arrangements, shall I?'

'Please.'

The thought of the nurse planning more killings circles in his mind after the call. Susan Weatherall was right: how many more victims might Sharon Cooper have slaughtered after Kylie and Mr Barnes, and probably the old lady Mr Barnes had befriended at Freshfields? He had arrived just in time to save Florence. It would have been easy for the nurse to go on to kill other Freshfields residents. Haunted by her words after her arrest, 'Think of all the others who need my help, trapped in their useless bodies and minds,' Noel was in no doubt that she had intended to carry out other murders. He remembered the murders carried out by the late Dr Harold Shipman, the serial killer of elderly patients in his care in Greater Manchester. He shared his thoughts with Sonia over an evening meal of fish, rice and peas which she had insisted he should share with her.

'By the grace of God, this nurse has been caught before she could commit any more murders. What she has done is terrible, especially for your ex-partner's mother and sons, poor boys.' Sonia sighed deeply and shook her head. 'But it's over. And I firmly believe your friend Florence will be less troubled by the Grey One now. The evil in the town has been suppressed today with this nurse's arrest. Perhaps you could phone Michelle later and see how the old lady is?'

Peering through the misty windscreen towards the road, looking out for Eddie's car, Noel still doesn't fully grasp what Sonia meant about the evil in the town being suppressed. But at least he can take comfort in the fact that Kylie's killer will face justice, and that the residents of Freshfields are safe.

He decides to give Eddie another five minutes. In the meantime, he will phone Michelle to see how Florence is settling in at Freshfields. He is honest enough with himself to know that checking on Florence isn't the only reason he wants to speak to Michelle. He'd also registered Sonia's sly smile when she suggested that he call her daughter.

His mouth is dry as he makes the call. Michelle picks up on the fifth ring. 'Good evening, Mr Reilly.'

He knows she is teasing him again about his formal address that morning and smiles. 'Hi. I was wondering – your mum thought maybe you'd appreciate a call – how is Mrs Mullins settling in? After the nurse was arrested? I mean, I might have phoned anyway...' Despite the chill inside the van, he feels a tide of heat rise up his neck and flood his face.

'Mrs Mullins seemed calmer. She didn't mention the thing again. And you could call me without my mother suggesting it.' There is a bubble of amusement in Michelle's voice.

'Yeah. 'Course. Well, that's good, then. That Mrs Mullins is more settled, I mean.'

'Yes. It's been quite a day.' Michelle hesitates. 'I don't make a habit of drinking in the week, but I'm thinking of opening a bottle of wine. If you are free...'

He takes a deep breath, aiming for a casual tone. 'I'm down at the pub by the river. Looks like I've been stood up. By my... brother,' he explains, keen to clarify that he doesn't have a date. He stumbles over the word 'brother': he has not yet fully adjusted to the idea. 'So, if you want to join me... Though I guess you won't have a babysitter for Joshua...'

'My oldest son is home tonight,' she says instantly. 'He'll keep an eye on Joshua. Give me half an hour, OK?'

'Great. If you get a taxi down, I could drive you home if you want a drink?' He clears his throat. 'That's if you're all right with me driving.'

'I'm sure I'll be safe with you, Mr Reilly. See you soon.'

Noel is grinning from ear to ear as he pockets the phone. A sudden burst of energy replaces the weariness that has dogged him throughout the afternoon. He waits another five minutes inside the van for Eddie, but is unsurprised when Eddie doesn't show. Even if Eddie already knew of Noel's existence, yesterday's meeting at their father's funeral was awkward. Noel jumps out of the van and locks it. On the other side of the river, the lights of the apartments shine brightly in the clear, starlit evening. He gazes over at them, struck by the contrast with that night only twelve days ago when he wandered along the foggy riverbank intent on taking his own life. He thinks of the nurse's contemptuous disregard for the value of life, and shivers. His own life might not amount to much – a struggling divorced handyman with a daughter he hasn't seen for months. But he now believes that life is God-given, and has a purpose. Sauntering across the car park to the pub, he admits to himself that the prospect of a drink with Michelle is another reason for his new hopefulness about the future.

Being a midweek evening, the pub is quiet. There are three young men drinking at the bar and two couples eating together at a side table. The combined odour of chips and beer grows stronger as Noel makes his way across to the bar. He orders a lime and soda from the friendly middle-aged woman and takes it across to a corner table.

Michelle arrives twenty minutes later, wearing a figure-hugging royal blue dress and navy diamanté court shoes. The outfit is such a contrast to the burgundy uniform she wears for work that Noel almost doesn't recognise her. She scans the bar and spots him, her face lighting up with her warm smile. His heart glows as she approaches the table. He stands to greet her, and she takes a seat on the padded banquette alongside him.

Noel wants to compliment her on her appearance, but finds himself tongue-tied. Somehow, he manages to ask what she would like to drink.

'A small Merlot, please.'

Noel orders himself half a lager along with Michelle's wine. He pays for the drinks and returns to the table, setting the glasses down carefully. He settles himself beside her, and inhales her perfume. He realises that he has never sat so close to her. His cheeks flush and he quickly raises his glass to his lips.

Michelle sips her red wine. 'Thanks. Your brother didn't show, then?'

'No.'

'Does he live in town?'

'In Oldford.'

'Right. Wouldn't you expect him to get in touch to say he couldn't make it?'

Noel tilts his glass so that the amber liquid catches the light. 'Too early to say. I only met him at my father's funeral.'

Michelle blows out her lips. 'Wow. You mean you didn't know he existed until yesterday?'

'No. I've not got my head round it yet, to be honest. Especially not after everything that's happened today.'

'What a time you've had.' She slides her free hand towards him on the banquette. Hesitantly, he places his hand over hers.

'Kylie's murder, losing your dad, finding a brother. Do you want to tell me about it?'

He turns to meet her sympathetic gaze and swallows. 'Are you sure?'

She nods her head. Released from the ponytail she wears for work, her raven hair is shoulder-length and lustrous. He imagines running his fingers through it. To distract himself, he picks at a beer mat with his free hand.

'I guess I should start here, then,' he says. 'The day Kylie died.'

And so he tells her everything, beginning with his despair that night and his vision by the river. He describes how he met Florence and Maureen, and talks about Florence's obsession with the Bright Giant and the Grey One, the phenomena of his own experience and of her research into the untimely deaths in the town. He explains to her about his troubled childhood and the reconciliation with his dying father, and describes the rocky relationship with his sister and the discovery of his brother. Finally, reaching for the cross in his jacket, he tells her of his new-found faith, describing Sonia's role in his spiritual journey, and his conviction that the Being he met is Jesus.

Michelle listens quietly, sipping her drink. When he finishes, she disengages her hand gently and looks deeply into his eyes. 'Tell me again what the Being said to you that night.'

Noel clears his throat. 'You have been chosen to right the wrongs in this place, to shine as light in the darkness. First, you will find your own healing.'

'That's what happened, isn't it?' Michelle shakes her head in wonder.

'Yes,' says Noel quietly. 'Yes, I believe it is.'

Michelle twists the stem of her empty wine glass between her fingers. 'And do you think you will be involved in the Master's business in the future?' she asks. 'Might this be just the beginning?'

'Maybe.'

'I see. Wow.'

They sit in silence for a moment.

Noel stares down at the beer mat which he has shredded as he told his story. 'I understand if you want me to drive you back now,' he says at last. 'I know how weird it all sounds, and if you don't want to... I mean, I know we're just having a drink, but I'd really like to get to know you better.' He stops, certain that she must be able to hear his heart hammering as he waits for her reply.

'I'd like to get to know you better too, Mr Reilly.' Michelle reaches for his hand again. 'Now, shall we walk? By the river?'

'In the dark?'

'Why not? You're not afraid of the dark, are you?'

'With you by my side? Never.'

Hand in hand they leave the warmth of the pub and emerge into the frosty evening. As they wander along the riverside path, Noel thinks that the moon and stars have never shone with such dazzling intensity. A brightness hangs over the river, a rainbow haze which is both mysterious and familiar to Noel. He has a deep unshakeable certainty that the iridescent glow is a promise that no matter what lurks in the darkness, whatever other wrongs he might confront, goodness and love will prevail in this troubled town.

Acknowledgements

I would like to thank the team at Instant Apostle for bringing this book to print. Special thanks to editor Sheila Jacobs, for her insight and suggestions which have vastly improved the novel from the draft first submitted. I am very grateful to the Instant Apostle team for a stunning cover design which perfectly captures the mood of the story. Thank you too to Tony Collins for kindly introducing the book to Instant Apostle.

Thanks as always to Neil and Alice who listened to my ideas begin to take shape during windy walks along the River Trent during lockdown, and to Alice in particular for her invaluable assistance in social media marketing ventures.